CASPIAN
RAIN

A NOVEL BY GINA B. NAHAI

Books by Gina B. Nahai

CRY OF THE PEACOCK

MOONLIGHT ON THE AVENUE OF FAITH

SUNDAY'S SILENCE

CASPIAN RAIN

A NOVEL BY GINA B. NAHAI

MACADAM CAGE

MacAdam/Cage
155 Sansome Street, Suite 550
San Francisco, CA 94104
www.MacAdamCage.com
ALL RIGHTS RESERVED

Library of Congress Cataloging-in-Publication Data

Nahai, Gina Barkhordar.
 Caspian rain / Gina B. Nahai.
  p. cm.
 ISBN 978-1-59692-251-8
 1. Jewish girls—Fiction. 2. Jews—Iran—Fiction. 3. Tehran
(Iran)—Fiction. 4. Deafness—Fiction. 5. Jewish fiction. I. Title.
PS3552.A6713C37 2007
813'.54—dc22

                                                          2007015663

Manufactured in the United States of America
10 9 8 7 6 5 4 3 2 1

Book and jacket design by Dorothy Carico Smith

For David, who always believed,
and for our children,
Alex, Ashley, and Kevin.

PART I

SHE'S SIXTEEN YEARS OLD—a young woman in a city with blue mountains.

She's walking to school with her books in her arms. She has on a faded gray uniform, a pale lipstick that she has had to hide from her parents and put on only after she has left the house. It's a golden spring morning, the light as clear as polished glass, the air imbued with the scent of poet's jasmine that blooms on slender vines everywhere in the city. The sun is just rising behind the tall maple trees that line both sides of the Avenue of the Departed, creating a gallery of light and shadows where the girl's image is by turns eclipsed and illuminated and eclipsed again—until she turns the corner onto the Square of the Pearl Canon and emerges into a sea of brightness.

As she steps off the edge of the sidewalk she feels a breeze, looks up in time to see a cloud of cherry blossoms rain down on her like a blessing. She lets out a cry of joy, opens her arms and turns full circle amid the flowers. Her books fall to the ground and her papers fly into moving traffic but she's laughing because she knows this is a good omen, a sign from the heavens that her luck has turned for the better. Any moment now, she thinks, providence will sweep toward her with a flap of its giant wings, land on her shoulder, and transform her life.

Once upon a time in a land of miracles.

When she looks down again, she's inches away from the shiny bumper of a car. A dark, angry man in a chauffeur's cap and uniform is leaning out the window and yelling that she should look where she's going, get herself killed under someone else's car if she wants, just don't mess up *his* tires. He doesn't frighten the girl at all. From where she's standing, she can see her own image reflected in the tinted black windshield of the car, see the flowers that have been caught in her hair, in the folds of her skirt, on top of her books that lie around her feet. The driver is still livid—hurry up and get off the road, you're holding up the boss people have work to do—but instead of moving out of the way, the girl leans closer to the car, peers through the glass at the passenger in the back seat. She has blocked the entire lane now, and cars are honking from every direction, but she takes her time picking up her books. God damn it girl, you're just a kid, you have no business causing a nuisance for people bigger than yourself, don't you know how to behave in civilized society? the driver yells again, but the answer is obvious.

This is what my father sees as my mother stands before him that early spring morning in the city of my dreams: he sees a girl of limited means and abundant spirit.

Of all the stories I will tell about my mother, this is the one I cherish most. I like to see her at the point of inception, the moment that would set the course for all our lives and all the stories that followed. And though I always know the end even before I have said the first word, I like the possibility, the promise inherent in each new telling, of a different finish.

THE GIRL ON THE STREET—her name is Bahar—would not stand out in any crowd. She's not particularly beautiful, or smart, or endowed with exceptional wit, but she has a zest for life, a wild and irrational optimism that is alarming because it is so out of sync with the reality that surrounds her. Her father—my grandfather—is a former cantor's apprentice who has not managed to rise to the ranks to which he had aspired, and who now sings at weddings and funerals instead. Her mother works in the house as a seamstress. She takes orders from rich Jewish and Muslim women, who send their maids to bring her fabric and thread and to pick up the work when it's done. The women hardly know the seamstress's name, don't trust her with anything more expensive than plain cotton or wool. They have her sew sheets and table-cloths, their children's school uniforms, their husband's caftan pajamas, and they're always complaining that she can't make a pattern to save her life, can't even cut a straight line, but still, she's honest and doesn't steal fabric, and she has mouths to feed; it's just a form of charity, this, and besides, no one charges as little as she does.

There's a son who has never worked a day in his life, who goes around in a secondhand suit and a borrowed tie. He pretends to be rich when everyone knows he wants for his next meal, lives off his parents instead of helping support the family. His one asset in the world is a deep baritone voice, and this alone has got him convinced that he should be an opera singer. He has never seen a real opera and wouldn't know where to go to see one, but he loves the idea of being allowed onstage so he can showcase his talents, earn the adoration of fans, become famous. As it is, he doesn't sing anywhere but at the homes of friends and relatives, and he only knows the lines to one song—a little-known and quite possibly mangled number he calls "Granada," which he sings in his sixth-grade English-as-a-second-language accent. The rest of the time, he sits on the roof of the Sorrento Café, on top of Pahlavi Avenue, sipping iced coffee that he gets for free from the waiters who humor him in the slower hours, reading government propaganda in yesterday's paper, and bragging to the handful of other patrons about a life they all know he does not lead and a future they know he will not reach. But what's the difference, really? It's all illusion if you think about it and who's to say what is or isn't likely. Wasn't Reza Shah an illiterate soldier one night and king of the country the next?

Real life, The Opera Singer likes to say, does not always rise to the occasion.

There's another son who died when he was only ten years old but who keeps coming back, dropping in on the family without any warning or invitation and staying for as long as he wants before he takes off and breaks his mother's heart as if for the first time. And a third one still—the youngest of the three boys and probably the smartest too. He realized early in life that there is no great advantage to being either poor or Jewish, and so he converted to Islam and married the daughter of a rich mullah who has promised him a great deal of money in this world and seventy-two virgins in the next. He's changed his name from Moshe to Muhammad, printed his picture in every newspaper in the city under the heading "Jadid-al-Islam"—new Muslim—and he's doing a fine job of convincing everyone he's worthy of his new station and newly acquired wealth.

Jadid-al-Islam's parents don't dislike him for converting as much as feel contempt for him: he couldn't tough it out as a Jew, they say; he chose the easy way out. Still, they can't shake the embarrassment his conversion has caused the family and so they go around pretending he's still a Jew, invite him to funerals but not weddings, ask if he could please leave the wife at home when he shows up on Cyrus Street where they live, if he could take off the Muslim *aba* when he comes around, think about his unmarried sisters whose chances at a good union have forever been spoiled by his selfishness.

The sisters' chances, in truth, had been less than stellar even before Jadid-al-Islam's conversion. The oldest one has already passed the age at which young girls become old maids. She stays at home plucking chickens and washing rice, waiting for the suitors who didn't call when she was fifteen and eighteen and who certainly won't call now that she's nearing thirty. She looks for them in the black lines cast by coffee grinds at the bottom of the fortune-teller's cup and in between the lines of Omar Khayyam's poetry, listens to her parents chastise her for not managing to find a husband, as if a man is something you buy at the fish market—put on your best smile and *someone* is bound to follow you home. But even they know there is more to her fate than meets the eye, that she's neither beautiful enough nor rich enough to be able to overcome her parents' circumstances or the damage her brothers have done to her desirability, and yet they blame her anyway, blame *her* and their own destiny, because, of course, they can't blame God—that would make them ungrateful and make *Him* angry; it could always be worse, you know, and besides, other girls they know have managed to find a husband in spite of their enormous flaws. Even Tamar, the cousin who's so dark everyone thinks she's Arab, eventually got married, and you know that's no small feat, given how fiercely Iranians hate Arabs, call them "rat-eaters" because that's what those savages do—they conquered half the world only to burn the books and tear the tongues out of the heads of any poets or philosophers a nation had produced and where are they *now*, oil money and all? Still wandering the desert with their camels and many wives, watching the world leave them behind.

The second sister, thank heavens, is married and has two kids, and she'd be just fine, really, she could have herself a good old time, if she didn't raise her husband's ire so often.

The husband is a doctor who barely made it into medical school—everyone knows this because the results of the college entrance exams are printed every year in the daily newspaper for the world to see—and who may or may not be a real doctor at all; he may be a hack, really, though he claims he's a "psychiatrist," treats crazy people as if a person's brain is like a bone you can reset or an appendix you can remove. Since when does the soul get cured with a couple of pills? Who died and put *him* in charge of saving the Lost anyway? Still, it's nice to have a son-in-law you can call "Doctor," even if he *does* lose his temper once in a while, beat his wife nearly unconscious right before the eyes of their children. After every beating, he takes her onto the roof of their house and locks her up in a room with a broken window through which a hundred pigeons fly in and nest. It's a drafty, frightening place—too cold in winter and dangerously hot in summer. The Psychiatrist keeps his wife tied to a pole, has a padlock on the door and the key in his pocket. Twice a day, he sends their children—a son and a daughter—to bring food to their mother, but he refuses to allow the neighbors or her family members to visit her while she's in confinement, leaves her there for several days until the house is overrun by dirt or he gets tired of the meals his nine-year-old daughter has to make for him in her mother's absence. Then he sends for his wife's parents to come to the house, gives them the key to the pigeon room so they can free their daughter. She emerges with her hair matted from dust and bird droppings, and her face and hands scratched from too many pigeons landing on her. She stands before him terrified and trembling, her eyes sewn to the ground because she can't stand to see her children looking at her in that state, and after a long apology to this healer of the human mind, sets about cleaning the house and cooking a meal before she's even allowed to take a bath.

Some families, I have learned, are stranger than others.

I used to like this—their strangeness—about my mother's family. It made them fascinating in the way that fairy-tale characters are fascinating—tragic to the core, but also mesmerizing. It never occurred to me, at first, that I might have inherited this strangeness, that I might have been born into the same weird spell and, with it, the solitude of the charmed.

⤜⤛

MY MOTHER—her name, Bahar, means "spring"—has the kind of brains no person with common sense has any use for: she can't add to save her life, can't comprehend even the most elementary principles of science. Yet she says she wants to go to university and become a teacher—a high school teacher of poetry and literature and all those subjects that are the domain of unemployed men and loose women. Bahar reads books about people who do not exist and actually thinks of them as real, collects pictures of American movie stars and makes a point of learning every detail of their personal life. She talks about Spencer Tracy as if he were her next-door neighbor, celebrates Grace Kelly's wedding to the king of Monaco as if there were a one in a hundred million chance, even, that this kind of thing could happen to her or, for that matter, to anyone she's ever likely to know. But then again, Bahar does actually believe she's going to marry a "person of substance"—"a rich man, with a celebrated name and social standing, someone of consequence, whom people know and *defer* to," she explains, with a straight face, to friends and family. It hasn't dawned on her that "persons of substance" do not marry girls who live one block away from the old Jewish ghetto of Tehran, or that girls from Cyrus Street do not become "of consequence" to anyone but, if they're lucky, their children—and maybe this is why she gets along so well with The Opera Singer, why she's the only one in the world who understands his delusions and treats them as if they were this morning's truth.

Throughout the school year, Bahar spends her lunch money on chewing gum and tamarind that she buys from orphan boys on the street. She buys lottery tickets as well—though her parents have forbidden her to do so time and again—because of course she's going to win millions with that *one* ticket she happens to have bought; just watch the evening paper you'll read all about it, they'll even print a picture of her waving the ticket in the air for the world to see: O ye of little faith. She'll bring the newspaper to school and show it to her friend, Angel, who has shared a desk with Bahar since they were in first grade.

Angel studies day and night, doesn't think she's ever going to get married, and certainly not to a prince. Like Bahar, she intends to go to university and become a high school teacher, to leave Cyrus Street and rise above her family's station, but she knows this will be a great challenge and is prepared to make the necessary sacrifice. Unlike Bahar, she doesn't waste time by going to the cinema, or by taking the long way home after school so she can walk past the boys' academy. She is from the kind of Jewish family that does not—as many others have done since Reza Shah opened up the ghettoes in every town and province across the country—downplay their Jewishness because they're tired of being looked down upon by the world. For these reasons, Bahar's parents approve of Angel and have allowed their daughter to visit the girl's house a few times. Other than that, they keep a tight leash on Bahar, worry about her excessive optimism because they know just the kind of disappointment it is bound to cause: they, too, had once been young and able to hope, and look what it did for them—the father's dreams of becoming a rabbi when he was well aware that a person must be born into that job, you inherit honor and respect from your parents; the mother's love for the son who died, her trust in Jadid-al-Islam, her faith that The Opera Singer would make something of himself. Look what it all brought them.

Bahar, though, keeps telling them they're wrong, they don't know what she knows, and what she knows is that she's going to do great things with her life, marry a great man and become of great consequence indeed, and that she's not going to give up, never rest or bend or stray from the path she is born to pursue till she gets what she wants.

Then she meets my father.

HIS NAME IS OMID. In Farsi, that means "hope."

He's twenty-four years old, the second son of a wealthy Jew. He has money to his own name, a job in his father's company, a very bruised ego: the girl he was engaged to marry has recently called off their wedding and now she is sitting by the phone, calling every person who ever knew her or Omid and telling them all about why she left him—because he is "devoid of emotions," she says, as if this were an actual medical condition, a biological deficiency that results in the lack of sensation in one's body. It's one of those expressions that has recently become popular in Tehran, especially with young women of a certain socioeconomic class—the kind who don't need to worry about whether they'll have a roof over their head or be able to feed their children. It presumes that having emotions is a desirable state akin to being rich, or good-looking, or even smart. Who else but a spoiled and idealistic girl who has never suffered hardship or worked a day in her life would give up a man in exchange for "emotions"?

Omid's former fiancée can get away with this—break up an engagement and know she'll find another husband—because she's the half-Jewish, half-Baha'i, only-child-so-she'll-inherit-all-the-money daughter of a man who has made more money than most. Among other advantages, the father's wealth has given him the impression that he can actually claim he's descended from royalty—never *mind* that he was a Jew before he converted to Bahaism and that Jews have been second class citizens in Iran since Islam first arrived. The former fiancée's grandparents, everyone knows, had sold boiled lentils and grilled chicken livers in the "Pit"—the central square of the Tehran ghetto, which is where all the Jews came from, the later protestations of some notwithstanding. The girl has a squeaky voice and short fingers, but she is otherwise attractive enough, and she knows how to handle herself in a crowd, how to endear herself to the right people and defend against the poisonous tongues of others. She spends her days at the beauty salon and the fortune-teller's house, taking three-hour naps in the afternoon and bathing in cucumber juice and rosewater, but none of that matters to Omid because he has never loved her, or desired her, or even felt particularly fond of her. As far as he's concerned, she could have been any one of a number of women deemed eligible for marriage. He was only going to marry her because that's what you have to do at a certain age—find a wife and have a few kids—and she was the one his parents had most liked.

So it isn't the end of his engagement that bothers Omid so much as the manner in which it has occurred—at the last minute, with wedding invitations already circulating, the whole town knowing that it was *she* who walked away. And there is another reason as well, though he would be hard-pressed to admit it to anyone, least of all his parents: as socially correct and well-connected as he is, Omid is also lonely.

He feels disconnected from the people who should matter to him most, incapable of caring enough for anyone to even *want* to establish a bond. He can't say more than three words to his older brother without feeling alienated and scorned, can't imagine having a conversation with his father that doesn't have to do with work. He loves his mother well enough, but she, more than anyone else, has always felt like a stranger to him. She's tall and thin, Mrs. Arbab, with a face as sharp as an ax, long fingers that she tends to for ten minutes every morning and that she soaks in warm paraffin at night. She wears white cotton gloves to keep the paraffin from staining her sheets, sleeps face up with her hair wrapped in a net and her hands folded on her stomach, so that from the foot of the bed she looks like a corpse laid to rest in one of those American films where the dead are put on display in open caskets in a church somewhere with carnations all around and well-dressed family members sitting in neat rows and displaying only the slightest level of grief because, what do you know, crying at funerals is considered unsavory in America: you're supposed to look aggrieved but not devastated. Americans don't *get* devastated, because they can do anything they want—without fear of failure or retribution; they're a different breed of human beings, those milk-and-honey girls and boys who grow up to be presidents and movie stars. Why would people like that ever feel anything even *close* to devastation?

Americans don't get devastated and don't lose their cool at funerals because they have no idea what real loss is. It doesn't affect them as completely, as irreversibly, as it does people in other parts of the world, and it certainly doesn't haunt them the way it does people in the East, doesn't pass from father to son for seven generations and sometimes more.

This—unaffected by loss—is how Omid's mother behaves at every funeral, except that she's not American and isn't sitting in church. Where she comes from the dead are buried naked in a shroud, without makeup and perfume and without their hair styled as if they were going to a soiree—leave it to Westerners to turn even a burial into a theatrical affair. The Iranian dead never do see the satin-lined inside of a casket, and they're lowered into the grave by relatives who sob till they faint, who even hire professional mourners to do additional crying in order to provide a respectable send-off.

Omid's mother, on the other hand, displays no emotion because she feels none. Her coldness has taught Omid to keep a distance not only from family members but also from anyone with whom he might have a chance of developing a real relationship. He deals with the living the way Americans do with the dead: elegantly and with grace, but without excessive emotionality.

When he sees Bahar on the street, he likes the bounce in her step, the way her hair curls into a single loop at the end. But there's something else that attracts him to her as well: he can tell, from her clothes and the fact that she's walking to school instead of being driven, that this is a girl who could be easily conquered, who would marry him in a heartbeat just because of who he is and what he can give her, who won't demand much—least of all, emotions.

He watches her cross the square and make her way into the alley that leads to the Persepolis School for Girls. He tells the driver to follow her. He sits in the car with his legs crossed and his suit jacket draped over the seat next to him so it won't wrinkle, and he lowers the window just enough to let out the smoke from the cigarette he has lit. It's obvious to him that the girl knows she's being followed. It happens all the time—young men or their mothers spotting girls on the street and following them to school or home, perhaps inquiring their name and, if they deem the family worthy, requesting a visit. They may never pursue her after that, or they may go back to assess her qualifications— her height and weight, her looks, her family's finances—in order to decide whether to extend the matter any further. It's been done like this forever, and it works well enough: marriages last because divorce is nearly out of the question; husbands are content because wives have no choice but to obey; and everyone knows better than to expect such a thing as "happiness."

All the way to school, Bahar keeps looking back to make sure the car is still behind her. At the guards' booth, she stops and whispers something to the attendant. Then she turns around, one last time, and smiles at Omid.

MY MOTHER, OF COURSE, is the one who told me about that encounter.
She knew that our lives—hers and mine—were forever entangled in a
single mesh, so she told me about that day and about many others as
well, gave me all the disparate, jagged pieces of that imperfect, forever-
changing truth that we call memory. With those pieces, I've tried to
create a single string of tales, each as complete and self-contained as the
next, that, I hoped, would illuminate for me a path to understanding
my parents:

"See the light falling like a blade through the trees where I walk,"
she said. "The glow of the metal on your father's car. See my brother,
ten years old and on his bike, racing through traffic as if he could fly.
See my sister with pigeon droppings all over her face; she looks like a
statue in the middle of a crowded city street, there's no hope in her
eyes, only shame for what she is and everything she'll never become—
and *that*, you see, is what I dread most: the end of hope, the setting in
of shame.

"See your father," she said, "so handsome he takes the breath away
from every woman who sets eyes on him. He can have any girl in this
town he wants, and yet he stops for *me*, looks through the windshield
and finds *me*."

"What were the chances, do you think, of *that* happening?"

It wasn't until later that I realized what those stories would mean
to me, how that fairy-tale world of ghosts and ogres and poor girls who
grow up to be queen would seep into every landscape I set my eyes on
afterward. They're always there, sometimes whole, often in bits—the
eyes that look into the sky expecting a miracle, the bits of white paper
scattered in the wind, the boys with the shaved heads and dirty felt hats
who peddle lottery tickets, it's *your* day, miss, buy one ticket and you'll

never have to wait for luck again.

And I see *him* as well—my father who stopped for her that day on the street, who brought to her the good fortune she had always known was hers. He's riding in the car when she's on foot. He has the advantage, the power to drive away or to stop, to .ndon her to her fate or to reach forward and pull her out of her universe of failed dreamers and of women who clean rice for a living.

❧

MRS. ARBAB LAUGHS when he tells her about the girl he has found on the street.

"I don't know the family," she says, meaning they're not worth knowing. Tehran's upper-class Jews are a selective group who pride themselves on socializing only with each other and with wealthy Muslims and Baha'is. They have no time for anyone who is not rich enough or attractive enough to be admitted into their midst.

"And anyway," she adds, "no self-respecting family would send their daughter to Persepolis if they could afford better."

They're in the parlor adjacent Mrs. Arbab's her bedroom—she on a white wooden bench with a pink satin cover, he standing behind her with his hands tucked into his pants' pockets. She has been peering into a large vanity mirror, trying to pluck her eyebrows before the sun goes down and deprives her of the natural light she needs to see every last hair, but now Omid is blocking that light, and this annoys her because it's already five o'clock and she has to get ready for a party that evening. She only needs three hours to do her face and nails, and she never leaves the house before ten o'clock, but she likes to get started early, and besides, she really thinks he should leave the matchmaking to her—he has already botched one union and cost the family enough face.

She leans toward the mirror and starts plucking.

"I want to find out about her anyway," he says.

She stops with the tweezers.

"What for?" she says, more confused than indignant, but careful not to frown because it leaves permanent lines on her face. She doesn't laugh too often either, and she says everything in a near whisper because she tries to keep facial gestures, which create wrinkles, to a minimum. She tapes her face every night when she goes to bed, pulls apart all the muscles and wraps a wide elastic band from her hairline down to her chin and back up. It's something she learned from a women's magazine she read in London once—the secret to Joan Crawford's youthful face. "What do you want to find out about her *for*?"

He says nothing, but he won't go away either, and now Mrs. Arbab's truly annoyed—here you are, you've already made yourself the talk of every beauty parlor in town, and now you want to give our enemies more rope to hang you with; you clearly have no clue how something like this will play out in public—but she knows that Omid is obstinate, and she really wants him to go away and leave her alone with her pancake powder and perfume, and so she says, fine, fine, I'll make some inquiries, don't ask me again, I'll let you know when I know, girls like this are a dime a dozen, no need to rush into anything, it's not like anyone's going to spirit her away anytime soon.

A month goes by without any mention of Bahar. Then Mrs. Arbab calls Omid into her room. She tells him about the seamstress who can't sew and the cantor who can't sing and, here's the topper if you still need more, there's a Jewish brother who pretends he's Muslim and a dead one who thinks he's still living—I'm not joking, these people are *particularly* stricken, even for *their* kind. Now can we please stop this awful game and spare me any more weird stories?

He says he wants to meet Bahar anyway.

She stalls for weeks. Then at last she sends a messenger to Bahar's father: A most eligible young man *may or may not* be interested in inquiring about your daughter. He *may or may not* come to see her, and he of course makes no promises whatsoever, but for the potential suitor to take the first step, to even make his identity known, you have to promise that, should a proposal be made, it would be accepted immediately and without condition.

It's Bahar's sacrifice to make—this bargain to swallow her pride in exchange for a good marriage. But she has already seen the car follow her, already knows she will marry the man she saw in the back seat.

❧

WHEN HE DOES COME to meet her, in the shiny silver car with both his parents, whose only intention is to point out to him every one of Bahar's faults, Omid is every bit as gallant, as handsome and charming, as she has imagined him to be. He wears a black pin-striped suit, shiny leather shoes, a gold watch. He shakes hands not just with Bahar's father, but with her mother as well, and he stands up every time the poor woman comes into or goes out of the room, which confuses Bahar's mother—because she has never been accorded this kind of respect and has no idea what to do with it—but also makes her like him enormously, makes her wish she, too, was young again and could dream of a man just like Omid. His refinement and sophistication, his smooth language and subtle gestures, make Bahar's parents sweat with embarrassment and curse themselves for not having a bigger house, or nicer furniture, or better manners.

It is true that the Arbabs are Jews, but that's where the similarities end between them and Bahar's family. Mr. Arbab's wealth makes him a person who deserves to be admired and envied. His wife's life of comfort makes it inevitable that she would have nothing but disdain for Bahar's mother—look at this woman, she probably isn't so old, but she looks decades older than I, her skin is cracked like the desert floor and she obviously hasn't heard of hair dye or she would have done something about that gray; it's people like *her* who give Jews a bad name.

Not for them—no thanks—these trappings of ghetto life.

Ten minutes into the meeting, Bahar's father excuses himself and leaves the room. He finds Bahar waiting breathlessly in the hallway, grabs her by both arms and says, this is insane, this man is too good for us, he'll never marry you, never leave the mansions of Northern Tehran to come take a girl from this crowded little street that's too narrow even for his *car,* and even if he *did,* even if he *were* stupid enough to choose you, he'd spend his life regretting it, you'd never be what he wants, never measure up.

In a rage, Bahar shakes herself free.

"You *want* me to be damned," she tells her father, "but it won't happen."

SHE'LL NEVER TELL YOU THIS, but her parents have barely noticed her all her life, have loved her only in the careless, absentminded way of parents who know their children will grow up to disappoint them. A girl, The Seamstress had said when her daughters were young, is her mother's worst enemy, a liability she must bear all the way into the grave. Then The Ghost Brother died and broke her parents' heart, and after that it became even more painful for Bahar's mother to see her and her two sisters, better to look away; there's nothing but trouble and shame where girls are involved.

Bahar's parents are not cruel people. They love their children as much as anyone else. They make sacrifices and shed tears with the best of them, but they also know the reality of things, want their daughters to know it as well. No point pretending otherwise.

Inside the room where the two families are meeting, Omid's parents think it's all over—that Omid is as appalled by what he has seen as they are, that he has recognized the folly of being here and, like them, can't wait to leave. Then Mrs. Arbab gets up and signals that it's time to go. Her husband kills his cigarette on the side of the plate in which he has been served peeled cucumbers that he has not touched because he couldn't bear to eat from these people's dishes, and that's when they realize that their son has lost his mind, gone crazy and needs to be locked up, because Omid shakes hands with Bahar's father, then with The Seamstress, and then he says, I've enjoyed meeting you, I'd like to come back if it's all right and meet the young lady next.

He returns to Cyrus Street alone. He sits across from Bahar in her parents' "good room," crosses his legs, lights an American cigarette. He tells her he has three questions.

"What is your favorite word?"

She's wearing a dress her mother had finished that morning. It's too large at the hips, pulls around the armholes, but she wears it as if it were a glamorous movie star gown. She's beaming with delight, thrilled to be alone with Omid. She doesn't take a second to think about his question before she answers.

"*Baran*," she says proudly, like an eager student on the first day of class. Rain.

He takes some time to process what she has said. He had expected a word like "duty," "honor," "loyalty,"—the kind of word he thinks a girl of her age and station would have on her mind, that she should have learned from her mother and set as a guideline for herself.

"Obedience," "Subservience," "Forbearance."

He drags on his cigarette and blows out the smoke, thinks, this one may have a cloud or two in her eyes, she must think she's a poet, but then again, she won't be hard to train.

He can tell that Bahar's parents have made improvements to the room since his last visit: the walls have been whitewashed by a coat of paint so fresh it still smells of wetness. The furniture has been rearranged, covered with pieces of red velvet where the upholstery is torn. The floor is covered with a better rug—probably borrowed—than what was there the first time. Someone has put a bunch of purple flowers on the windowsill.

He looks away from the flowers and smiles indulgently at Bahar. Clouds maybe, he thinks, but also great innocence.

"What is your favorite thing to do?"

Again, she doesn't hesitate.

"To leave home in the morning."

Now, he's genuinely disturbed. He shifts in his chair and rests his cigarette on the edge of an ashtray, tells himself he may indeed be making a mistake, that he may have misjudged this girl. He's imagined her as the kind of wife who would be happiest at home, cooking and raising children and agonizing over her choice of fabric for the drapery. He can't see why she would want to run out of the house in the morning, or where she would go.

On the other side of the window, a young boy is riding a bicycle around the fish pool. It's an old and rusted piece of junk, that bicycle, and it squeaks as it goes. Omid has no idea who the boy is. He doesn't know anything about Bahar's siblings and doesn't want to find out. It's clear to him that she will stop seeing them once he marries her, it's simple enough, really, why complicate matters by actually meeting people you won't have a thing to do with. Still, the noise of the metal rubbing against metal is making him want to grit his teeth. He waits a few minutes, throws an angry glance or two in the direction of the yard, and when Bahar doesn't get up to ask the kid to go away, Omid decides to leave.

He has one last question.

"What is your favorite color?"

THE SECOND TIME my parents meet alone, he brings her three sheets of fabric.

He has spent weeks fighting his mother and older brother, fighting also his own doubts about whether Bahar is indeed someone he can live with, or take out in public and show people. She's clearly not as docile as he had imagined she would be, and she does display a certain hardheadedness, a certain defiance of convention, that is the very opposite of what Omid had expected. But then she *is* only sixteen years old—young enough to be malleable—and who's to say? She may even pass for more than she is, make a place for herself among the wives of Omid's friends and relatives, get invited to their twice-and-three-times-weekly card games and their daylong trips to the hairdresser and the tailor and, more and more now, those spas where a scam artist with a quick tongue and a bunch of color brochures from some American company will wrap women's thighs and hips in bandages till they look like mummies, leave them to sweat in a steam room till they're as dry and dehydrated as the dead but also, miraculously, a few pounds lighter than when they came in.

Mostly, though, Omid has watched his father for clues as to how far Mr. Arbab is going to let him go with Bahar, how long he'll wait before he steps in with one exclamation that will supersede all the bickering and bargaining that goes on between his wife and son and which he normally ignores—let them fight it out, they're all fools. But though he's clearly revolted by what he has seen and learned of Bahar's family, Mr. Arbab doesn't seem too opposed to her becoming Omid's wife: She's not beautiful, but not bad-looking either, he has said. She seems rather bright, and certainly eager, he has observed. And then, there's this, he has told Omid, fixing him directly with that gaze of his that could melt a rock: one gets in life what one most *deserves*.

It's not a secret that Mr. Arbab thinks little of Omid and his potential. His silence about Bahar, however, is not a sign of indifference. Nor is it an indication that he plans to capitulate to his son's wishes. It is really a taunt, a gauntlet he has thrown and that he is waiting for Omid to pick up: show me you're man enough to stand up to your mother, to go against convention, to risk my ire—even if it means you're going to ruin your own life.

Omid has come back with gifts for Bahar.

"Close your eyes," he tells her, and unfolds a white lace—so heavy it sighs as it rolls off his arm—on the chair.

"Close your eyes again," he tells her, and drapes pink taffeta over the lace.

He watches as she runs her fingers across the fabric, as she brings it to her face and lets it rest for a second against her cheek. He thinks then it's always going to be so easy—to give Bahar so much happiness with so little effort, to spread it like a veil over the imperfections of her life, to hide her inadequacies and his own inability to love.

He tells her he has had a tough time finding the third fabric. He has sent his driver, Hassan Agha, into every store on Ferdowsi Avenue more than once, and in the end he has had to order the fabric from abroad.

"What is your favorite color?" he had asked the last time they met, and she had answered, "Caspian green."

Green the color of emeralds, of the forest leading to the Caspian, of the sea at high noon.

She has never been outside Tehran, doesn't know what the sea looks like except from pictures. She has no idea what it's like to breathe the salty air, to sleep in sheets weighed down by humidity and wake up with sand in her hair. But she has read about the Caspian in many books, and she can imagine it well enough. She knows just what color the mountains will be, how the water will be like glass, silver in the sunlight, reflecting the gold of the rice shoots in the fields along the shore.

"You are never the same," she has told Omid, "once you have seen the green of the Caspian."

Close your eyes one last time.

BEFORE HE PROMISES her to the Arbabs, Bahar's father sits her down for a talk. He tells her she had better think this over real good, because there will be no going back from here on—I give them my word and you'll be *his* forever, even if he changes his mind the next day, if he never gives you a ring or doesn't marry you or, may God make me mute for saying this, if he decides to divorce you and send you home to me.

I want you to understand this and think about it before you jump feetfirst into the fire, girl: you and I are not like *his* kind of people; we don't have the same rights, can't take the same liberties. And here, child, is the rub, what I want you to comprehend with that no-good head of yours: this marriage is not going to take place, this man is too good for us, he'll never marry you. I don't know what Omid's game is, but it doesn't matter, because the minute I go to them and say yes, she's yours, she'll kiss your hands and be your servant and earn the privilege of being your wife—the minute I say that, you'll be marked as his, spoiled and tarnished beyond repair. And even if he *did* give you a ring and a promise, even if he *were* stupid enough to choose you, he'd spend his life regretting it; you'd never be what he wants, never measure up.

She laughs at him with that childish abandon that has always made her parents' heart quiver with anxiety. She's been reckless and unreasonable all her life, but now, she's also blinded by joy, giddy with the prospect of escaping her destiny once and for all.

Listen to me, girl, I'm drawing the line in the sand for you. This is the point of no return: you can go ahead and promise yourself to him, but if you do, there's no coming home tomorrow or ever. You'll leave my house in a wedding gown and the only way I'll ever let you back is in a caftan shroud—*dead*, that is—because we could never live down the shame and infamy of divorce, and you won't have any other place to go either. A divorced woman has no rights, no family, not a penny to live on. What *then*?

But even as he says this, the father knows that Bahar is doomed—she's going to say YES, and he's not going to stop her, how could he? Who, in his place, would be able to walk away from such a deal, to turn his back on the chance—granted, it's one in a hundred million—that his predictions will *not* come true, that his daughter will indeed live happily ever after, and that *he,* who knows so much about disappointment, will for once be blessed?

HER PARENTS BORROW money to pay for the engagement party. They spend weeks fixing up the house, buy new chairs, prepare food for a hundred. They're mortified that Omid's friends and family will come down from their mansions, see the circumstances in which these other Jews live, and arrive, once again, at the obvious conclusion that some people are naturally inferior to others.

They're also terrified that Omid will come to his senses while there's still time, call off the wedding, and leave them with a debt they will take years to repay and a daughter who's been "stained" and will therefore be unsuitable for marriage. Still, you can't spit good fortune in the face and so they tell themselves maybe this is going to work out after all—maybe this is God's way of paying them back for everything he has taken away—so they pray hard and press ahead with the preparations.

The house can't accommodate more than three dozen people comfortably, but Bahar's parents have asked the Arbabs to invite as many guests as they like, and they have invited all their own relatives as well—it's what you do, there's no avoiding it. They have prayed that the most embarrassing relatives will not show up, but of course those are the first to arrive and to place themselves in areas where they are most likely to be noticed. At the last minute, they even give in to The Opera Singer's wishes and hire a guitar player to accompany him when he sings "Granada." The man arrives in impossibly tight blue jeans and a shirt that's open halfway down to his navel, and he will spend most of the night sitting idly or helping himself to servings of fried chicken and rice, because every time he plugs his guitar amplifier into an outlet, it blows out all the power and immerses the house in darkness.

"Invite as many guests as you like," the parents have asked Omid, yet he arrives nearly alone, accompanied only by his parents and his older brother. When he walks in, the women in Bahar's family scream in delight and ululate to ward off the evil eye. They throw rose petals at him and rush forward to shake hands with his parents, welcome, welcome, where is everyone else? And still, they take a few minutes to understand what Omid means when he says, this is it—these are all the guests I have invited tonight, I didn't want to impose, I thought we'd just have everyone else come to the wedding. Slowly, the realization sets in that something is very wrong—someone is being insulted here, and it's clearly Bahar and her parents, because let's face it, the groom didn't want his friends to see this house, to see his wife's relatives, but then again, who can blame him? Look at him, he's a prince; and that mother of his, she acts like Queen Victoria, for God's sake, she won't even shake hands with anyone lest her manicure get ruined.

Bahar, though, chooses to ignore the calamity that is being played out.

She comes up to Omid in a knee-length dress her mother has sewn with the pink taffeta he had brought. She has her hair down on her shoulders, and she's painted her nails the color of the dress.

Come inside. I will give you my best intentions and all my hope.

He gives her a five-karat diamond ring, an antique watch, a diamond necklace. He sits next to her all night, watches her dance but refuses to join in, makes no excuses for his parents when they leave early, though it's only eleven o'clock and dinner has barely been served. This is a great insult, to leave your son's engagement party just when it's getting off the ground, this isn't America, you know, where parties start and end before midnight, Americans may do a lot of things well, but having parties is not their forte, in this country, a good party doesn't end till the sun comes up.

At the end of the evening, Bahar asks Omid if he likes her dress. He nods gently and smiles.

"We'll have a *real* tailor work on your clothes from now on."

THE REAL TAILOR is an Armenian woman named Alice who has a two-month waiting list for new clients, and who has never been known to deliver a dress on time. She's sharp-tongued and dour, imperious with the rich, indignant with the less wealthy. She acts as if she were doing them all a favor—taking their money and making them wait three months for a dress—and her clients have bought into this wholeheart-edly. They sit in her parlor from midday till evening, sipping Turkish coffee—made by a fourteen-year-old peasant girl Alice has bought from the girl's parents for the price of a bed and three square meals a day—exchanging diet recipes and the details of the latest scandal in town while they peek at each other's fabrics and devise ways to outdo everyone else in good taste and beauty. They measure their own and each other's social standing by the length of time Alice makes them wait before they are admitted into the atelier, and they'll talk about it that evening at the parties they will go to, create or ruin reputations by reporting on how a client was received by the Armenian.

Alice will make Bahar wait all day.

She knows who Bahar is because Mrs. Arbab has called to make the appointment for her—my son is marrying well below us but we need the dress to be up to standards, and I wouldn't dream of having it made by anyone but you, but really, I can't go there with her, I know it's cus-tomary, everyone does it, but spare me this agony, would you please, just let her come alone, or with one of her weird relatives.

Bahar arrives early, her wedding lace folded neatly in a bag, her smile so bright and confident it puts Alice on alert that she's a person who needs to be reminded of her true station in life. She leaves Bahar in the waiting room—have a seat, I'll see if I can make time, you're the first to arrive, but I'm expecting other customers, they have priority—and disappears into the atelier.

Other women arrive in groups of two and three. They've all heard about Omid's engagement, and so they sit across from Bahar, examine her openly and without pretense, even talk about her out loud with one another. They ask her pointed questions: Are you here alone? Didn't anyone want to come with you for your first fitting? Doesn't Mrs. Arbab ever take you anywhere?

Bahar answers politely but with too much enthusiasm—indicating that she's glad to be here even if she *has* been slighted by her future mother-in-law, that she's prone and vulnerable because she doesn't know yet how to arm herself against the scrutiny and judgment of the society she intends to be a part of. Her weakness makes the women dislike her even more, gives Alice permission to keep her waiting all day.

Every hour or so, Alice opens the door of her atelier and looks into the waiting room, exchanges greetings with new arrivals, then motions for one of the women to come inside for a fitting. She knows Bahar is a bride-to-be, and should therefore be given preferential treatment, but she ignores her anyway, closes the door on her and her sad little plastic bag without even bothering to indicate how much longer Bahar will have to wait. The other women see this but do not interfere. Some of them even feel sorry for Bahar, wish Alice would accord her more respect, but they're neither brave enough, nor caring enough, to risk alienating Alice by rising to the girl's defense. So they smoke More cigarettes, leaf through year-old issues of *Vogue* and talk about the incompetence of their maids, the cheekiness of their cooks, the habitual lateness of their chauffeurs. They watch Bahar from the corner of their eye and ask themselves how much longer she's going to sit there, pretending she doesn't know what's going on, she must be hungry, for God's sake, it's four o'clock in the afternoon and she hasn't had lunch, just tea that Alice's maid brings around on a tray every half hour or so and that Bahar drinks with too much sugar and too many dates—the stuff is fattening but she probably has no idea.

They watch her and shake their heads. What is it about being poor, they wonder, that diminishes a person so entirely? That attracts tragedy?

Invites loss?

At five o'clock, one of the women finally takes Alice aside and tells her this isn't right, this poor girl has been patient enough, you may not owe *her* any respect, but you can't insult the person who sent her to you. Then Alice calls Bahar into her workshop.

She has closed the door for every other one of her customers—to give them privacy as they undress—but with Bahar, she leaves it halfway open.

"Take your clothes off," she says. "I need to see what I'm dealing with."

Bahar puts her bag down on a table and looks at the open door.

"Let's go," Alice urges. "I'm tired. I want to call it a day."

Tentatively, Bahar takes off her skirt, then stands in place and looks at the door again. The women in the waiting room pretend they're busy talking to one another, but Bahar knows that they'll all look at her the minute she turns away. She asks Alice if she can close the door.

Alice takes Bahar's arm and leads her to the mirror.

"You think no one's seen a naked girl before?" she asks.

Bahar takes off her shirt and climbs, in only her underwear, onto a platform in front of the full-length mirror. She stands there as Alice takes her measurements, and tries not to look in the mirror where she knows she will see the other women looking back at her. Alice's hands are cold and angry. They push and poke at Bahar, and if she reacts by pulling away, they come at her more aggressively.

The women are watching.

When she's done with the measurements, Alice takes the lace out of the bag and spreads it on a table. "Not bad," she says. "What do you want to do with it?"

She picks it up and wraps it around Bahar's body, starts to pin it here and there so as to devise a style. One of the pins pricks Bahar's skin. She pulls away instinctively. "That hurts."

Alice doesn't stop what she's doing.

"Hold still!" she commands, but suddenly, Bahar is defiant.

She steps off the platform so she's at eye level with Alice.

"You're poking too hard," she says, "and you should close the door."

Alice puts down her pincushion and stares at Bahar. She hasn't expected the girl to challenge her, certainly not before an audience of other customers, and so she can't let this go without setting the balance in her own favor again.

"Get back on the platform," she says in a measured voice, but Bahar won't move. Her eyes are red and her lips have turned white with anger and she just stands there, looking afraid of Alice, and even more afraid of what she, herself, may do.

"Get on the platform," Alice says again, "or go home."

They glare at each other. Alice clutches the wedding lace in her fists. She wants to give Bahar time to contemplate the consequences of alienating her—of throwing a fit here, in front of all those women who will bear witness, that very evening in all the parties around Tehran, to the fact that Omid's new bride-to-be is a shrew with a temper. Slowly, she takes Bahar's arm and, digging her nails into her skin, shoves her back up on the platform.

"Now hold still," she commands. "A girl like you should be grateful just to have been allowed *in*."

In the mirror before her, Bahar sees a young woman, erect on a box in an airless room bathed in the sinking afternoon light. Around her, half-made gowns and naked mannequins lie on the backs of wooden chairs, on the arms of a blue velvet sofa, on the surface of an etched glass coffee table. Beyond them in the waiting room, a dozen women watch silently as she stands in surrender, arms stiff at her sides, face inundated by tears of humiliation and rage.

SHE WILL ALWAYS REMEMBER this—how she was attacked and belittled by a woman who should have been helping her, how she backed down and let Alice win, how the other women saw this and left to tell about it. As much as she tries to believe that she did the right thing, that she took the high road and refused to act in a manner unbecoming a bride-to-be, as much as she tries to believe it didn't mean much—it was one hour out of a lifetime and who remembers it, anyway, but Alice and I—Bahar can't forgive herself her weakness.

In a world defined entirely by the domination of the mighty over the weak, Bahar has thought she could rise from her beginnings and, on the strength of a good marriage, traverse the boundaries into the land of the strong. Only after she has become my father's wife, given him all the goodwill and optimism she can muster, proven her abilities and her talents and still found herself waiting at the gates—only when the boundaries have proved immutable—does she understand the limits of what hope can do.

That's where the rage came from.

I think now it was this rage—my mother's inability to prevail over the forces she had once believed surmountable, the shame she felt for not having fought back at first, and later not fighting enough—I think it was this rage that made her unable to accept my limitations, to accept *me* with those limitations. I think it was her sadness at having sold herself for a wish, her dreams that rose like ships in the night, lit up and glorious against the reality of what she would be able to attain—I think it was those dreams that, in the end, kept us apart.

She has turned a corner—that day when she arrives with her wedding lace in her hands and the promise of a new destiny wrapped in gold around her ring finger—turned a corner and found herself near the top of the world. She is capable enough to stand the height, fearless enough to keep climbing, and yet she can see, right there in Alice's mirror, that any minute now, she will come up to a precipice.

THE PRECIPICE, even before my parents have married, is a self-possessed, quiet stranger with dark eyes and an even darker past.

Omid sees her for the first time in the Aramaic Brothers' jewelry store in the lobby of the Tehran Hilton. He has come to the jewelry store to buy a gift for Bahar, to bring to her at the henna ceremony a week before the wedding. He's standing at a display case across from the Younger Aramaic Brother, who is helping him select the right piece for the occasion. Omid has his back to the door, and he's looking at a bracelet that the Younger Aramaic Brother has laid out on a black velvet pad—this is a great deal; it's the best we have had in a long time; it may be expensive, but it's worth a lot more than what we're asking—when he feels a shift in the brother's voice, then hears him stop mid-sentence. Omid looks up from the bracelet; the Younger Aramaic Brother is staring at something behind Omid. His eyes have softened and his face is devoid of its usual intensity and he clearly has no memory of, or interest in, what he was doing only seconds earlier.

Omid has known the Aramaic Brothers for some time. They have been in business for thirty years—since they were eight and nine years old, respectively, and their father pulled them out of school to teach them the jewel trade. They're in the store seven days a week, and they make house calls for a select few. They know their customers' tastes and financial status, and they know everyone's secrets as well. They know which married man is sleeping with what woman, which wife is covertly selling her wedding ring to finance her daughter's dowry, which mother-in-law has insisted on the cheapest, most flawed stones for her son's wife. Most of all, they know how to keep a straight face, show no surprise or disapproval or moral outrage at even their customers' most dreadful secrets, because every stone, of course, has a thousand stories to tell.

The Aramaic Brothers, Omid has found, never betray an emotion, and that is why he is so intrigued, that day when he sees the Younger Aramaic Brother smile in blissful wonder, about the source of the man's delight. Omid is too well bred to turn around abruptly and look for the object of this bewilderment, but he does feel an unmistakable shift in the mood within the room, as if a certain balance had suddenly been interrupted, and then he hears a woman greet the Older Aramaic Brother.

She has a deep, quiet voice, and she speaks in formal, deliberately distant language. She sits down at a table directly behind Omid and waits for the Older Aramaic Brother to open the safe. Here they are, they arrived last night, I wanted you to be the first to have a look, they're magnificent, really, five karats each, pink diamonds are rare, you know, the woman who wants to sell them is in debt and has to let them go. Omid turns around.

She is, of course, beautiful. She has slick black hair, white skin, dark eyes, and long legs and those other features that define what is most desirable in a woman. But she has something else as well—an air of aloofness, a strange confidence that is unnerving merely because it is so unusual in a woman, a seeming detachment from anything that might reach or hurt ordinary folk. She's wearing a white, sleeveless dress and a pair of snakeskin shoes. Her hair is pulled back from her face, exposing the side of her neck, the curve of her shoulder, the tip of her collarbone. She doesn't look at Omid at all, but he has the sensation that she knows he's there, staring at her. She picks up one square-shaped earring, then the other, holds them in the palm of her hand, puts them back on the table.

"Show me what else you have," she commands the Older Aramaic Brother. He goes into the back where the safe is, and returns with a box full of jewels. He lays them out, one by one, on the table before the woman. Here's a necklace that I made for the Shah's sister; she changed her mind at the last minute and took something else. Here's an original

Van Cleef, a Rolex with a diamond bezel, a pink sapphire bracelet that's an exact replica of what the sultan of Dubai gave to one of his wives. The woman looks bored.

"Thank you for this," she says, and picks up her purse. "I'll send word if I decide I want anything."

She shakes hands with the Older Aramaic Brother, nods at the younger one, and walks right past Omid without looking at him even once.

THE ARAMAIC BROTHERS tell Omid what little they know about her.

Her name is Niyaz. She's staying at the hotel with her lover—an older man with a sailor's skin and an endless fortune he has come upon purely by chance. They are both Iranian, but they live most of the year in Europe. She's Muslim; he started out as a Jew and then quickly crossed over—because of his money and his good looks—into that most coveted of all spheres, the place where a man's religion and ancestry are immaterial, where he is accepted and envied regardless of his beginnings. Long ago, he gave up home and country and bought a house in the mountains overlooking Lake Lugano in Switzerland. He spends his winters at Gstaad, his summers on a yacht on the Caribbean. He plays backgammon in the casinos of Monte Carlo, owns the largest private collection of Fabergé eggs. He speaks seven languages and knows his wines and he certainly knows his women as well: God knows he has slept with enough of them in his youth, and probably still does, but then he has managed, in his late forties, when other men lower their ambitions or simply retire back to their wives, to score his biggest conquest of all.

Rumor has it that Niyaz was only fourteen years old when she became the man's lover. She is, by all accounts, faithful to him in every way, but he hasn't married her and she doesn't seem to mind this, denies, in fact, that she would ever want to commit to him beyond the next hour or the next day. So she lives with him in sin without bothering to hide herself, and yet, instead of being stoned or spat on or at least shunned for her immoral ways, she is the darling of Tehran's high society and the object of admiration by both men and women, and there's no telling how she pulls this off, no way to make sense of it except to say that God loves some people more than others.

Outside the store, Omid leans against the white marble wall of the hotel lobby and lights a cigarette. Inhaling the smoke, he closes his eyes and waits to feel the tobacco sting before he exhales. He tells himself he should have more control of his senses, that he's a grown man about to be married and can't afford to feel like a teenage boy on his first encounter with a girl. He's seen beautiful women before—some even more beautiful than Niyaz—and he's barely been impressed by them beyond the moment, barely felt any desire for them at all. Even now, it isn't so much Niyaz's good looks that he thinks about as much as the detachment with which she treated everyone in the store, her aloofness when she had looked at the stones—none of this matters to me, I don't need *it* and don't need *you*, nothing anyone can say or do will ever touch me, I am, in every way imaginable, beyond reach.

This is just as well, Omid tells himself. Leave the woman to her lover and think about your own wedding that's coming up. But even as he determines never to look back on this day and at that woman, he knows there's more at play here than he's ready to believe: something inside him has moved, just a millimeter, but enough to ensure that he won't forget.

THIRTY-TWO WOMEN come to Bahar's house on the morning of the henna ceremony. They bring jars of quince syrup and milk and honey, rosewater and ceruse and lavender and henna. They stand in the yard singing old Persian love songs until Bahar is ready to leave, and then they sing louder and ululate as they walk with her in a procession that begins on Cyrus Street and ends at Silk Road Alley, where the women's public bath is located.

At the bath, they feed Bahar homemade sweets and cherry syrup, paint her hands and feet with henna, give her advice on how to conduct herself in her husband's bed, how to make sure she conceives many sons, how to win over a reluctant mother-in-law. At dusk, they send word for their men to come to the house—the bride is ready and the festivities are about to begin.

She wears a dress made from the Caspian green taffeta.

She sits in the courtyard amid a circle of women and young girls, on a chair she has decorated with white ribbons and paper flowers. Her mother drapes a hundred-year-old veil of embroidered silk on Bahar's head, puts a large glass bowl on her lap. One by one, the guests come up to Bahar and say a prayer. Amid loud singing and the shrill sound of women ululating, they press a silver coin on the bride's forehead. She smiles and thanks them, then tilts her head forward and lets the coin peel off her skin and fall into the bowl.

When all the guests have had a chance to make an offering, Omid takes his turn. He stands before Bahar inside the circle of women, under a shower of flower petals and white and green sugar drops while in the background her father plays the violin to a chorus of guests all singing "On This Moonlit Evening." He bends forward and kisses Bahar on the crown of her head, opens a little velvet box, and hands it to her with a blessing. May it bring you good fortune.

It's the bracelet he had seen in the Aramaic Brothers' jewelry store. Bahar gasps in delight, bounces to her feet, and throws her arms around Omid's neck—thank you thank you I know I'll wear it always in happiness and joy, we'll be the best couple in the world, you and I— but he only smiles and helps her put the bracelet on.

She pulls him by the hand—dance with me—but he's too composed, too detached from his surroundings to become embroiled in such manifestations. He stands aside and watches Bahar be swept away by the guests. She's dancing with her arms up in the air, the green of her dress a dark silver in the moonlight, and he can see that she's looking for him through the crowd, that she wants him to see her and perhaps even admire the way she looks, but this only makes him pull farther away. Slowly, he makes his way into the back of the yard, then out the door and into the street that is dark and quiet but for the sound of the festivities in the house. Outside the door, he stops and breathes the night air, looks at his watch, and wonders how much longer the party will go on, when it will be proper for him to leave. He's thinking about the sadness that filled his heart the minute Bahar opened the jewel box and saw the bracelet, the envy he felt at the sight of her unremitting joy, that he feels every time he hears her laugh in that unrestrained way of hers, or talk with that endless, indestructible faith she has—God only knows why—that she will love and be loved, desire and be desired. Until recently, Omid has never felt that kind of joy, never known it was possible. He's used to people who keep their emotions in check— tamed and measured and disguised till one can hardly tell the difference between happiness and sorrow, hope and despair. It's only when he saw Niyaz at the Aramaic Brothers' store that he felt the haze lift from his heart, felt the sting of desire—fierce and scalding—in his flesh.

Behind him in the house, the music spills off the violin that Bahar's father is still playing, runs into the alley like a narrow stream, and maybe the music is what attracts the dead to the world of the living, reminds them of their unfinished affairs and inconsolable mothers, because there he is again—the ten-year-old boy in the faded black shirt and torn pants Omid had seen in the courtyard the day he first spoke with Bahar. He's sitting on top of the neighbor's wall directly across the street, dangling his legs carelessly in the air, and smiling at Omid with that wide, exultant grin.

❧

WATCH HIM CAREFULLY—The Ghost Brother. There's a reason why he keeps coming back, not just to his parents' life but also to Bahar's life, a reason why he refuses to leave.

You might be called ignorant or stupid, lunatic or delusional for claiming you have seen him, or you might pretend you haven't seen him at all—enough ghost stories, we're living in the age of reason, the dead behave differently nowadays. Still, you only have to look at him to see the extent of his earnestness, the dogged innocence with which he haunts the living no matter how much they try to escape him or deny his existence, and you can't help but wonder what deep and unrequited longing brings him back.

He had had a name, of course, before he died, but hardly anyone remembers that now or even knew it when he was alive. He was just another one of the hundreds of little boys who grew up on the streets of South Tehran, playing soccer without shoes on and getting into trouble with his parents and teachers because he couldn't sit still long enough to learn anything. His hands were always blistered from the three dozen strikes of the principal's ruler he received almost daily, and his body was bruised and sore from beatings by bullies around town, but he had those onyx black eyes that smiled no matter what was happening to him, that hair that was straight and dark as a raven's wings, and he might have proven to be smart, even—had he lived long enough for anyone to put him to the test.

He had done reasonably well in school for a couple of years, but the more challenging the lessons became, the more distracted the boy grew, and after a while he was spending more time in the principal's office—standing on one leg, his face to the wall, his hands raised in the air until he turned blue in the limbs from poor circulation—than in the classroom. So he started to skip school, which must have suited the teachers just fine because they didn't report his absence to his parents. He had this ancient, rusted bicycle his father had bought for him years earlier from a neighbor who had moved up in the world and left Cyrus Street, and he took to riding the bike all around town, from dawn to dusk, seven days a week. By the time his parents found out what he was up to, he had already missed a month of school, and maybe this is why they let him be, didn't force him off the bike and back into the corner of the principal's office, which is where he would have ended up, no doubt about it, now that he was so far behind. They did warn him many times not to ride the bike on the street—there are too many cars these days; you'll get run over—and once or twice his father even confiscated the bike, chained it to the metal pump in the corner of the yard that in earlier days had pulled water from a well, and told him he could have it back only if he promised not to go into the street with it. But The Ghost Brother had cried and begged, and a few days later, there he was again, pumping the pedals with those skinny legs of his that never seemed to tire, and sometimes he even closed his eyes and stretched his arms out to the side as he rode, let the wind slap his face and chest and stomach till he looked, from a distance, like a bird in flight.

The man who hit him had only just learned to drive. He saw the boy riding in front of him and honked the horn to get him to move away. He also put his foot on the brake, and this is when he realized there *was* no brake; the car was old—get out of the way, boy, for God's sake, pull over, this thing's coming at you and I can't stop it can't stop it, even when I pull the hand brake, why do you think I'm honking the horn at you like this? But then there he was, the boy, riding his bike on the tip of the car's front fender, raised in the air, and tossed onto the asphalt, where his head cracked open like a ripe, red pomegranate.

WHAT SHOULD HAVE been the end, however, turned out to be only The Ghost Brother's beginning.

Thirty days after they buried him, his family gathered in the house for prayers when they heard the sound of bicycle wheels squeaking and of a rusted chain scraping against metal in the courtyard. They dropped their prayer books and rushed outside, saw nothing, and went back inside. They heard the sound again the next day, and the day after—in the courtyard first and then out in the alley, where it quickly faded into the din of cars and pedestrians, only to return late at night when the family was preparing to sleep.

"It's *him*, " Bahar had cried. She was six years old. "He's come back."

Her words had driven her mother to tears—if only it were so; it's only our ears that are ringing; this is the age of cars and television, the dead don't rise from the grave anymore—but Bahar was not one to be deterred by logic, and so she kept running after the sound, searching for her brother in every corner of the house, calling his name as if he were a stray pet she could guide back home.

One Friday afternoon, heat was melting the asphalt on the street and cracking open the watermelons in people's kitchens. Bahar's father lay face up on the floor of their "good room," trying to find in daylight the sleep that evaded him at night. Her mother sat at her sewing machine, making white cotton shirts that her rich clients' sons would wear in a few weeks when school started. Bahar heard the sound of the bicycle and ran into the yard, followed it to the fish pool that was round and deep and overrun with algae and frogs. The frogs croaked all night and hid in the algae during the day, but you could see the tadpoles—thousands of them—swimming in the water like a dark moving cloud. Bahar looked into the water and saw the dead boy.

It broke her heart to think that he was so alone, he had crossed the line with such audacity, had come home to seek the comfort of his mother's embrace.

Take my hand, she yelled, leaning toward the water. He smiled and clenched her wrist. She tried to pull him out, but instead she felt him tugging at *her*. She tried to free herself, resisted till she felt her scapula about to tear out of her back, but the boy was the stronger of the two; he lifted her off her feet, headfirst, and into the pool. Her lungs began to fill with water and her hair was becoming tangled in the viscous moss, and she was swallowing the tadpoles and the algae and still, The Ghost Brother kept pulling her in deeper.

And she would have drowned, make no mistake, but for her cousin Tamar, who happened to walk into the yard at that very moment, saw Bahar in the pool, ran up, and saved her from The Ghost Brother's mischief.

Come quick Bahar has drowned.

SHE WILL TELL OMID about this—her near-drowning, how it made her realize she wanted to live, to do something important with her life, leave a mark of herself after she was gone. He won't believe half of it, of course, and who can blame him? This isn't the kind of thing that would happen at the home of a "person of substance." Young boys who live on Pahlavi Avenue do not ride their bike when they are supposed to be in school. Even if they did, they wouldn't get hit by a car, or turn into a spirit and haunt their family. On Pahlavi Avenue, six-year-old girls know how to swim because they have pools—*real* ones, swimming pools with marble edges and tile floors—in their yards, and if anyone did fall in, the water would be clear blue and sparkling, free of algae and whatever else Bahar thinks she had swallowed that day and claims she vomited for a week after.

To Omid, the story will mean only that Bahar's parents were stupid and ignorant for not teaching their children how to swim. He will not understand why Bahar would even confess to him such an embarrassing truth. But she will go on about it nevertheless. She'll admire Tamar's intuition and her quick and levelheaded actions, bemoan the pain her own mother must have felt in the few minutes when she thought Bahar dead—the poor woman has just lost a son and now she's losing a daughter as well. She will even describe with regret how the stack of little white cotton shirts her mother had been working on was overturned in the rush to the courtyard, how her mother had had to wash and iron the shirts before they could be delivered to her clients.

Bahar will tell Omid of everyone else's pain but not of her own. She won't tell him that she became terrified of water after that day, that her parents didn't celebrate her return to life nearly as much as they had mourned their son's loss, that, given the choice, they would doubtless have wanted *him* to be the one who survived.

And she won't tell him this either—because she's afraid that he won't believe her, and even more afraid that he will: Deep in the pool, as she sank into the mud, Bahar had heard a silence so frightening, it would haunt her for the rest of her life. It wasn't the silence of the dead, she would think to herself later, because there is nothing quiet about dying and nothing quiet, either, about an afterworld that keeps spitting its inhabitants back into this one the way it did The Ghost Brother. There are worse fates, she believes, than dying, greater tragedies than not being. What Bahar had heard that day in the pool, what made her run for the rest of her life, was the sound of a voice that, though uttered, would not be heard.

I'm drowning here, look in the dark and see me.

THE WEDDING IS HELD at the Officers' Club downtown, in a gilded ball-room where, for many years, the Shah's closest friends and most trusted generals have gathered to celebrate important occasions. Omid's parents have not made a secret of their disregard for the bride-to-be, but nor have they spared any expense or effort in the planning and execution of the party: they have standards to uphold, friends to impress. They are part of a social hierarchy that depends on every member's ability to rise to, or above, the financial level attained by the others. So they've invited seven hundred guests, decorated the ballroom with red and pink roses grown especially for the occasion by the city's premier florist, who has a rose farm in the city of Esfahan where the best roses grow, and they're serving champagne and caviar at the reception preceding the dinner. Bahar's relatives have been assigned the area farthest from the stage, and that's where they've gathered, wide-eyed and envious, watching the "people of substance" and wondering out loud what stroke of luck, or genius, or chicanery has helped them rise to the station they now have.

The women on Omid's side of the family are all aglitter with silk and jewels. Their hair is pulled up in a beehive and sprayed stiff. Their eyes are painted in dark shadows, their eyebrows plucked to a single row of hairs. They have striking faces and heavy frames—the kind of beauty that has been fashionable in this part of the world for centuries but that has recently been challenged by French and American movie stars with tiny waists and skinny legs. Their men drink heavily and smoke cigarettes, discuss business and politics, joke with Omid that he's a man condemned, you're walking to the gallows and you don't even know it, son: these are the last moments of freedom you'll ever know, so go ahead and enjoy. They all wait for the bride.

She arrives in the silver car with the shiny fenders, driven by the same chauffeur who had yelled at her through the window that day on the Square of the Pearl Canon. A white silk runner stretches from the street up the front steps of the building and into the main hall. Along it, young women stand prepared with little gold braziers that hang from a chain, and in which the coal is red hot and ready. When the car arrives, they throw handfuls of wild rue seeds onto the coal, swing the braziers on their chains so that the smoke from the seeds rises around them like a fog. The driver bounds out of the car and opens the door for Bahar—be careful, ma'am, your gown is delicate let me help you out, just hold on to my hand.

Here she is, the lucky one, look at her gown, it's French lace with crystal beads, it must have cost a fortune to make, and what about that necklace, those Aramaic Brothers sure know how to set a large stone. She's barely seventeen but who knows what spell she's managed to cast on Omid, what poison or powder she had him consume so he would lose his mind in this way because, let's be frank, who but a madman would pick *her* among all the other girls he could have?

She walks up the steps.

Look at her, she's nothing special, that makeup doesn't suit her and she wobbles on her shoes, she obviously doesn't have practice walking on heels, it's the *little* things that give away a person's breeding, but then there you have it, it's all in the stars, a person's destiny is carved on her forehead before she's born and *this one*—this girl right here—is for sure blessed.

She enters the ballroom to cheers and gasps.

OK, so his parents have thrown a magnificent bash and they've given the girl some substantial jewelry, but haven't you heard, they've refused to buy Omid a house, they're sending him and the wife to live in that place they built years ago along the Alley of the Champions— the one they wouldn't live in for a single day, that they never even furnished because the neighborhood went to the dogs before construction was completed on the house, and *that,* my dear, is the true measure of what they think of the bride.

On the stage, a robust young woman dressed in black sings in a voice so powerful it fills the room like a mammoth wave and makes the glass tremble on the windows and the chandeliers. She calls to the groom to come and greet his bride and so Omid goes to Bahar, takes her hand, and leads her toward the dance floor.

"Come dance with the new couple," the singer commands the guests, and Bahar's head is spinning with joy, her heart aches with pride and her eyes strain to see everything, to take in every inch of the room and every person in it so that she will remember this moment and this night for the rest of her life.

The singer belts out a measured but heartrending story of two lovers who are separated by fate and will reunite only in death. Omid takes Bahar past the tables that are covered with red satin, the chairs draped in red gauze, the red and pink flowers everywhere. The lights are dim and the air is heavy with the scent of cigarette smoke and perfume as Bahar and Omid begin to dance. Around them, the crowd forms a wide circle. Bahar's mother emerges from the back, out of the shadows where she has been banished, and throws a handful of rose petals at her daughter. Someone else does the same thing, and a third person, and then the dance floor is covered with red and pink petals and still they dance, Omid in his black tuxedo, Bahar in her white dress and her white, transparent veil, dance in circles that, Bahar believes, will never end.

No one knows how my father met Niyaz again, or how he ended up becoming her lover. In time, he will tell Bahar and me about that first encounter in the Aramaic Brothers' store, and about the effort he made after that day to forget about Niyaz. But he won't speak of the months he spent searching for her, or of their first conversation, or how it was that he, who had never felt deeply for anyone, suddenly would do anything for a woman he barely knew. When he utters her name, the lines in his face will become deeper with pain and his eyes will darken with emotion, but he will never speak of her except as an absence—someone without whom nothing he has is worth the price of keeping.

Without the advantage of knowing the facts, Bahar and I will be left to fill the blanks on our own, to imagine who or what this other woman could be, how she could wreak such havoc upon our lives. The mystery infuses Niyaz with a power we can't beat: One minute she's a stranger in a store my father has walked into. The next minute she owns us all.

PART II

THE HOUSE ON JUNE STREET sits on the corner of a lopsided alley that curves and twists and limps along for three narrow blocks before it ends abruptly against the front door of the Spanish Academy for the Arts in Tehran. The school is in a converted mansion that had once served as a residence for the wives and children of Fath Ali Shah Qajar—the second monarch of the Qajar dynasty who had, in his day, kept a hundred and sixty wives and more than a thousand eunuchs in his harem at the Palace of Roses. He had also kept a hundred tailors, countless biographers and jewelers, and a host of astrologers and soothsayers, whose job it was to determine the most opportune moment for every move the Shah ever made. Fath Ali Shah had fathered so many children from so many wives, he went his entire life without ever setting eyes on many of them, and still he sat, year after year on his throne in the Palace of Roses, and watched the procession of virgins hunted down and brought to him by his emissaries from every part of the country. Because he was a good Muslim who believed in the sanctity of the flesh, he would not touch the virgins without having married them first. Islam, however, allowed a man only three "permanent" wives. The others had to be married on a "temporary" basis—which, for an ordinary man, might mean anything from fifteen minutes to a lifetime. The Shah, of course, married all his temporary wives with a ninety-nine-year contract—not because he had any use for them, really, after the first few nights, but because he could not allow any other man to touch what had once been his. He built the mansion that later became the Spanish Academy in order to house his older, more discarded wives. For the wives' servants, he built a row of cramped and airless houses behind the mansion and along the Alley of the Champions, and he continued to marry virgins and send them away until he had produced sixty sons, and forty-eight daughters, and then he went and died, leaving his offspring to fight over his empty throne.

The fight over succession was settled by the British, who had controlled Iran and stolen its resources for far too long to allow a raggedy bunch of princes to determine its future, but the struggle over the Shah's inheritance—money and jewels and land—went on for decades. Over time, the abandoned wives' mansion was sold to the Russians, then to the French, and then the Americans, who were the last of the great powers to help themselves to Iran's oil reserves. Then the mansion was purchased by a middle-aged German couple who had come to Tehran by way of Buenos Aires—ostensibly on a "diplomatic mission," though they barely ever left the house or received any guests—and who brought with them seventeen trunks full of old linen and expensive art, a teenage daughter who claimed she was the world's leading dancer of the Argentine tango, and a ninety-year-old parrot who spoke German and Spanish like a native.

By then, the Alley of the Champions was overtaken by down-and-out immigrants from the provinces who came to Tehran looking for work, bankrupt merchants who were hiding from their creditors, and old opium addicts who preferred the dark, airless houses built in the last century to the more modern ones with big windows where the light invaded their peace. Where the alley met June Street, there was a one-acre, square lot where Mr. Arbab had built a house in the years before the Second World War. He had intended for the house to be a residence for himself and his family, but he never did occupy it for even a single night because construction was interrupted first by the Second World War and then by massive shortages of building materials that resulted from the Allied occupation, and by the time the house was finished, Mr. Arbab had become too rich to live anywhere near the Alley of the Champions. So he left the house empty and locked up, and he might have sold it at some point or simply left it to drown in dust, but Omid went and married a girl without a recognizable name or a dowry worth keeping, and then his parents decided that June Street was exactly what their unworthy son deserved—let the fool live downtown in the swarm of cars and donkeys, of sidewalk vendors and squatters who make their home in the open skeletons of buildings under construction, who cook their food on open fires, wash their laundry in the gutter and hang it out to dry from exposed metal beams. Let him and the girl step out of the house every morning and find seven beggars already camped out on the sidewalk with their sick infants and crippled spouses on display, pleading meekly for help—I'm hungry, sir, God will love you if you feed my children, and if you don't, He'll curse you and your offspring, your sons will go blind and your daughters will become whores.

Bahar, at first, does not know that Omid has been given the house as punishment for marrying her. She doesn't understand that her in-laws have snubbed her by sending her to live on June Street. It's yet another sign of her humble origins that she is enthralled by the house from the moment she first sees it, is actually grateful to the Arbabs for having allowed her and Omid to live in it. It will be some time before she understands why Mrs. Arbab sniffs and looks away, or why Omid's brother and his wife smile so smugly every time Bahar thanks them for the house. Even *this*, they think, is more than she could have aspired to.

❧

FROM THE STREET, all you can see is the red brick wall that surrounds the garden, the giant mulberry and persimmon trees, and the top floor of the house, which rises higher than the wall. Inside are three bedrooms, a living room with a gold-leaf painted ceiling, a dining room with a round balcony that overlooks the yard. There are porcelain tubs in the bathrooms, a fireplace in the kitchen, sunlight everywhere you look: all the doors, even the one leading into the kitchen, are made of etched and mirrored glass. They reflect not only the inside of each room and the light from all the windows, but also the images cast in the other doors—creating an endless echo of shapes and colors that go on for as far as the eye can see.

Bahar walks through the house with her arms stretched out like wings, makes pirouettes under the skylight in the hallway, puts flowers on the mantelpiece and on the side tables next to her and Omid's bed. She walks with Ruby—the maid who is married to Hassan Agha, the chauffeur, and who gives him more grief than any one person should have to endure—to Drug Store—the newly opened market on Perse-polis Avenue where you can find the latest in imported American goods. She buys Revlon nail polish and a subscription to a pirated translation of *Les Misérables* that will be delivered to June Street in weekly installments by a young man with light blue eyes and a Turkish accent.

She sets a table with new china and lace, wears high heels and a short dress, sits down with Omid for their first home-cooked meal.

They've been married a week.

She tells him she can't wait to see her family members' faces when they come to the house to visit, can't wait to tell her friends about her new life when she goes back to school next fall. She says she's going to study hard and be a good wife, she's confident she'll get admitted to university even though the entrance exam is designed to keep out all but the smartest and most hardworking students. She says she'll make Omid proud.

"I don't know what you mean," he interrupts.

"I mean I'll do my best in every area," she explains enthusiastically. "I'll be a good wife, so our families will be proud of us.

"And I'll be a good student as well," she continues, "I'll get good marks—"

He interrupts her again. He says there's no question of her going back to school, or going to university; she's going to be his wife, stay at home, tend to her responsibilities, and do whatever it is that wives are supposed to do.

He tells her he really has no intention of having her "people" come to their house—they serve no purpose, he says, bring no social or economic ties that could be of use, they're ghetto folk, that's all, and best left there.

She's still smiling when he says this, because she hasn't had time to interpret the hardness in his eyes. She hasn't seen what has been obvious from the start, and now she's stunned by what she hears, by the stern expression with which he utters those words—I'm going to say it once and only *once*, open your ears and learn quickly.

He goes back to eating his rice.

She draws a breath from somewhere far away and mumbles through her astonishment, "I'm going to be a teacher."

He keeps eating as if he hasn't heard her at all, or heard something that doesn't merit an answer.

"I've always wanted to be a teacher," she says.

It occurs to him that she may not be the kind of girl who's easily "trained," who surrenders a fight. He thinks about the day he saw her on the street, how she had stood, impervious, before the driver and his barrage of insults.

"You're going to be my *wife*," he answers, and hopes she'll understand the definition. She doesn't.

"I have to see my family."

He frowns now and puts his fork down on his plate, wipes his lips with the napkin on his lap, and pushes his chair away from the table.

"You're my *wife*," he says. "You'll make your own family." The finality is his voice makes her shudder.

"We're a modern couple," she says. "We can do things differently."

He looks at his watch and wonders how much longer this dinner should go on, when it will be proper for him to get up and go read the afternoon paper in his study. He tells Bahar he has never thought about being part of a "couple," and isn't about to consider it now, or he wouldn't have selected a girl so different from himself in upbringing and background.

He sees the devastation that his words have brought to Bahar and is surprised to find that he's moved by this. He wants to tell her it's going to be all right, things will work out one way or another, but he knows this would be a lie, she's in for a rude awakening—this girl who has never left South Tehran but who dreams of Caspian rain. For now, he decides not to engage her in any more conversation, tells himself, what's the difference, he's already married her, she'll just have to learn the ways of civilized folk and become a person he can take with him to parties.

But she won't give up.

"I thought I'd finish school," she says, and her obstinacy makes him shudder. "I've promised myself I'd *become* somebody."

He glares at her. As moved as he is by her vulnerability, Omid can also feel his own helplessness grow larger.

"I want to *become* someone," she says again, and this is more than he's going to put up with.

"You've done that," he says, "by marrying *me*."

She sits at the table with her red painted nails and her dark eyelashes. She's staring at the roses she has cut that afternoon, thinking about the meaning of what has just happened, and already, you can see the light fading in her eyes.

AFTER HE'S MARRIED, Omid looks for Niyaz everywhere he goes. He finds himself accepting invitations he might otherwise have turned down, arriving early and staying late on the off chance that she might walk into the place as she had walked that day into the store. Every once in a while, he hears her name mentioned by women who utter it in awe, or by men who despair because they know they will never so much as lay a finger on her. He stops at the Aramaic Brothers' store whenever he's in the area, and they know why this is, know he has come to find out if she is in town and staying at the hotel, and so they give him the best advice they can—this one is beyond reach, my friend, who can compete with that lover of hers? And maybe it's best this way, maybe some things *should* stay out of reach.

Omid believes them, but he can't stop himself from searching. He takes Bahar to most of the gatherings he is invited to—they're newly-weds, and she's eager to go along, to meet everyone and make friends—but she only manages to embarrass him with her lack of sophistication, the small and large differences that exist between her and the other wives. She wears the fancy dresses and shoes she has bought with his money, but she lacks the poise and the elegance to carry them off, moves more like a schoolgirl at recess than like a lady holding court. Her skirts wrinkle the moment she sits down, and her makeup is either smudged or too heavy, but it isn't only her appearance that gives her away; it's something deeper and more difficult to define—a certain zeal she has for things in general and for Omid in particular, a fervor she demonstrates for being with him, not only in person but also in spirit—we're a team, you and I, and together we are going to build a life more beautiful than anyone has ever lived. It's as if they had never had the conversation that had so disappointed her; as if she had no inkling of what he plans for her, or how little he's prepared to give her.

She's too enthusiastic when meeting new people, too expansive in her praise of them. She shares her thoughts about Omid and their marriage with the other women at the parties they go to, stands with them as they smoke and drink and smile absently at her over-the-top excitement, or at the many stories she tells about her strange relatives and their substandard lives—tells them, one can only assume, because she doesn't realize how strange her people are and how bad they make her look. That's lovely for you, my dear, very quaint, the women condescend, but Bahar can see the disdain in their eyes, so she becomes deflated and confused and aware that she has extended herself too much and in vain.

Still, it doesn't occur to her to keep a distance from those women, to learn to treat them with the same cynicism with which they treat each other. She won't stop talking about her family as if they were people she should be proud of, won't stop heaping praise on her in-laws as if they weren't aware of their own perfection. She's innocent and sincere—yes, willing to help anywhere she can, to forgive a snub and respond with kindness because that's what people do when they're from the ghetto or barely out of it; they *expect* to be snubbed—and this may be a quality that would be forgiven in another time and place, but among Tehran's new elite, who have forgotten their own ghetto past too well, it only provokes condescension.

Your friends' wives look down on me, she tells Omid in the car as they ride home from those parties. Her voice then is small and bewildered, and she tucks her hands between her knees when she speaks, looks down at her shoes like a fourth grader before the school principal. They don't think I measure up, she says, and Omid knows this is true. She's a good girl, and she means well, but he can't really blame the other wives: Bahar's behavior makes her an automatic target, and at any rate, none of this concerns him, really, all he wants is for her to fade away and leave him to deal with his own frustration over having wasted yet another evening looking for Niyaz. So he throws a tired glance at Bahar and offers the only bit of wisdom that comes to mind: Don't try so hard.

SHE TAKES THAT ADVICE to heart and tries to overcome the sense of foreboding that descends, like tiny particles of dust visible only through a shaft of light, every time she and Omid are alone together. She tries to engage him in conversation and finds that he's distracted, tries to get close and feels him recoil. She smiles at him, and when he smiles back, his eyes are empty of emotion. He does not see her, she knows. Doesn't even *try* to see her.

How do you become a star if no one is looking?

Every few weeks, she brings up the matter of the school again, and he has to repeat what he's already told her—it's out of the question, it's never going to happen, just look around and you may understand what I'm telling you. He's not being cruel or unusually strict with her, he believes, he's only doing what everyone else does—what should, in fact, be done. No self-respecting husband with his kind of money would allow his wife to go to school—to sit in a classroom all day when she should be at home, doing whatever it is that wives do. He can't let her go to university and become too smart, or turn into a raging communist, as most students seem to do these days. He can't let her work because that would make people think he's got financial woes—why else would a woman leave her children and her maids and the daily luncheons that keep her so busy, only to go be an employee somewhere else?—which would damage the family's social standing.

Bahar, too, knows that Omid is right. She knows he's never promised her anything he hasn't delivered. Yet she can't let go of the notions she has nursed in her head all her life, and she certainly can't remain passive and accept the fate he's handing down to her.

After every setback, she tells herself to be patient, to give him time to adjust to married life, and to think about what he will and will not permit her to do.

She calls her mother on the phone and says that all is well in her new life. She asks about The Unmarried Sister, who has finally given up on dreams of normalcy and enrolled in a secretarial course at the local branch of the ORT American Academy for Girls. She asks about Jadid-al-Islam, who has recently begun to sport a beard and to wear an aba, so that he looks every bit like the mullahs in his wife's family, and he acts like them too—plays with worry beads all day long and sticks his chin to his chest when he speaks, rolls his eyes up in their sockets, and fixes his weird and unnerving gaze on his interlocutor as he drags every word for emphasis. No doubt, her mother speculates, he's preparing for his father-in-law's death, transforming himself into as suitable an heir as possible. And he's preparing for his own father's death as well, because he knows he'll inherit what little the man may leave behind— the wife and other children be damned. It's the law of the land: the person who converts to Islam becomes the sole heir of even his most extended family members. You could have a third cousin die, and he could have a hundred sons and grandsons, and still, you get to inherit every bit of the man's money if you're a convert.

They talk, too, about The Pigeon Sister, who is spending more time than ever locked up on the roof. We must save her from The Psychiatrist, Bahar tells her mother, but she knows that there's no way to do this, that her family has no influence with him and that community leaders—the rabbis and elders and all those men who have so much to say about every subject in the world—won't get involved in "domestic" matters. Civilians don't believe in telling a man how to discipline his wife, and the police would laugh if anyone asked them to interfere with a husband's authority. The only way The Pigeon Sister would be saved from her husband is if he killed her, or if he threw her out of the house and back to her parents', where she would spend the rest of her life in infamy, unable to see her children or to look other women in the eye.

Some things, Bahar's mother laments, never change.

Bahar has heard her mother say this all her life. She's heard other people say it as well. It's a fact, everyone knows it: happiness is transient; tragedy is what this world was founded on—how else to explain all the horror, all the wars and famines and betrayal and backstabbing you read about in the Torah and the Koran?

She hangs up the phone and struggles to contain the sense of panic that fills her every time she thinks about her own future. She spends hours talking to Ruby, who knows Omid's family inside and out and doesn't mind telling Bahar how it is—you're green and inexperienced, ma'am, those people are laughing at you and they'll keep laughing unless you learn quickly how to become just like them. She tries to teach Bahar to cook Muslim-style (meaning with more elegance), tells her she must get rid of her ghetto accent, to stop going on about school and that foolishness of being a teacher, if you want to have a happy marriage, learn how to make your husband happy in bed.

Bahar calls Angel, her friend since first grade, who will understand her determination to pursue her dreams. She hasn't seen or heard from Angel since the night of the henna ceremony, when she stood in a corner of the yard for an hour and then left without saying good-bye. She skipped the wedding without an explanation and hasn't called even once after that, but Bahar knows they're still the best of friends.

Angel's mother answers the phone and says, Angel is busy, call back another time. She says the same thing the next time Bahar calls, and again the time after that. One afternoon, Bahar asks Hassan Agha to drive her to Angel's house.

She wears a pretty dress and high heels, orange Revlon lipstick, hoop earrings. She wants her friend to see her happy and composed, wants her approval, perhaps even her admiration. She rings the doorbell and waits, rings again and announces herself in the intercom.

Angel comes to the door. She looks tired and pale, like she has been studying all night. She doesn't invite Bahar into the house.

"We can't be friends anymore," she says without introduction.

She's standing with her hands folded on her chest, and she looks pleased with herself, looks like she has waited for some time to deliver this punch.

"We have nothing in common," she proceeds to explain. "You're a married woman."

She says this as if being married were a sin.

"My parents don't want me to talk to you anymore. They say you'll corrupt me with the things you know about men."

She's punishing Bahar for leaving Cyrus Street—marrying above herself and her friends.

"Besides," she says, "I'm off to university next year. You'll always be just a wife."

BAHAR TRIES, but can't resign herself to not going back to school. She takes driving lessons and reads pirated translations of American novels that she buys from Drug Store, hires an English tutor, learns to sew by following instructions in *Burda* magazine. She invents every excuse possible to explain to her family why she hasn't invited them to her new house or gone back to Cyrus Street even once since she got married. She asks her in-laws to dinner and spends three days preparing. They arrive late and leave early, conduct private conversations in her living room without allowing her to join in. They comment on every flaw, every shortcoming in her presentation. These are all things she should have learned from her mother, they tell her to her face, things that come naturally to a woman with the right kind of upbringing.

She invites other guests as well—Omid's friends and their wives, his cousins and business associates—and tries even harder to do things as they should be done. Still, her guests can detect "the Jewishness" in her food, in her manners and accent and choice of words, and this puts them off and makes them offer excuses the next time she invites them. June Street, they say on the phone in the blithe and informal manner they have adopted since they have become rich, is too far downtown for us to travel at night. There are too many potholes in the asphalt, too many beggars knocking on the car window every time you stop at a light. Air pollution is worse down there; a person's clothes will be coated with soot the minute he steps out of the car. And anyway, my dear, I understand Omid himself is hardly ever at home.

Her heart sinks at that last comment, but she contains the hurt, suppresses the doubt, with the same dogged hopefulness she has upheld throughout her life. One morning, she goes to Omid as he stands shaving in the bathroom.

"I'm seventeen years old," she says. "All my friends are still in school."

He's bare-chested in front of the mirror, using an old-fashioned razor, which he prefers to the electric ones because it gives his skin a smoother feel. They've been married six months.

He pulls the razor down across his cheek in a slow, straight line. Then he turns on the faucet and rinses the blade.

"Your friends are not married."

He's not angry or impatient—just detached.

"Yes, I know," she says, and then stops to think. She's standing behind him and to the right, so they can see each other in the mirror, and she's holding a silver hairbrush that she picked up without thinking, to contain her nervousness. She presses the handle in her hand and struggles to find the words to express what she feels.

"I'm lonely," she says, as if this should bear any consequence for him. "I think I should be in school."

He turns on the faucet and rinses the blade again.

"You decided to get married."

There is a finality in his voice, an unfeeling, indifferent conclusiveness that is greater than the sum of his words.

She swallows hard and shifts her weight on her legs. Around the handle of the hairbrush, her nails dig into her palm, but she doesn't feel them at all.

"Yes, I know," she says, "but I think there is a lot I can do if only I were given the chance. I think I can be a good teacher."

"I don't care what you *think* you can do," he answers, and this brings tears to her eyes, makes her despise him suddenly and with all her heart. "Whatever it is, you'll have to do it at *home*."

He doesn't say this with any passion, or rage, or vindictiveness. He probably won't remember this conversation an hour from now. It's not important enough—what happens to her—for him to dwell on at length, and this is precisely what he wishes she would understand, that he chose her because he wanted a *wife*, maybe a child or two—so he would fulfill whatever his role was supposed to be as a husband, so he would, once and for all, settle the matter of his domestic life and know that he'll never be challenged, or disturbed, or called upon to be part of a "couple," or to rescue anyone from "loneliness."

"I didn't think marriage would be like this," she says. "I thought we were going to make a life *together*."

He turns around, suddenly animated, and snaps.

"If you're disappointed," he yells loud enough for the servants to hear, "pack your bags and go home."

She throws the brush at him. It flies past his face and lands on his image in the mirror, then drops into the sink. A minute later, the mirror begins to crack.

THERE'S A KNOCK at the door, then a man's voice asking if he might have a word. Niyaz looks at her watch. It's two in the afternoon, and she's headed to the beauty shop to prepare for her evening with The Lover.

She opens the door on the Older Aramaic Brother. He's wearing a linen shirt and no tie or jacket, like he's going to spend the day at the beach instead of a jewelry store. But that's how he dresses all the time; he abhors formal clothes, and his clients are used to this by now. Niyaz hasn't been to the store since she returned, but he's smiling at her as if they only saw each other a day ago.

"I've brought you something," he says, and hands her a black velvet jewel box.

His voice is neutral, devoid of any overtones and insinuations.

"I think you'll like it," he says.

She looks at the box in her hand, then at the Aramaic Brother. He knows what her question is, but he's not answering. His silence means he can't reveal the identity of the person who sent the gift.

"They're good stones," he says. "I'd keep them if I were you."

She puts the box in her purse and walks to the elevator with the Aramaic Brother. She's been back in Tehran for only a week, staying at the Hilton, but the city has gotten to her already. She feels bored and overwhelmed at once. She doesn't like the constant intrusions, the small-town mentality that drives so much of the conversation and the activity of the people here. She runs into an acquaintance wherever she goes; her phone rings all the time with one invitation or another; The Lover, who is patient and attentive when they're alone together in Europe, stays away entire nights, playing cards and backgammon with old friends.

In the lobby, she shakes the Older Aramaic Brother's hand, then walks out to the car. She rolls up the window and closes her eyes, which are already burning from the smog. She thinks about the beauty shop—a gaudy, overcrowded new salon owned by a flagrantly homo- sexual prince, heir to yet another fallen dynasty, who prefers the com- pany of rich, beautiful women to the day-to-day drudgery of managing the fortune his father has left him. He especially loves to see Niyaz, sends for her, in fact, as soon as he learns that she's in Tehran, extending every favor and courtesy without ever letting her pay. She thinks about the evening ahead, how it will be exactly the same as last night or the night before: a large, glittering party in some mansion or other, beau- tiful women wearing enormous jewels and gowns in the latest fashion from Europe, men with fantastic fortunes who can have any woman they want, a host of singers and musicians and film and television actors who get paid just to attend the party, a back room with large pil- lows on the ground, bubbling hookahs, unlimited amounts of opium.

She opens the box. There's a pair of square, pink diamond ear- rings—she recognizes them from the last time she was at the store— but no card. She knows, from the look on the Aramaic Brother's face, that they're not from The Lover. It's not the first time she has received such a gift from an admirer who wants to impress her with his wealth and generosity before he makes his identity known. In the past, she has always returned the gifts, never even felt curious about who had sent them. This time, she finds herself wondering what they'll look like against her skin, how The Lover will feel when he sees them on her and realizes she has accepted a gift from another man.

She thinks back to the day she saw these earrings at the store. She has a vague recollection of a man in a dark suit—a shadow, really, and maybe she's imagining it now, but she can almost feel the intensity of his gaze, how he had made a point of not looking at her at first, and then wouldn't stop staring.

She puts the earrings on and looks at herself in her compact mirror. Against her skin, the stones take on a darker hue.

THE DAY OF THE FIGHT, Omid doesn't come home for lunch. Bahar waits till two o'clock, then calls the office. His secretary is a young Muslim woman who resents having to work at all, and resents even more the fact that she's working for Jews. She tells Bahar she has no idea where her husband is or why he hasn't come home or called—I only work here, I don't babysit my boss, but my guess is, if he hasn't told you where he is, it's because he doesn't want you to know.

Frustrated, Bahar goes into her bedroom and lies down for her afternoon sleep. She dreams she's back in her parents' house, lying face up on the dirt floor of the yard with Angel beside her. They're talking about what they're going to do when they're grown women, how their lives will be different from those of their mothers or even their older sisters. A few steps away, Bahar's father is playing the violin. Bahar keeps talking to her friend, but the violin becomes louder and more insistent every minute, and soon enough, it drowns out her voice completely.

She wakes up and gets out of bed. She can still hear the music from her dream, and it bothers her so much she turns the tap on in the bathroom and throws cold water on her face so as to sever the ongoing connection with the dream. But the music is still there, like a memory she can't shake off, or something that has overrun the confines of the past and is intruding into the present. It's much louder, in fact, much more intricate and masterful and harmonious than any song her father has ever played, and then she realizes that it's not a memory at all, that it's coming from the outside—from the direction of the Alley of the Champions—so she goes to the window and looks outside.

In the alley, a few people are standing at their doorsteps, exchanging baffled looks and peering incredulously at the yellow house, where, for over two decades, the inhabitants have maintained an eerie, exaggerated silence. Still others are coming out of their homes, and after a while they all gather and talk. Then a man breaks away from the group. He's been appointed as emissary—let's find out what this is all about, this music is strange, it sounds like a woman screaming in pain, or maybe in delight, but either way, it's too loud and rather shameful.

He goes up to the yellow house and rings the doorbell. He waits, rings again. When no one answers, he starts banging with his fist, looking back at the two dozen others who've slowly approached the house but maintain a safe distance in case one of those Nazis overreacts to a simple call by a neighbor. At last, the door opens. A woman appears in a long dress and exchanges a few words with the caller, then closes the door. The man looks baffled. He rubs his head and walks back to the group.

An hour later, the news is all over town: The Nazi couple has died. They have left all their affairs in order and chosen the time and manner of their death. They killed their parrot first, then drank a glass of poison each.

The young woman—ostensibly their daughter, but who really knows?—was in the house while all this was going on. She knew of the plan ahead of time, and approved wholeheartedly—why wait for illness and old age to destroy you when you can go out in style?

She has called the undertakers and doesn't need help from the neighbors.

She appreciates the sentiments, thank you, but she's not, at all, chagrined by the loss.

The music she's playing is an Argentine tango.

✤

AT HOME, Bahar can barely get Omid to speak to her. He comes and goes more or less like any other husband, sits at the table and eats the meals she has cooked, curtly answers questions. He takes her to some parties, goes to others alone. He knows that she feels isolated and unfulfilled—she makes no secret of this: she must have told him two dozen times—but he doesn't care. He wants her to stop whining about seeing her family—I've told you that they're not welcome here and that I won't go to their place either, what about this don't you understand?—but of course, she doesn't. Every Friday morning she fights Omid for permission to go to Cyrus Street for Sabbath dinner. Every Saturday, she declares she's going to invite her family to the house, threatens to do so against Omid's wishes—you're their son-in-law, you owe them the respect, they're people just like everyone else.

Obedience, subservience, forbearance.

One Friday afternoon, she puts on a new dress, picks up an expensive handbag, and asks Hassan Agha to drive her to Cyrus Street. She has been married a year.

In the car, she puts her knees together and leans her legs to one side, the way those glamorous women do in the movies, settles into the back seat for the ride. She wonders what Omid will do in retaliation for her disobedience. She knows he won't beat her; he's too refined for that. Her own father had beaten her mother in the early years of their marriage, and he still does from time to time, when she says something stupid or talks back to him. Her father is not a cruel man. He doesn't hurt with the intention to inflict real injury. And he's not violent like The Psychiatrist who, sooner or later, is bond to kill his wife or cause her permanent brain damage.

Some "people of substance" beat their wives as well, bt they do so behind closed doors, secure in the knowledge that the wives will keep their secret—will deny it, in fact, if word gets out to the community through a disloyal servant—and they know enough to understand this isn't a civilized way to behave, and at any rate, Omid is too dispassionate a person, too detached from whatever concerns Bahar, to lose his temper in that way.

So she knows Omid won't beat her, but he is, after all, a husband. Defying him will have consequences. And yet, as fearful as she is of Omid's response, Bahar is more afraid of the confinement to which he has damned her so casually.

Close to her parents' house, she sprays herself with perfume and lights a cigarette. She doesn't really smoke and doesn't know how to inhale, but she wants her hair and skin to smell like that of the other women in Omid's circle—the ones who wear Tufts hair spray and Clinique makeup from America; who live, it seems, only to be beautiful; who spend their afternoons preparing for the evening and their evenings charming one another, then ride home at dawn in their fancy cars, close the curtains in their bedroom, and sleep through daylight.

In South Tehran, she watches the street slip past the car and feels her heart expand with joy at the thought that she is no longer *from* here— that she has escaped, can ride into and out of it anytime she wants.

She gets out of the car at the top of the alley that leads from Cyrus Street to her parents' house. She tells Hassan she'll walk the rest of the way.

"As you wish, madame."

He stands with his heels together and his back erect, head tilted slightly down to avoid eye contact. "I'll be right here when you come back."

He watches her walk away.

"Be careful with the potholes," he warns without irony, as if he didn't know she grew up here.

Bahar ambles slowly toward old neighbors' homes and the groups of children who have seen the car and want to know who's in it. She kisses every one of the women on both cheeks, greets the men with utmost correctness, ruffles the children's hair. She spends an eternity inquiring about the health and well-being of each family. She can tell she's looked up to and envied, yes, but she can also sense the resentment, the not-so-subtle reproach—you're not one of us anymore, we don't trust you—with which her old neighbors address her: "We're well, thank God. Can't complain, though I'm sure *you* are much better, then again, I see your husband's not with you, I don't believe he's ever come to see your parents after you got married, does he think he's too good for these parts, or is this a new way of doing things, a young married woman going places by herself?"

It's a strange and unforgiving club—this world Bahar has left behind: the only way to belong is to be damned.

THE UNMARRIED SISTER opens the door and offers Bahar a contemptuous smile.

"You're overdressed," she says. "You must have thought you were going somewhere special."

Their mother rushes out of the kitchen.

"Take your husband to the good room," she says in her most sophisticated accent, because she thinks Omid is there also, "I'll bring some pomegranate juice." She wipes her hands on the front of her dress, pushes her hair off her face, and does her best to look presentable to her son-in-law.

"Her *husband* isn't with her," The Unmarried Sister remarks. The words are so loaded, they obviate the need for further explanation.

The Seamstress looks puzzled, but only for a second. Then her shoulders droop and her chest deflates and she says, to no one in particular, "Naturally. It's *beneath* him."

Though they haven't seen each other for a year, The Seamstress doesn't kiss Bahar in greeting. She hardly ever kisses her daughters. She'll kiss other women, once on each cheek, as is customary, but she has been angry with her daughters all her life—angry because they are girls, and she knows they'll disappoint her—and she carries this into every contact and conversation they have with each other. She just goes back into the kitchen and resumes rolling garbanzo-and-meat balls with fresh cumin and dried lime. She's slightly overweight and aging badly. She has a round face, thinning hair, large brown spots on her once-fair skin. Her breasts sag and her hands have become wide and masculine-looking. They grab hold of things—a raw chicken, a set of plates, the little box of makeup Bahar has bought at Drug Store and wrapped carefully, and which she gives her now as a gift—firmly but without grace.

She turns the box over and examines it. "You're still wasting money on useless things," she says by way of thanks.

Bahar takes off her expensive dress and changes into one of her mother's loose-fitting gowns. In the kitchen, she chops parsley and dill and spring onions, mixes them into white rice and sets them on the fire to steam-cook. She cuts the feet and heads off chickens that have been kosher-killed and plucked only hours earlier, and fries them with garlic and lemon juice. Her father is in the "good room," drinking glass after glass of hot tea brewed with cardamom and counting his debts on an abacus. He talks to himself out loud—about how his life would have been different if he had managed to raise better sons, forced The Opera Singer to find work instead of posing like a dandy without a dime, prevented Jadid-al-Islam from converting, never bought that bicycle for The Ghost Brother. He asks Bahar to find a husband for The Unmarried Sister, refers to Omid in the formal language reserved for strangers or people who command great respect.

There are only four of them in the house, but they stack fifteen plates on the small dining table: The Opera Singer will surely want to eat once he gets home from the Sorrento Café, and The Psychiatrist might bring The Pigeon Sister and their children, and besides, it's Sabbath, you never know who's going to drop by unannounced; you can't offend your guests by being unprepared, or starting to eat before they've arrived. The Seamstress brings out a tray of garbanzo-and-meat balls, which she has cooked in chicken soup and sprinkled with powdered black lime, then wrapped into lavosh bread with fresh basil and radishes. Traditional Jewish-Iranian food, served on Sabbath, and that most Muslims have never seen or tasted.

They wait.

At nine o'clock, The Opera Singer arrives. He never has enough money to pay for food at the Sorrento Café, and the waiters won't let him linger at the table for as long as he wants. "And besides," they remind him every week, "aren't you a Jew? Don't you people eat at home Friday nights?"

When he sees Bahar, he beams with genuine pleasure.

"*There* she is!" he announces in his tenor's voice, "*The one who got away.* We thought you had abandoned us for good." He laughs good-naturedly and pulls a chair up to the table, starts to eat before any prayers have been said.

Bahar has changed back into her party dress.

"Nice dress," he observes. "Sit down, I want to tell you about the important person I met today at Sorrento."

He's mentioned meeting "an important person" countless times in the past, and he's completely sincere, not at all bothered by the fact that he has been meeting "important persons" now for upward of a decade and they have yet to discern his enormous talent and help him become famous.

The Seamstress goes into the yard to look for possible visitors. She comes back with two of her husband's aunts—widows who can't bear to spend Sabbath alone. She packs some food and takes it to the house of a sick neighbor. She has called The Pigeon Sister's house twice already, and no one picks up, which could mean they're on their way over, but it's getting late, he's probably just locked her up again and pulled the cord on the phone. At last, Bahar's father says the prayers for wine and bread, and then everyone sits down. They eat quietly, with only the sound of their spoons touching the edges of the plate, and even The Opera Singer takes a break from talking for a while. They're thinking about The Pigeon Sister, wondering if she's hungry, if her children are afraid, or alone, or begging their father to let his wife back in. They're thinking about Jadid-al-Islam, who is probably spending the evening with his wife's mullah relatives, cursing Jews louder than anyone else in order to prove he's a good Muslim.

Bahar's visit has reminded everyone that nothing has changed on Cyrus Street or in their family. One of them has married up, it is true, but the glow of her triumph won't reach as far as they might have hoped. It has always been like this for the Jews of South Tehran: every turning point has led to another loss; every expectation, to more disappointment. They can't even escape their destinies in death, they're thinking, just look over there and you'll see the proof—The Ghost Brother who's come to call again, who's standing in the door frame, looking hungry and tired and so alone that it makes you want to cry. You know what he wants is for you to ask him to come in, to sit at the table—come back, we believe in you still—but you can't do that because he's all about death and tragedy, this one, to invite him in would be to bring disaster into your house and let it loose into every corner like a blind rabbit on the run. And so they all stare at him for a while, pray silently that he will get tired of standing there and go back into the night where he came from, and when he doesn't, The Seamstress finally gets up, stumbles across the room to the door, and, crying silently, closes it on her dead son.

IT'S LATE when Bahar leaves her parents' house. At the top of the alley, the silver car glows in the moonlight like a promise. Bahar feels her heart expand when she sees the car, when she remembers that it will take her away from this place, carry her through the dark city streets that widen and become cleaner the farther they get from South Tehran.

Hassan opens the door and helps her in. Then he sits behind the wheel and backs the car out in a straight line from the top of the alley into the middle of Cyrus Street, where he has enough space to turn around. It's the beginning of winter in Tehran, and the trees are bare, their trunks and branches as luminous as spirits in the night. The sky is already taking on the purple hue that warns of snow, and so Hassan turns on the heater, puts his window down a crack to let in some air. Then he says, "*Family* is a good thing."

He has never really spoken to Bahar before, so it takes a moment for her to register what has happened. He has said only good morning and good night, yes, ma'am, at your service—even if I *do* know better; you're the boss's wife, you can make any decision you like, even a wrong one, only your husband and your in-laws have a right to deny you.

"Yes, of course," Bahar answers eagerly. "Family is a very good thing."

He keeps driving with one hand on the steering wheel, his eyes fixed directly ahead, and doesn't react. She wonders if Hassan has heard her, if he's still waiting for a response, so she leans forward, rests her hand on the back of Hassan's seat, and says, loudly and with greater enthusiasm, "You're right. You're absolutely right."

She sits back and crosses her arms on her chest, squeezes herself into the corner against the door so he can't see her flushed face in the rearview mirror. She wonders if she has given the wrong response, or if he's just ignoring her—because servants do that, she reminds herself, especially the ones who've been with a family a long time; they feel entitled to have moods and opinions, they misbehave, or they act like the boss doesn't exist.

But Bahar knows she's nobody's boss, even if Hassan *does* accord her respect.

She stares out the passenger-side window and tries to forget that any words were exchanged between them at all. She can tell they're at Conquerors' Square because she can see the statue of Reza Shah—army boots and general's cape and that eternal frown that had commanded such fear within the nation—and she shudders at the thought that she'll soon be at home, that she'll have to face Omid and the consequences of her defying him.

Family is a good thing, Hassan has said, emphasizing the first word, and it occurs to her that she might have missed his real meaning: *Family is a good thing, madame, it's important to protect it, here you are, you've started your own family, perhaps you should do better at keeping it intact.*

The passenger-side window is dark. Bahar watches herself in the glass: the large brown eyes with the ends tipping downward; cheekbones that are too flat; a mouth that opens too wide when she smiles, making her look like the simple girl that she is. For the thousandth time since she has married Omid, she wishes that she looked better—looked like someone else, someone he would reckon with, that he would like more. She had never minded her looks until she went out into society with him and met all the women who were so much more beautiful than she—who had been selected as wives by their rich husbands precisely because of their blue eyes or blond hair; because they were tall, or voluptuous, or ever so confident: women who caught the eye and made Bahar feel inferior in their presence.

She looks away from the window and leans forward in her seat again.

"Do you ever see *your* family?" she asks, more to reassure herself that he is not ignoring her than because she wants to know.

He looks back at her in the rearview mirror, and now she knows she has touched a nerve, because he looks deeply indignant. He parts his lips to say something, hesitates, then goes on.

"My family, madame, is *your* family." Then he turns his eyes back to the road.

"Yes, of course," she mumbles, feeling mortified because she realizes that there was indeed more to what he had said than she had grasped before, that this is why he looks so disappointed: he thinks she's slow and stupid.

Hassan, she knows, has worked for the Arbabs since he was nine years old—since his father brought him to Tehran from their village of Araak and sold him on the street corner to the first person who stopped. Hassan's parents had had four daughters and three sons. They gave their daughters away to rug weavers, who used them from ages five or six until they became adults and went blind, or died of tuberculosis. They sold the boys as farmhands, or laborers, or servants in the homes of wealthy people in Tehran.

That was thirty years ago, before Omid was born. Hassan has worked for the Arbab's through the Second World War and the Allied occupation. He has watched Omid grow up, watched him run barefoot in the yard while his mother demanded that he come inside, or put some shoes on, you'll step on a nail and die of tetanus, damn this country, with all the germs it breeds it's a miracle anyone's still alive and standing up, Hassan go grab that child and hose down his feet, tie him to a chair if you have to but don't let him run around like some filthy peasant boy with hooves instead of feet.

He stops the car at the front gates of the house, gets out, and opens the door for Bahar. He doesn't look at her as she steps out. He waits till she has found her key and put it into the lock before he gets back into the car to drive to the end of the yard, where he parks every night on a gravel patch under an awning. She watches him drive away, stands with one hand holding the key that is still in the lock, and that's when she knows that it's Omid whom Hassan had been warning her about in the car.

He's still out there—the peasant boy who is charged with guarding the prince—watching Omid run toward danger and trying to bring him home.

EVERY AFTERNOON at the hour of sleep, the woman in the yellow house opens all the windows and plays her wild, breathless music on a giant gramophone till she has awakened every soul on the Alley of the Champions and June Street. She plays the music at other times too, without regard for her neighbors or for the Islamic calendar that forbids music and dance and other displays of immorality during certain parts of the year.

Forever patient with foreigners who command respect and indulgence among Iranians merely because they come from elsewhere, the people on the Alley of the Champions toss and turn in their beds for a good two weeks, hoping she will stop the racket on her own before they finally complain to The Tango Dancer. If you don't mind, miss, we're trying to get some rest over here, we're working people, you see, we rise early and stay up late, we don't have the luxury to plan our day around the schedule you follow with your gramophone.

She looks at them with her charcoal eyes—dark hair and cherry lips and a dozen gold bangles on each wrist—in those long dresses with the necklines that make even the most insolent of God's subjects look away in embarrassment, and says not to worry, music is good for the brain, you'll get used to it, a day will come when you won't be able to sleep *without* it. The neighbors shuffle home in their nightshirts and rubber slippers, scratching their heads and struggling to understand how this hitherto obscure young woman they had barely seen and certainly never thought of, suddenly metamorphosed into the local bully. They go back the next day and ask politely, become rude, threaten. Once or twice, they even call the police, but it's futile because the police are afraid of The Tango Dancer and don't want to confront her: she may be a German spy like her parents, or an informant for the Shah's secret police. Who are we kidding here, the parents were Nazis in hiding, since when do diplomats live on the Alley of the Champions, and this daughter may still be connected to something dark and dangerous and at any rate not worth tackling on the meager salary they receive from His Majesty's coffers, or the few hundred tomans in bribes they extract from ordinary citizens in exchange for performing their duties.

The spy story, Bahar knows, has surrounded the occupants of the yellow house since they arrived in Tehran a quarter century ago. To those who had asked their business in Iran, The Old Couple had said only that they were "diplomats," without explaining what country they represented or what ambassadorial mission they thought they could fulfill in that crumbling fortress with their strange daughter and their bilingual parrot. They did look like diplomats, all right: like the thousands of Nazi operatives who had suddenly appeared in Iran during the Second World War, when Reza Shah had aligned himself with Hitler, and the ones who arrived later, to hide from their crimes.

Before they moved into the house, The Old Couple had sent three men to scrub the walls with lavender and lye and to unload trunks full of linen and silver and art. The men later reported that the linen looked like those things you see in the movies—stark white and paper-stiff and ostensibly hand-stitched by cloistered nuns in some monastery in the Alps. What is it with those Christians anyway? Sending their women into a cave only to sew sheets and napkins—how does *that* serve God? The silver bore different initials, none of which matches the owners', one of the men had told them—I may be illiterate but I can tell just by the shape of those letters. And the paintings must have held inordinate value, because The Old Couple kept most of them wrapped and locked up in a closet in a darkened room. The ones they did hang on the walls, they protected from light by putting wooden shutters on every window—what is it with people from Europe? Why do they keep their houses so dark?—and were fastidious about keeping the shutters closed and the doors locked at all times.

They also installed barbed wire and broken glass on top of the walls, and for a while they kept a large, black dog that was trained to kill or disable anyone who happened into the house uninvited. The dog was poisoned by traveling salesmen who wanted to knock on The Old Couples' door and sell a few things without being torn apart by some rabid creature, and the linen quickly succumbed to the gray air and gasoline-infested winds of South Tehran, but the paintings remained intact—looking old and expensive and every bit as stolen as the crown of Nader Shah on a pauper's head.

The Old Couple were blond and tall and Aryan-looking, spoke English with a European accent and not a word of Farsi for years after they had arrived. The girl they claimed was their daughter had Gypsy skin and raven hair, spoke only Spanish when she first arrived, but switched to Farsi within a few short months. She never went to school or tried to get married or behaved in any way like a normal woman. She admitted freely, even proudly, that she was a dancer—which is the same, really, as a whore, albeit a more sophisticated one. She said her specialty was Argentine tango—what's the difference, ma'am, tango is tango: they stomp their feet and clap their hands and rub their bodies against each other in plain view. She even claimed she had once earned first place in a tango competition in South America—isn't that where that Jewish Nazi hunter was looking for Mengele?

She never displayed any attachment to The Old Couple, and certainly did not pretend to mourn their death, having observed not even an hour of what should have been a yearlong period of prayer and abstinence. She said they had written a will and left instructions for burial—just like a German, to be so organized even in death. One morning they had dressed in their best outfits, drank a glass of poison each, and laid down on their bed holding hands (they killed six million, what's two more, even if it *is* themselves?).

The Tango Dancer went to the burial dressed in white, a hot-pink camellia tucked into her hair, and wasn't at all upset that, except for a handful of kindhearted employees who had performed various tasks for The Old Couple over the years, no one had cared enough to show up. The next day, she hung a handwritten sign outside the front door of the yellow house, offering dance and music lessons and announcing the imminent opening of the Spanish Academy for the Arts. Why she thought such an enterprise might succeed in a country where music and dance had long been considered the gateways to prostitution, in a neighborhood where most people struggled to meet basic survival needs and had no money to spend on acts of moral turpitude, was beyond anyone's comprehension. She threw away The Old Couple's bed and turned their room on the ground floor into a dance studio. She tuned the piano in their drawing room, opened the locks and the shutters—the paintings can go to hell—and waited for her students to call.

FROM HER ROOM on the top floor of the Tehran Hilton, Niyaz can see the Damavaand peak of the Alborz mountains. Her bed faces the window, and she likes seeing the mountains as soon as she opens her eyes, likes it so much she sleeps with the curtains open, awakens with the first light of dawn and watches the sky change color as the sun rises. Often, she goes to bed only an hour or two before daylight, and so she'll close the curtains after a while and go back to sleep, wake up again in the afternoon, and quickly leave her room, which, by then, is starting to feel cramped and airless.

She has stayed in this room twice a year for nearly a decade. It's paid for by The Lover, rented twelve months at a time whether or not he is in the country to use it. He also keeps a car and a driver in Tehran, and he places them at Niyaz's service whenever she's here. He pays all her expenses, brings her gifts, treats her to anything she wants even if he's not spending time with her—if he's in Europe, or South America, aboard his yacht, on a plane, in some famous hotel or legendary house. In return, he asks for nothing and commits to even less. They are each free to come and go as they please, with whomever they please: it's the secret to the success of their affair, the reason they've stayed together for as long as they have. They're civilized people who know that life is too dear, too fleeting, for archaic conventions and petty displays of possessiveness.

She sits up in bed now and leans against the pillow. She's naked to the waist, her skin glowing warm against the whiteness of the sheets. She has on the pink diamond earrings Omid had sent to her months earlier, and she knows this pleases him, knows he has given them to her with joy and would give more—anything, really, just say the word. His innocence amuses her. She looks over at him in the bed. He's awake but silent, watching her. He looks at once ecstatic and crushed, like someone who has had the misfortune of seeing his greatest dream come true.

She tells him she would almost live in Tehran permanently just to see those mountains every day. She likes the country, the landscape, well enough, she says; it's the *rest* she can't stand. She can't bear the constraints of a religion and a regime that govern a person's every act and thought and emotion, that define good and bad in stark terms and profess to know the difference in every case. She hates the way this so-called morality sucks the life out of the living. She's not a person who can be governed by others; she's not one who can be owned.

She picks up the phone on the nightstand and calls down to the lobby, orders American coffee and ice water and a pack of cigarettes. She's not afraid that Omid will be seen with her in the room, that word will get out and reach The Lover. She knows he won't confront her on this if he found out—he's too proud for that, and anyway, who's to say how many other women *he* has brought into this room throughout the years? It's true she has never been unfaithful to The Lover before, though she has had countless opportunities and with men who surpassed Omid in almost every regard. It's true, also, that she's not particularly impressed with Omid—not enough, anyway, to jeopardize her relationship with The Lover. For all her independence and aloofness, all her self-imposed solitude and the distance she maintains with everyone but The Lover, Niyaz has known, for years now, that she won't be the first to end the affair. She's been with The Lover since she was a young girl; he's all she has, really—her only friend and only family. Before she met him, she had lived alone nearly all her life, since she was five years old and her father sent her to an English boarding school that was really an orphanage for children of rich people who didn't want to be parents. She managed well enough back then, has managed just fine with The Lover: he set the rules, difficult as they were—no marriage, no monogamy, no living together except for limited periods of time—and she met the challenge with unusual grace. But lately, she has begun to resent The Lover's kind tyranny, the fact that he knows he holds all the cards and has her at his mercy. She's tired of all the traveling, the hotel rooms, the days and weeks when she doesn't hear from him and knows not to call. Lately, she has begun to wonder what it's like to be loved more than desired—to be *wanted* enough to keep.

BAHAR GOES TO CYRUS STREET every week, and after a while it becomes routine—the fight on Friday morning, the nervous departure in the afternoon, the days of silent treatment Omid retaliates with. He comes home late every night now, skips the hour of the afternoon sleep. He lies in Bahar's bed without saying a word to her, and in the morning, sits at the dining table and eats his wheat flatbread and butter and honey, drinks his tea, and acts as if she doesn't exist. His silence makes her anxious. She's always watching for it to rise or ebb, and she doesn't realize—yet—that it's only half borne of anger, that, most of the time, he ignores her because he's thinking of Niyaz.

This isn't the life I signed up for, she tells him, but it doesn't matter. The only person who hears her and responds is Ruby, the maid, who has her own very set ideas on how a marriage should be conducted, and who feels strongly that Bahar is going about it the wrong way.

"You can't make a man do what you want by yelling at him," she explains. "You've got to seduce him first, make him happy where it counts before you start asking for things."

She tells Bahar she should produce a child already, learn to behave like other wives and start spending her days at the tailor's and fortune-teller's, at the hair salon and the movies and those endless luncheons that people with money host for whatever reason they can think of: when one of them loses a few kilos on a grapefruit-and-cigarettes diet or buys a piece of jewelry she can't wait to show off; when their infant daughters sprout their first teeth or their sons get their first hair cut— no offense, ma'am, Jews do some *strange* things, they pray all their life for a son, and when he's born, they cut off his penis and keep him looking like a girl for three years. Rich women are imbeciles, as far as Ruby can tell, but they're welcome to their petty lives and boring parties if it keeps them out of the house and out of the servants' way. She also believes that Bahar should stop whining about school and work and that whole business of "becoming someone" before she has children: I'm sorry, ma'am, if I don't shed too many tears for you, it's just that people are dying out there of hunger and disease and loneliness, and you've got a man who pays for your every meal and buys you everything you want, so what if he doesn't want you to become prime minister? If I were you, I'd worry less about school and more about where he goes at night and why he won't take you with him and how come you're not pregnant after all the time you've been married?

Bahar's family, it seems, shares Ruby's concerns about Omid and the state of the marriage. Every Friday night, her father looks at her with apprehension and asks if there is a reason why she leaves her husband "alone with strangers" only to come to Cyrus Street. Her mother asks without irony if she is intent on ruining her life by remaining childless, and The Unmarried Sister hints that Omid must be sterile, or sleeping with other women, or, dare she say, with one of those men who prefer the company of boys.

Have a child, they say, before you get too old. But Bahar says she doesn't want to yet. What she doesn't say is that Omid has never mentioned a child either, that he sleeps in her bed but not *with* her—not unless she asks, and then, only halfheartedly.

THE PROBLEM IS, she can't believe this is going to be her fate. One summer day, she puts on a simple white and yellow dress and a pair of flat, white canvas shoes—the kind young women wear to school. She combs her hair straight and pulls it into a ponytail, goes out with no makeup at all. Hassan is away driving Omid. She takes a taxi to the Persepolis School.

The summer session is for the students who have failed a class and must do remedial work before they are promoted to the next grade. In the yard, Bahar sees a few of her old classmates. They surround her and ask to see her wedding ring. They want to know what being married is like. Before she has had a chance to answer, the principal spots her from his office and comes outside.

"What are you doing here?" he wants to know.

"I've come to enroll for twelfth grade."

"Enroll *whom*?"

"Myself."

The principal glares at her. He knows who she is—the girl who married Omid Arbab—and he would treat her more kindly if the husband were with her. He sizes her up, notices her red nail polish.

"I see you like to paint your nails."

She realizes she should have wiped the polish off before she came here, but now it's too late, so she puts her hands behind her back and swallows her anxiety.

"I was a student here not too long ago."

He doesn't say anything.

"I missed the last three months of eleventh grade because I got married. I'm hoping I can make that up this summer, start twelfth grade in the fall."

He's still giving her that you're-too-big-for-your-britches-but-I'll-cut-you-down-to-size stare.

She opens her bag and takes out an envelope. It's money she has saved from her household expense account.

"What's this?" he asks.

"First month's tuition." She offers him the envelope.

"Does your husband know you're here?" It's a rhetorical question, meant to embarrass Bahar, remind her that she can't deceive the principal.

"Yes." She tries to keep her voice from wavering.

He raises an eyebrow at her. "Really?"

He knows she's lying.

"In that case, he's going to have to call me himself," he says. "I need his express permission, and even then, I'm going to tell him I think it's a bad idea."

She hesitates a moment. She's weighing her chances of winning with this man.

"I have the money," she makes one last attempt. He doesn't move.

"Go home," he tells her. "Your student days are over."

❧

HER PARENTS, too, keep telling her to go home.

Go on to your husband, don't raise his ire don't defy him even if it is to come see us; he's a man after all and he wants his wife at home or one of these days he'll send you packing and then you'll show up here with your divorce papers.

Bahar holds on to the money she had saved up for school and uses it to sign up for a secretarial class instead. She'll learn typing and short-hand and proper manners for answering the phone, she decides, and once she is adept at it all, she will convince Omid to let her work at his office. She may not become a teacher but she's going to have a career nevertheless.

She waits every day till Omid has left for work, hides her wedding ring in her purse, and rides to the class in a cab. She won't tell Ruby where she's going, which arouses suspicion—whatever it is you're doing on the sly, ma'am, you're wasting your time, this town is not as large as you might think, people know your husband and his family: one of these days, you'll be found out and then he'll lock you up.

Three weeks into the course, Bahar is at a typewriter, practicing furiously, when the teacher comes up behind her. "I understand you're a married woman."

The teacher is also a woman, but she is older—in her fifties—and possessed with that bizarre and horrifying cruelty so common among people who, although feeble in their own lives, have been bestowed with some level of control over the lives of others. She's hovering over Bahar with her hands on her hips and her eyebrows knotted, and it's clear she is not pleased with what she has found out.

"Where is your wedding band?"

Bahar drops her hands into her lap and looks down without answering.

"Some relative of your husband's saw you walk in here this morning from the street," the teacher explains. "They told him."

Bahar nods, defeated.

"You should be ashamed of yourself."

Bahar nods again.

"He's sending the car for you," the teacher says. "Wait outside."

❧

SHE FIGHTS for a few more months. One Sabbath, she's sitting at her parents' dining table, so sad she can't swallow her food, when The Opera Singer puts an arm around her. He's clean shaven and looking fresh, smells of coffee and Aramis Cologne. He has just met an "important person," a man who produces the most successful pop music program for Iran's only TV station. The man is Jewish, and he's looking for new talent. They've had a good chat. The Opera Singer is hopeful.

He tells Bahar that he knows all about desire and disappointment. He knows what it is to want something, to want it so bad that you refuse to give up, even in the face of overwhelming odds. He knows about dreams and the price of chasing them.

"But here's the thing, you see: you can hope all you want. It doesn't mean you're going to win," he says. His smile is the saddest she has ever seen. "You can bend fortune's back, but you can't break it."

Suddenly, she realizes she has been wrong about him, that they have all been wrong about him. He's not a dimwit who has remained blind to the futility of his dreams. He knows he's going nowhere with the singing, that none of his plans or contacts or many boasts will ever amount to anything. He's only going on with the charade because he has no idea what else to do, no inkling of who else he *could* be, and this is what he wants to spare Bahar.

"Sometimes," he says, "you must kill one dream in order to save another."

Bahar is eighteen years old. She gives up hope of going back to school or working, and decides to have a child.

PART III

IT WILL BE DIFFICULT, later, for me to keep sight of the person that she was, to reconcile the tenderness she showed me at times, the faith she held in me, with the disappointment she directed at me when I failed, the force of her disapproval when I disobeyed.

She was not a bad mother.

I know this because I watched her, in the days of my early childhood when I depended on her for my very existence and later, from a distance borne of silence and disenchantment and regret so deep, it defined us to the core.

Like the pauper who buys a fish with the last of her money, takes it home, and in its stomach, finds the most precious pearl in the world; like the beggar's daughter who is sold for a song at the slave market, taken to the king because she is so beautiful, and made queen; like all the men and women in the fairy tales she had heard as a child and which she had so doggedly believed in, my mother knew she could be *more*.

So she lived in a state of perpetual loss—the runner who gives her all to the race and always comes short. She couldn't give up the fight and couldn't quite win and so she was caught between the pride of battle and the shame of defeat. And in that state, in that place where rest was impossible and wanting led only to more sorrow, she bore me expecting that I, at least, would not fail.

What if you bet your whole life on a single wish, and lost?

❧

INSIDE THE MATERNITY WARD at Varjavaand hospital, three dozen people are standing in a hallway, waiting for news of the birth. They've come because they know Bahar is going to have a boy, they are certain of it: that's what the fortune-tellers have seen from the moment she began to show, and what Omid's aunts have detected every time they studied the way she stood up from a chair—with her right leg in front of the left, because the right is the stronger of the two—and besides, Mr. Arbab demands that his sons produce heirs, and his wife can't stand girls. It's one of the things she prides herself for: the fact that she has no daughters, she thinks, means that she's "chosen," that she's somehow better, or more complete, or at least *entitled* to more, than most.

But now Bahar is crying in the delivery room, and a nurse is telling Omid and his parents that they were all wrong, that the fortune-tellers' tarot cards and the friends' coffee grinds and all the other barometers of a baby's gender were wrong as well—it's a girl, ladies and gentlemen, but don't lose heart, it happens every day, at least she's healthy and the mother is young, she'll have other children and they may turn out to be boys.

Bahar, though, keeps saying there's been a mistake. She's sure she was carrying a boy; she won't know what to do with a girl—she's already selected a name for her son and bought him a trunk full of clothes: little blue vests, white shirts, navy and red jackets. She has washed the clothes by hand, folded and stored them in the drawers of a brand-new chest made of yellow wood with pictures of little boys playing with bears. A dozen times a day, she has opened the drawers and looked inside them, smiled at the thought of dressing her son in those clothes, of pushing his carriage down the street and stopping only to let strangers admire his good looks. She has enjoyed the first bits of kindness and even halfhearted respect from Omid's relatives since she was married—she's going to be the mother of his son, after all; she can influence his future. She has even enjoyed the first bits of attention from Omid. But now she's going to lose all that, she's fallen from grace, never to be trusted to do right again.

One by one at the hospital, my father's relatives come up and shake his hand, pat him on the shoulder and mumble something about "the next time," then shuffle away. My maternal grandparents stand, hat in hand, before the Arbabs and whisper to them what they know to be a lie: that having a girl is a blessing in disguise, that girls are more loyal to their parents, that they are the ones who will be there to care for you when you're old.

All this offends Omid in a strange way. What's wrong with a girl? he wants to know. Who said a person should have only sons? But the others smile at him as if he were someone who's staring death in the face and claiming immortality; they nod pensively and walk away. And so he learns quickly this is a losing battle—let them think what they want, he can't worry about changing people's beliefs. His heart is elsewhere and he has enough trouble keeping himself engaged and present in the moment. So he tells Bahar's mother that he has to rush back to the office, he'll be back later to see the baby.

Bahar cries so hard, the patients in the adjoining rooms request a transfer.

SHE WILL TELL ME this time and again—how she cried on the day I was born and for so many days afterward while she was in the hospital, how she fell into despair every time the nurses brought me to her or she tried to imagine what lay ahead for us both. Late at night, when the other patients were asleep and the visitors had left the hospital, she will tell me, she would walk the halls and wonder how she was going to overcome this new reality.

And she would cry again later, when she came home from the hospital and realized that Omid had not changed at all; that having a child had not brought him any closer to his wife or made him any more interested in his home life. That I, who should have lured my father back to his family, had failed from the start.

That she had even fewer options now—now that she was responsible for my well-being, was disadvantaged for having given birth to a girl.

"I made a mistake," she will say in the matter-of-fact voice she uses when speaking of things that hurt her most. It's the way her own mother had spoken to her daughters: life is hard; it's harder for women; toughen up and get used to reality. It was the best her mother could do for her, Bahar will tell me—to rid her of any and all illusions about what lay on the road a woman must travel. But I think it was a punishment as well, that their mother punished the girls—for *being* girls—by planting in their heart the seeds of fear and disappointment, taking away their hope, condemning them to the same fate she, herself, had suffered.

I'm four, eight, ten years old—my mother's only child, the source of all her heartbreak.

My name is Yaas.

I have hazel eyes and white skin—hence my name, which in Farsi means "poet's jasmine." But you don't have to look far to see that the name doesn't suit me: the breed of poet's jasmine we call yaas is a tiny flower with infinitely delicate petals and an uncommonly fine fragrance. It grows on a vine with very thin branches that break easily and require a trellis or some sort of support in order to grow. I, on the other hand, have the kind of resilience that would allow me to survive on my own and under any circumstance. It is true that I have tiny bones—thin ankles and wrists, a face and body that look more like a pencil sketch of a child than a complete picture—but I'm a girl, and this alone makes me indestructible: every woman I know, even the ones who refer to themselves as "thinking people," which means they understand more than most women but not as much as men, believes that girls are like weeds; they grow anywhere, survive any illness and misfortune, even if you don't want them to.

I know, too, that I've been born with a second disadvantage: I have red hair and freckles—features that are considered unattractive by Iranians. People in this country like blond hair and green eyes. They want women who look like a foreigner—which means a "Westerner." They'll forgive dark hair if it's straight and shiny, and they may, on occasion, tolerate olive skin if it belongs to a woman of exceptional beauty. But they have no time for red hair and eyebrows, or orangutan eyelashes, or for little brown spots on a girl's cheeks and on the bridge of her nose: that kind of look belongs to Jews from Esfahan, and to other deviants whose origin and bloodline, sadly, cannot be ascertained.

To compensate for my shortcomings, Bahar teaches me to read before I have started school. She expects me to speak and walk and eat "like the daughter of a person of substance," tells me I must have great ambition, that I must dedicate myself to achieving goals no other girl my age would dream of reaching. Study hard, she says, be the best in your class. Don't marry young, don't give up a chance at going to university, don't *ever* depend on a man for your livelihood.

She dresses me in yellow and blue and red, but not pink. She hates the color pink, and the bows and ribbons and red patent-leather shoes with the tiny black-and-white roses on the clasp that I stare at every time we go to the store. She buys me sensible shoes instead, complains that Omid is undermining her efforts at raising me properly when he brings me dresses and dolls from his overseas' trips.

"These things will make you vain and self-absorbed. They'll distract you from what you need to accomplish, take your mind off studying when you're at school," she tells me.

Her own mother, she says, forbade her daughters from looking in the mirror more than once a day, lest they became too vain and "difficult to control." She says this as she sits in front of her vanity mirror that's lined with tubes of makeup and bottles of perfume, as she paints her eyes and nails, dips her hair in beer to add body, and rolls it in tight loops around tiny curlers. She puts on shiny silk blouses and flowing velvet skirts that she has spent weeks making, wears bracelets and earrings and narrow pumps with needle-thin heels, and if Ruby points out the irony in it all—you deny the child everything you want for yourself—Bahar will fly into a rage, scream that this is all there is for her to do, this is what *she* has been reduced to, but she's damned if she's going to let her daughter fall into the same trap. If I so much as touch one of her silk scarves or a single white satin glove, she snatches it out of my hand and warns that I must stop focusing on frivolities, must be diligent and do well in school, because that's the only way I'll "become something."

I am the part of her that she dislikes and resents—the "natural disadvantage" that has made her, at twenty-three, a person with no options.

And maybe it wasn't so hard, at first, for me to live with the disappointment and the distance, to know my mother more as an absence than what I later wished she could be: a hand that would hold me in the dark, fight the demons I was unable to fend off, keep me from falling. Maybe it became more difficult—Omid's not being there, Bahar's blaming me because she *was*—when I began to suffer other losses, to feel the distance grow between me and my parents, to understand that it was permanent and inevitable. That's when I would reach for Bahar and Omid and find them each standing on the edge of an even greater divide—of longings and desires—his, hers, mine—that opposed each other.

Maybe I wouldn't have done what I did, caused this damage I can never undo, if I hadn't been so alone in the dark.

It's important that I remember this.

✣

NIYAZ IS SITTING ALONE on the terrace of a café in Monte Carlo. It's Sunday afternoon, the end of summer, and her skin is golden brown from all the days she has spent lying in the sun. Most of the tourists who have crowded the city for the past three months are gone, so the street is quiet. Across from her in the café, a group of young people are drinking beer and laughing at a comment one of them has made. They're locals, Niyaz can tell, because they're dressed as if they don't care where they are and who might see them, and they don't look around every few minutes. One of them—a black African in a stark white shirt that sets off the beauty of his skin—leans over and kisses one of the girls on the lips.

Niyaz has chosen a table near the back of the terrace. She orders coffee and lights a cigarette, thinks about how she hates the end of summer, how it reminds her of departure and loss—the vast, unbroken solitude of her childhood and early youth, of cold farewells and long plane rides and months of endless confinement to the dark, forbidding halls of that all-girls boarding school where the nuns beat her because she was pretty. She grew up in that boarding school. Her father was a rich aristocrat with a well-publicized opium habit that consumed all his energy and left no time for raising children. Her mother had divorced him and gotten married again, to the Iranian ambassador to Indonesia. Niyaz was five years old—an only child—when her mother left for the Far East. Soon after that, Niyaz was shipped away to England.

The waiter appears with her coffee and a glass of water. He asks if "Monsieur" will be joining her.

"Soon," she says, and flicks the ash from her cigarette, looks up to see that the waiter is staring at her again, standing with his arms limp and his face painted with that bewildered look he gets every time she comes into this café. She smiles, revealing a row of perfect while teeth, and perhaps a certain indulgence for the longing of a man who has admired her for so long.

The Lover arrives in a metallic blue sports car, drawing stares. He walks into the café clearly aware that the air around him changes color when he moves. He passes the young people without a look, smiles broadly when he sees Niyaz, and kisses her on the forehead. The waiter rushes to the table—what a pleasure to see you again, Monsieur, may I bring you a glass of champagne, would you like to see a menu, or will it just be drinks this afternoon?

The Lover reaches for Niyaz across the table. She lets him hold her hand but remains impassive.

"It's been too long," he says.

He's been away most of the summer—on his yacht, with a Lebanese friend, circling the Caribbean. He had invited her to Monte Carlo, but soon after she arrived, he decided he wanted to sail on his yacht. He had asked her to join him—you've come all the way from Tehran, you might as well come along—but she could tell he didn't want her to go and so refused. She could have left then for Paris or London, Beirut or Cairo, or any of the other cities where The Lover has friends who would take care of her, or she could have gone back to Iran, to Ramsar on the Caspian shore. But she hated the idea of packing up for another place, and so she had stayed put. In the first few years she had spent with him, she'd liked The Lover's lifestyle—the constantly changing landscape, the sense that they were staying ahead of time, cheating the clock, escaping age and atrophy—but now she wanted to see the seasons change in one place.

She tells him she has stayed in Monte Carlo nearly all summer. She left only once, for California, where she spent two weeks in a small town by the Pacific—Spanish missions and red-tiled roofs and the names of Catholic saints on every street. She rented a house on the beach.

The Lover has been to America before and doesn't think much of the country or its people. He thinks the ocean is too cold, the people too unsophisticated. He finds Los Angeles tacky, New York too gray. He has no time for the middle-aged waitresses in blond wigs and nurses' shoes who pour black coffee into thick mugs and shove them at the customers across linoleum countertops in noisy coffee shops with vinyl-covered seats in every city. Or for the men in golf pants and white Cadillacs who order enormous steaks in brightly lit restaurants, drink whiskey, and talk about the price of oil and the movements of the stock market while their wives swap recipes and boast to each other about their children.

"I bought the house," she tells him, her voice suddenly naked. "I wanted a place where no one knew me."

When her father died, his family didn't bother to tell Niyaz. She found out months later, at summertime, when the headmaster at her school told her she couldn't return to Tehran because there was no one there for her to go to. She learned later that her father's family had tried to steal her inheritance, but they failed because the money had been entrusted to a close friend who was given the task of guarding it honestly till Niyaz was of age. She was nine years old when her father died. She spent that first summer with an old English couple—friends of the headmaster—who lived in the countryside near Kent. The husband was a veteran of the Second World War who still saw people being blown up everywhere he looked. He walked around the house nearly naked all the time, looking for his pants, his shirt, his socks and shoes, until his wife took him by the hand and led him into their room, showed him yet again where he had left his clothes, and dressed him like a child. It was the first time Niyaz had seen such warmth between two people, the first time she had been in a house where the owners had lived for decades.

She takes a sip of her coffee and lights another cigarette.

"I'd like to stay in one place for a while," she says to The Lover, "see if I can spread roots."

The Lover knows about Niyaz's desire to stay put. He knows, too, about the man who has been pursuing her in Tehran—about the jewels and orchids and fur coats he sends to her. The Lover isn't jealous of this man, doesn't feel threatened by him. He knows Omid is no match for him, but he thinks he might be just what Niyaz needs—someone to break the fall when The Lover leaves her.

By the time they finish their drinks, the weather has turned cool, and she shivers lightly in her sleeveless dress. They sit together for a while longer and watch the movement on the street. He looks at his watch—six o'clock—and says something about a backgammon game later that night at the Casino de Paris. He pays the check and they walk out together. For a while, they stand on the sidewalk and look at the sun that is blood-red-orange against the horizon. He turns to her one more time, sees that her eyes are filled with tears. He takes her face into his hands, kisses her eyes, her lips. Eleven years and no promises.

He gets into his car and drives away without a word. She doesn't let her tears fall, won't indulge in the ordinary rituals of parting and loss.

THE NIGHT of their seventh anniversary, Omid doesn't come home at all.

They have been fighting for weeks, Bahar having confronted him at last with rumors she has tried to, but can no longer, ignore, and it terrifies her that Omid denies nothing, that he says only that he's doing his best—let me be, this isn't the way I *wanted* things to work out but the more you probe now, the more you'll drive me away.

I gave you my life but you've denied me yours, she says, and he knows this is true, knows he has humiliated her by the public way in which he has conducted his affair with Niyaz. The affair itself is excusable, certainly understandable: no one expects a married man, least of all one with money, to swear off other women. Even penniless husbands who can't afford to keep a lover will have one-night stands with cheap whores or loose women from time to time. The more pious ones, who believe extramarital sex is sinful, will take advantage of the Islamic provision under which they can enter "temporary" marriages. So Omid doesn't blame himself for being unfaithful to his wife, but he is aware that he should have kept his relationship with Niyaz more discreet, spared his wife the humiliation of being abandoned so openly and for a woman so very superior to her in every way.

He never would have loved Bahar, people are saying, even if there *were* no other woman.

He calls from the office that evening and tells Bahar not to wait up for him. She has prepared dinner for them, and she's wearing a new robe made of red polyester and black lace. She bought the robe because she thought it looked like something Joan Crawford would wear in one of those black-and-white films where the women look glamorous even in their sleep. She likes those films, those movie stars who were once nobodies—just common girls from ordinary American families who happened to be spotted by someone important when they were eating ice cream; that's all it takes, she knows: one break, one lucky turn of the wheel, and a girl can be famous around the world. Bahar has a drawer full of pictures of movie stars in her bedroom dresser. The pictures are on postcards that come in packs of twelve; they are connected by perforated lines and can fold into a stack and open like a fan. She looks at the pictures all the time, shows them to me as well: here's Rita Hayworth, who married a Turkish Khan; here's Marilyn Monroe, who sang at John F. Kennedy's birthday; here's Elizabeth Taylor with the purple eyes and the many husbands; here's Grace Kelly, who played the part of a princess in a film and ended up becoming queen in real life.

In the store where she saw the robe, Bahar had imagined it was a magic cloak—put it on and you, too, will become a legend worthy of your own postcard—but Omid hasn't even mentioned the anniversary on the phone, and she knows he won't notice the robe either.

She'll never wear the robe for Omid after that. She will use it as a housedress, walk around in it as she cooks and sews and gives Hassan Agha the shopping list for the day.

She stays up half the night, falls asleep near dawn, and wakes up when she hears him come in at nearly nine o'clock. She remains in bed and closes her eyes, lies motionless as she listens to his footsteps approach in the hallway. Suddenly, she knows that he's coming to talk to her, to tell her something she doesn't want to hear. Go back, she prays silently, let me sleep through this, I'm not ready, I'll never be ready.

He comes up to the bed.

She sits up and pulls her knees to her chest. She hugs her legs and lets her hair fall to the side of her face, so that it shields her eyes from Omid's.

"I'm not doing right by you," he says, and she hears the night in his voice, hears the thrill of the hours he has spent with Niyaz and the sadness he already feels for being away from her.

Yes, it's true, you're not doing right by me, she wants to say, but you took away all my other options and left me with this, and you can't take this away as well, no matter how much we both don't want it.

Instead, she starts to cry.

He sits in front of her on the bed, touches her knee with the tip of his fingers.

"Don't!" she screams. His gentleness is a warning to her that he's about to deliver a blow.

"Don't you say it! I'll never accept it, never let you force me away."

In one violent motion she gets out of bed and bounds, barefoot, out of the room. She runs down the stairs and into the yard, sobbing, and there she stops, facing the house, panting and crying at once, ready to run again—into the street, even, if she has to—to run far enough that he can't catch up with her and say what he's come to say.

THEY WILL GO ON this way for many years. They will stop poking at the truth, settle for an empty and insidious peace that leaves their outer selves intact but eats at their insides from the marrow out. Bahar determines to stay the course, bets on the other woman tiring of Omid, or on Omid giving her up, coming back to his wife and daughter as other stray men have done before him. She is not one to surrender a fight—my mother who has raised herself out of South Tehran by the sheer force of believing. It is true that the lines of battle have shifted for her, but she still intends to win.

If he doesn't love *her* enough to return, she bets on Omid loving his child enough.

Did he love me enough?

I remember the way he looked at me when I saw his car pull into the yard at the end of the day and ran to him through the garden and toward the back gates, where he stood and waited, smiled at me even if my clothes were dirty or my uniform was torn. He wasn't disappointed by my "raggedness"—as Bahar would have called it—wouldn't get angry if I touched his white shirt with my ink and pencil-stained fingers. He didn't ask me if I had done well in school that day, didn't send me away to finish one chore or another. He would give me his hand, and we would walk together back to the house, and for the few minutes when we were alone together and away from my mother's eyes, I believed that my father loved me enough.

Did he indulge me, as Bahar said, expect so little of me, because he had no interest in what happened to me?

When we walked in, the house was like a hollow chamber, empty but for the single, overriding truth of my parents' anguish, of my mother's wounds and Omid's cruelty and the looming—forever looming—

shadow of the woman who was the cause of it all. I knew better than to hold my father's hand inside the house: it would mean taking sides with him, abandoning Bahar, who counted on me as her only ally. I knew better, too, than to follow him into his room, or sit with him while he read the paper, or wait to eat dinner with him. But I watched him from a distance the whole time he was at home, and I could see when he looked at me that his eyes were calm and accepting, and before he left again—to see *her*, we assumed, though he never did say—I made him promise he would be there when I woke in the morning. He kept that promise most of the time.

I remember how handsome and elegant, how very sad he looked as he left our house again at night. I remember how he paused at the end of the hallway, long enough for me to believe he had changed his mind, that he was going to stay this time, before he closed the door behind him.

I imagined him alone on a wide, bare street, driving toward her, expecting that she would fill, with her beauty or her charm or all those other qualities that only *she* possessed, the wasteland of guilt and loneliness he carried away from our house.

He *did* love me; but he loved Niyaz more. It wasn't a fair fight; not one I was equipped to win.

In no time at all, The Tango Dancer has become the most notorious of the Alley's residents, the one person everyone seems to hold in equal scorn but about whom no one can stop talking. She's like a curse they are not able to get rid of or ignore.

She plays her music at any odd hour, and she tells the people who complain that sleep is overrated and futile—you've been given a brain and the means to utilize it, you're not some pigeon who should stop the minute it gets dark. Imagine how much more you could do if you didn't sleep so many hours. She seems to go days without sleep herself, drinking cup after cup of Turkish coffee that she brews unusually strong, no milk or sugar, so that it pours from the pot like mud.

Twice since she began terrorizing the Alley, she has come home to find her windows smashed and her gramophone bludgeoned to pieces, but she has only gone out and bought another one the next day. Everyday, she rides the bus north to Pahlavi Avenue, where the richest people live, and there she puts up signs that announce "a revolutionary new method of learning music and dance, taught by the world's premier artist of Argentine tango. Try one lesson and you will never doubt again."

Most of the time, the signs go unnoticed. They fall off the trees where she has stapled them, or are torn off the walls of shops and houses where she pastes them without the owner's permission, but every once in a while they do compel some well-meaning parents to put their young boys or girls into a car and drive them down to the Alley of the Champions. Sometimes, the cars stop at the top of June Street, pause for a moment, then turn around and go back in the direction they came from. Once or twice, some foolhardy parent has actually taken a chance, accompanied a child into The Tango Dancer's dance studio, then rushed out to tell their spouse and their friends about the Spanish or German or whatever she is woman with the gold bangles in South Tehran, who reeks of cigarettes and is believed to be a spy—I bet she's there to keep an eye on the subversives who penetrate the low-income neighborhoods, she probably sleeps with the men she spies on, what else is she going to do? It's not like she's actually going to have steady students at that place.

Sometimes, The Tango Dancer rides the bus all day. She sits by a window with her back to the passenger next to her, smokes cigarettes, and stares at the moving scenery from one end of town to another and back. People get on and off, and sometimes they try to talk to her, but The Tango Dancer pays them no mind, just remains in that seat until she's alone with the driver and he stops the bus on June Street, opens the door, and says, end of the line, sister, even stray dogs and wild gypsies have gone home.

She emerges from the bus looking pale and distracted, like someone who knows she's about to be assaulted by an excruciating pain and is afraid to face it alone. Then she goes into her house, with the vast, empty rooms where a shah's hookah-smoking, slowly-rotting wives once sat and watched their own end approach, brews a pot of Turkish coffee, and puts her music on.

Once, she returns from her bus journey with a man.

She doesn't know the man's name or where he comes from. He's just someone who was riding in the seat next to her, who stayed on the bus as long as she had and, for most of that time, cried like a child. He looks about twenty years old, and you can tell he's Zoroastrian because he has that Indian-black skin that's so different from the black Arabs' in the south of Iran. He wears a pair of house slippers for shoes and has no belongings but the clothes he has on. His father has thrown him out of the house that day—disowned him because he had wanted to marry a Muslim girl. Shame on you, boy, you might as well spit on your ancestors' graves, don't you know how Muslims have persecuted us Zoroastrians for centuries? How they raped and robbed and drove your people off their land and into hiding all the way to India?

The Zoroastrian has nowhere to go and no money, no friends or family who would provide him safe harbor from his father's rage, and the girl for whom he has reduced himself to this state—well, it's not as if any Muslim parent would approve of a union with nonbelievers either—*her* parents have her locked up and beaten, they will find her a suitable husband within days, if not hours, and she will marry whomever they say because she knows the alternative would be death at the hands of one of her own male relatives.

The Tango Dancer has three empty rooms on the second floor of her house. She tells the Zoroastrian he can live in one of them, pay rent when he finds a job. She knows that what she's contemplating—a single woman living under the same roof with a man she is not married or related to—is tantamount to heresy, but if that bothers her, she betrays no sign of self-doubt. She's used to being the outcast, wouldn't *want* the approval of her neighbors even if it were offered.

No MATTER HOW MANY TIMES I ask or how much I want to, Bahar will not let me grow my hair. She won't let me wear a barrette, or a bow, or the smallest ribbon, or even an elastic band. Once a month, she spreads a white sheet on the kitchen floor, puts me in a chair in the middle of the sheet, and cuts my hair to within inches of my scalp. She does this, she says, to "downplay your weak point," doesn't mind that the haircut, coupled with the trousers and shorts she prefers for me over skirts, makes me look like a boy. When someone mistakes me for a boy— "your son" this and that—she looks at me and laughs, as if this were an inside joke she and I both enjoyed.

"No such luck," she will say, and I'll feel like vanishing, like taking a wide brush and painting myself invisible.

I dream of having long hair—shiny, silky hair that I can pull back into a ponytail like the girls I see in American television shows every night, the ones with cute noses and slim, strong legs, who get into trouble in each episode and always emerge unscathed, who will grow up to be beautiful women, become famous, marry a king. I avoid looking in the mirror because it reflects an image that looks harsh and masculine to me—someone I don't recognize or want to be.

She's cutting my hair again one Friday morning in August, a week before I am to start second grade. She's wearing the red and black robe that she bought for her seventh anniversary. I sit with my back to the window that overlooks the dusty servants' yard on the side of our house. Through it, I can feel the midmorning sun, see the light that is heavy and white. It blazes against the mirrored glass door directly in front of me and makes me squint when I look up. Around me on the floor, wisps of red hair fall from Bahar's scissors onto the sheet.

I hold my hand to the light and watch the halo it forms around my fingers, try to believe my mother as she tells me this is the best way to wear my hair—neat and tidy and easy to maintain; you won't have hair in your eyes when you look at the blackboard in the classroom, and besides, it's hot out there, you'll feel cooler with short hair.

When she's done with my hair, she picks up the sheet by the edges and shakes it through the open window. Hair falls from the sheet like dandelion seeds in the wind. I stand by the chair and watch as she folds the sheet and puts it away, rinses the comb and the scissors and stores them in a drawer.

She's young, and pretty, I think, and so very brave for enduring her life of disappointments as she does—on her own, with anger as her only weapon, without abandoning me in the process. I want her to look at me so I can say this to her—that I love her for what she is and for what she does for me—but she's engrossed in her task and seems unaware of my presence.

She goes back to the sink and washes her hands, takes a bowl of ground beef out of the refrigerator. She mixes in two eggs, a handful of bread crumbs, a spoonful of flour. Then at last she looks toward me and says, "Go wash up."

Go clean your room; put your toys away; eat your lunch, you're being wasteful; look at your hands, they're black again, haven't I told you not to pick berries from the tree, and why are your clothes so wrinkled again, are you turning cartwheels in them or what?

There's always something to do. Something that will send me away from her.

I go into the yard and stay as long as the heat will allow me. I help Hassan Agha water the lawn, pick the sour grapes off the trellis behind the greenhouse and eat them raw, their skin coated with dust. I climb the mulberry tree and pick its fruit till my hands are sticky with the juice. From where I sit on the tree, our house looks like an aging fortress surrounded by an ever-growing city that has tried, but never quite managed, to engulf it.

In the servants' yard, Ruby squats over an enormous pewter tub with lavender-blue water where she's doing the day's wash. Come here, kid, sit next to me I need help wringing these clothes, you might as well learn how to keep a decent house, God knows *I* never did, I'm a Kurd, I should be riding on horseback and hunting wild game instead of scrubbing floors.

Ruby has been this way—brazen—since the day she married Hassan Agha and came to work for the Arbabs. She has the rosy cheeks and fleshy body of a girl who has been raised on cool mountain air and tender lamb's meat, the white skin and light eyes, the presumptuous manners and earsplitting laugh of a rebel who has, by sheer resolve, made a life for herself in Tehran. She is, she's proud to say, a calamity of a maid. She's dangerous with a broom, poison in the kitchen, reckless enough with the dishes to make certain she is not often asked to wash them. She has been fired from more jobs than she can count, and she admits to this freely and not without some pride—I'm not the servant "type," she says, as if she were talking about the color of her skin or her genetic makeup; as if some people are born maids and some aren't.

Ruby, though, says what she thinks and takes orders from no one—least of all her husband, who would be crushed if he learned of the extent to which his wife holds him in disregard. He knows she is less than pious, of course, because she smokes every kind of cigarette she's offered, pours arrack on ice and drinks it down like quince-seed syrup on a hot summer day. She eats *haram*—even pork—as if she had no idea what "forbidden" means, and swears like a streetwalker, which, many people say, is in fact not so far from what she is: she spends all her free time on the street. She stands next to the vendors who sell chicken livers and lamb testicles broiled on skewers over a small brazier, and chats with every customer or passerby who comes along, tells everyone she's waiting—waiting for a good man to whisk her away from her crusty old husband and her awful, demeaning job.

She stands up from the tub now, and pulls one of Bahar's dresses out of the water. It's short-sleeved, with red and white checks and a flat, round collar. It emerges from the water like a mermaid rising from the sea, hangs above the white, soapy surface with its tail still submerged, dripping pink and gurgling bubbles. Ruby folds the dress in half, submerges it in a second tub with clear water. Rings of pale crimson loop around it in contiguous circles and turn the water red.

I help Ruby wring the clothes one by one, then hang them on the clothesline and fasten them with wooden clips. The sun is so hot I can feel it parch my skin. I put my cheeks and eyes to the wet fabric of the clothes I'm hanging and let them cool my face, take my shoes off and stand by the tubs as Ruby overturns their contents on my feet. I drink from the hose, hold my head under the running arc of clear water until my hair is dripping. Around me, steam rises from the scorched ground and evaporates in the blinding glare of the wide, silver bottoms of the upside-down tubs that lie in the yard like a pair of luminous drums.

Ruby dries her face with her sleeve and stretches.

"There," she points with her chin to a large box of Tide and a smaller one of Blue Nile bleach. "Take those into the basement for me and put them some place easy to find."

The basement is separate from the house, accessible through a set of steps from the servants' yard to a small landing. There, a pair of double doors with a lock that hasn't been used in years lead down a short staircase and into a vast and cavernous room where sunlight doesn't reach. It's a spooky place full of dust and echoes and the smell of stale air. Forever cooler than the rest of the house, it attracts large yellow lizards and shivering gray mice, birds that fly in when the door is open and subsequently can't find their way out, and stray cats that come in from the street to birth their litter, and leave the wet, trembling creatures to starve in the dark until all that's left of them are piles of bones and balls of short, gray-blue fur. Every once in a while, Hassan Agha comes in and sweeps away the dust and the carcasses, the bits of dry leaves and the rats' droppings. He tidies up the boxes of soap and bleach and naphthalene that Ruby stores there, stacks the pieces of broken or unused furniture, the old magazines and paperback editions of bad American novels that Bahar had bought at Drug Store, the suitcases full of old clothes—mine, hers, Omid's—that she doesn't have the heart to throw away. He hoses down the floor and the walls so that the smell of wet cement mixed with dust and soot and spider webs permeates the place for days and makes Ruby cough and gag and curse her husband's obsession with neatness.

I'm not afraid of the basement. I go into it often, on Ruby's orders or on my own, like an adventurer on a risky and frivolous expedition undertaken mainly in order to escape the inadequate reality of the immediate world. On days when my parents scream at each other in the house, or I hear Bahar crying alone behind the locked door of her bedroom; when we set the table for three and wait in vain for Omid to come home so we can have what my mother calls a "family meal"; when I see the look of disappointment on Bahar's face or hear her tell Ruby, or her mother, or near-strangers she engages in conversation that she couldn't possibly have another child, her husband is rarely at home, he barely touches her, he even sleeps in another room most of the time, he's put a bed in his study and moved his clothes there, but let me tell you, this may not be a bad thing, suppose I got pregnant and had another girl, what would I do with two daughters and a husband who's not there—on days like that, I escape into the basement and lose myself among the three-legged chairs and moth-eaten costumes, the naked, blond-haired dolls that my mother won't allow me to play with and unused cowboy guns and dirt trucks I have only feigned interest in so as to please her.

"Enough with fairy tales and glass slippers," she says whenever she takes my dolls and puts them away in the basement—she, who collects pictures of doe-eyed movie stars with red lips and curled hair, who consumes with zeal and without the slightest bit of skepticism the surprisingly similar "confessions" of brokenhearted young women who go public, once a week, on the pages of a magazine called Modern Ladies:

they were virgins all; they fell in love with bad men, lost control of their senses, and gave in to temptation, became unchaste and therefore unworthy of marriage, so their men left them—what choice do the men have? They can't marry girls who are not virgins; they'd be fools to trust girls who didn't have enough honor, enough self-control, to resist the men.

I pick up Ruby's boxes and go down the steps, through the double doors, and into the almost-complete darkness, which I navigate by memory, my heart beating wildly in anticipation of the blue giant or the scabbed and mangy stray cat I may come upon at any moment, until I reach the middle of the room and find the long piece of rope that, when pulled, brings to life the single lightbulb screwed into the ceiling.

Around me, the walls are gray and bare and covered with soot. The floor is concrete. Thick, elaborate cobwebs hang from the corners of the ceiling and look almost incandescent in the faint, flickering light.

I put the boxes of detergent and bleach next to the bottles of lye and the industrial-strength alcohol, the rat poison and disinfectant, the plastic bag full of soft sponges and abrasive pads. After that, I go on with my usual exploration. I look inside the unmarked boxes and battered suitcases. I find the bits of fabric left over from Bahar's sewing projects, yellowed and disintegrating pages of the serialized translation of *Les Misérables* she read when she first got married, recipe books that couldn't teach her to "cook like a Muslim," and the dozen or so newspapers whose front page features Jackie Kennedy in various outfits, on trips in foreign countries where she's trailed by hordes of local women who adore and admire her because she is the wife of an American president and she wears those pearls and sunglasses and outfits that none of the adoring women could ever afford.

Bahar's dowry chest is here. I pull it out of the shadows and into the middle of the room, under the lightbulb, and open the lid. Moths fly out, translucent wings beating soundlessly, from between dresses and nightgowns and linen handkerchiefs with narrow lace borders. I take out the pink, lopsided dress Bahar wore to her engagement party, the honey-colored blouse and light gray skirt she had on the first time Omid came to Cyrus Street. I find the white shoes she wore to her wedding, which gave her blisters that bled. Her wedding dress is not in this chest, but I find her veil, pull it out till it trails on the dusty floor, hook it into my hair. I slip my feet into her shoes and walk down the aisle the way I've seen brides do in American television shows—head high and bouquet in hand and church music playing on an invisible organ. Then I find the green dress she wore the night Omid gave her the bracelet he bought at the Aramaic Brothers' store.

Caspian green.

I take out the dress and feel its perfect surface, the fabric that smells—have I imagined this?—not of mothballs and dust, but of the perfume Bahar wore to her henna ceremony. I watch the way it reflects the light in waves of green, the way it lies heavy and cool, against my skin. I open the zipper in the back and step into the dress with the wedding shoes still on. I put my arms through the armholes and close the zipper as far as I can and then I turn a pirouette—duckling to swan—imagining I'm Bahar dancing on a floor of rose petals in a palatial hall with a thousand people watching.

She's on top of the steps, looking at me.

There it is, the dress that embodied all her hope and optimism—that she wore when her heart was as light as a sparrow and her faith was solid as gold—worn by a seven-year-old in a moth-eaten veil and stained high-heeled pumps, in a dusty basement in a sweltering town where loneliness reigns.

I stand still, terrified that she's angry, feeling I've stolen not just her identity, but also her happiness. She stares at me for an eternity without saying a word. Then at last she says, "I've been calling you. I must have called you a dozen times."

THE MAN RUBY goes to see every afternoon is a thirty-eight-year-old Assyrian shoe salesman who thinks he's a rock-and-roll drummer— "Like Ringo Starr of the Beatles," he tells people, "think of me as the Persian Ringo Starr." He lives alongside the Zoroastrian on the second floor of The Tango Dancer's house—another tenant she has taken in without regard for what it will do to her reputation. He goes by the stage name Artemis, after the sidekick in the American television show Wild Wild West, wears his shirt unbuttoned halfway down to his navel, and carries a pair of black drumsticks wherever he goes, in case he's overcome by the urge to play the drums while he's standing in line at the movies, or having drinks with a friend, or out on a clandestine date with a girl. In the shoe store on Shah Reza Street, where he works, he keeps a Polaroid of himself handy at all times—"in case a 'person of consequence' in the industry comes in, notices Ringo, and asks for a headshot. You have to be ready for luck wherever it calls."

His family has pointed out to Artemis on more than one occasion that the kind of luck that turns an obscure working-class Iranian into Ringo Starr of international fame does not, as a rule, shop for shoes on Shah Reza Street. The only person of consequence who has ever gone into the store, they remind him, ended up killing another customer over a pair of shoes they both wanted. The killer was a general in the Shah's army. He didn't like that the other customer was walking away with *his* shoes—we have only one pair in your size, sir, and unfortunately, that gentleman tried them on first. So he pulled out a gun and put a bullet in the man's head, took the shoes, and walked out without paying or fear of retribution.

This is the land of the mighty; the weak should know their place.

None of this, however, has made an impression on Artemis or

weakened his resolve to dedicate himself to his life's ambition. In The Tango Dancer's house, he stays up all night and sleeps till noon, speaks too loudly, and includes a curse word in every sentence he utters. He leaves his clothes and shoes, his necklaces and comb, and even his toothbrush anywhere he pleases, except in his own room, because this is how Ringo Starr lives, how all the rock-and-roll musicians behave— they have people picking up after them every minute of the day, so they go out of their way to make a mess; it's an image thing, you have to *look* the part before someone will *give* you the part.

His behavior offends the Zoroastrian and annoys The Tango Dancer, but to Ruby, it's an extension of something already fabulous and captivating. She talks about Artemis every chance she gets, says his name the way other women utter Clark Gable's and Errol Flynn's— with her eyes glazed over and her voice filled with awe. Look at him, he's so magnificent, so young and talented, and he's so smart, he has such ambition!

Every afternoon as soon as Bahar lies down for a nap, Ruby rushes downstairs into a room we call The Triangle. This is a dark, lopsided space on the ground floor, directly under the staircase, with a doorway so small she has to bend in order to cross it. It's used for storing non-perishable food items—rice and oil and flour, sugar cones that have to be broken into small pieces by special pliers, the kinds of staples that become rare in wartime and during famines and that can mean the difference between starvation and survival. In it, Ruby has placed an old sofa, a mirror, and a small wardrobe full of dresses she knows Hassan Agha will not discover because he would never think to look here. She changes out of her work clothes into a short, low-cut dress, trades her opaque chador for one that is sheer enough to expose her bare legs, and goes into the street. She returns an hour or two later, tired but starry-eyed. She wipes off her makeup and changes outfits, then resumes her daily litany of complaints about any work Bahar has asked her to do.

"Go make sure your mother's sleeping," she tells me one day as she checks herself in a foggy mirror she has nailed to the wall of The Triangle. She has large plastic curlers in her hair and wet nail polish on her toes, and she's painting her lips with a tube of lipstick the color of fresh blood. I go upstairs and listen outside Bahar's door. I can hear the ceiling fan running, and I know the curtains are closed, because the light that seeps from around the door into the hallway is muted and pale. I go back and report my findings.

"It's OK," I tell Ruby. She's wearing a pair of gold high-heeled sandals now and has put a fake beauty mark on the side of her mouth. She pours perfume onto her chest and neck, pulls at the top of her dress so that more of her breasts are exposed, and picks up the sheer chador.

"If anyone asks, I've gone to the corner store for a tub of butter."

I don't know how anyone could believe that Ruby would dress this way just to walk to the store, but I'm more intrigued by her boldness, the confidence she has that she won't get caught no matter how flashy her clothes or outrageous her mission. I watch her go out the yard door, then I race up the stairs and into our dining room on the second floor, on the side of the house that faces the street. There is a large mahogany table here that seats eight, a heavy wooden chest where Bahar stores her china, and next to that, a metal heater with a brown shell and a grill that gathers dust all summer and overheats in winter. Beyond them all is a round balcony with a wrought-iron railing. Often in summertime, I sleep on this balcony to escape the heat. I hide a transistor radio under my pillow and fall asleep to its sound, wake up several times a night to watch the city.

From the balcony, I see Ruby enter the Alley of the Champions with her flowing chador and gold sandals. I see her move through the crowds of pedestrians and beggars and street vendors, the women who hiss at her as she walks by—look at her, she's such a whore, she's going back to that Nazi's house, I wonder which one of those men she's sleeping with today or is it both of them in one afternoon?—the stray animals and kids on bicycles and old people sitting by the open gutters. She stops to talk to some people, but never for an extended amount of time. Then she goes up to The Tango Dancer's house, knocks on the door, and vanishes into it like a wax figure in the blazing afternoon sun.

They are an odd and solitary bunch, The Tango Dancer and her tenants—disparate exiles whose only common ground is a deep and unrequited loneliness so profound, it surrounds them like a halo.

I think now this is why I was so mesmerized by them all, why I was drawn to them like a sleepwalker to the piper's tune, why I saw in that crumbling house of thwarted hopes and out-of-reach ambitions the echo of my own and my parents' lives.

WE SPEND EVERY New Year's Day at the Arbabs', but we celebrate Jewish holidays with Bahar's parents. The Arbabs do not believe in excessive displays of religiosity. They observe Yom Kippur because it's the holiest day of the year and because if they didn't, they would be considered cowards by their friends—you're afraid you'll starve if you don't eat or drink for twenty-seven hours. But they don't see the point of Rosh Hashanah, because they already *have* two New Years every year: the Christian one, which they observe by throwing a large party, drinking champagne, and kissing one another at midnight; and the Persian New Year, which takes place on the first day of spring. They have Persian counterparts for Shavuot and Sukkot as well, and they prefer those because they're modern Jews who believe themselves Iranians first and Jews second. Never mind that most Muslims in the country see the matter differently—that they believe Jews are not Iranian, they're imposters and spies, sent here by Israel to take over the country like they've taken over America, to get rich off the sweat of God-fearing Muslims. And never mind, either, that Jews had been second-class citizens in Iran for centuries before the Shah came to power and liberated them from the ghettos and the poverty they had been condemned to by the mullahs.

The Shah likes the Jews; he likes Zoroastrians and Baha'is and Christians as well. It's the mullahs he can't abide, and that's because he knows the mullahs are after his throne, they want to rule the country and rob it blind—those dirty, illiterate men with black beards and grease-stained abas, trained by other mullahs in those rat-and-roach-infested seminaries in Qom. They collect tithe and use it to buy real estate and antiques and women, teach their students to hate everyone but their own. Up until thirty years ago, they terrorized the Jews and intimidated the ruling monarch, but all that changed when the Shah's father became king: he banned the chador, ordered men to shave their beard and don Western-style suits instead of abas. And when the mullahs objected, he arrested a thousand of them and hung them all in one day from gallows erected around the city.

So the mullahs can say what they want about Jews not being Iranian; they can say that Jews are untouchable, that they drink the blood of Muslim children. They have no power in this country, are no match for the Shah and his American-trained-and-equipped army. And the Shah protects the Jews, does such a good job of it, in fact, that the mullahs are saying he's Jewish himself. Because of him, many upper-class, Western-educated Muslims have embraced the Jews as well. Some of them actually *believe* there's no difference between a Jew and a Muslim; others are sophisticated enough to pretend as such. In exchange for this graciousness, "Jews of substance" downplay their Jewishness and take pride in being Iranians first. Instead of a Star of David, they wear gold plaques with the figure of the Shah engraved on the surface. Instead of Hanukkah and Passover, they celebrate Christmas and Easter—holidays that are more festive, more attractive to the eye; they don't require a person to starve, or to give up bread, or to relive forty years of bondage in one week. That's what the Arbabs do.

Bahar's parents, by contrast, do not have the luxury of choosing their holidays. In South Tehran, Muslims and Jews take their religion seriously and practice it regardless of the difficulties it may cause. They're used to a God that demands sacrifice, not one that hands out decorated pine trees and colored eggs in painted baskets. Nine years after she has married Omid, Bahar is still shocked at the sight of the Christmas tree the Arbabs put up every winter. She can't understand why her mother-in-law swears on the holy Koran instead of the Torah.

"Let's not forget we're all Jews," Bahar tells Mrs. Arbab once and immediately regrets it because it evokes a disdainful look and a smile, and then Mrs. Arbab answers, "Yes, but some of us are not *ghetto* Jews."

She takes me to Cyrus Street every Friday night and on every Jewish holiday. "Don't talk about your father," she tells me every week, "not a word about that woman, don't tell anyone that he and I fight."

It isn't unusual for her to direct my speech or habits. What *is* unusual is the way she talks about me with her family members.

She refers to me as if I were an outsider who can't be trusted, an Arbab in flesh and in spirit—be careful what you say around her she'll repeat it to her father, lower your voice she can hear you, she may be my daughter but she sympathizes with *him*, she won't take his side openly but I see it in her eyes, she doesn't condemn him for doing what he's done to us, she clings to him no matter how much he ignores *me*, whoever said a daughter is her mother's worst enemy sure got it right.

It will be years before I can put words to what happens between Bahar and me when we're with her parents: she has left Cyrus Street and paid the price by being treated as an outsider whenever she returns. So she points to *me* as the real outsider—look at her, she's an Arbab, she has her father's features, she's loyal to him no matter what, not like me who hasn't forgotten you at all, don't you see how I come back every week?

I walk into my grandparents' house hoping I will find the way, each time, to make them forget that I'm my father's child.

One night during Passover, I walk in on a conversation between Bahar and her aunt. They're in the kitchen with their backs to the door, facing the stove, where they're frying chicken in lemon juice with onions and saffron. I've been given the task of setting the table, so I've come in for the plates and the flatware.

"I'll never forget how your mother miscarried at eight months because she was frying chicken by this same stove," Bahar's aunt remarks.

I've heard about the miscarriage before, but don't know what connection it had to cooking or that stove, so I pause and listen.

"It was a neighbor's wedding," the aunt goes on. "Everyone was helping with the food, but your mother was too pregnant. She shouldn't have stood on her feet all those hours, but they had given her twenty chickens to fry, and she did every last one. When she finished, she sat down and drank a pitcher of ice water. That did it. The heat from the stove, the cold water. It stopped the baby's heart."

Bahar remarks that it's inconceivable to her that a parent could suffer the loss of a child and still go on. "I don't know how my mother did it."

The aunt nods. "I know," she says, turning off the flame under the skillet. "I know. I lost one myself." She wipes her hands on her apron and turns away from the stove. "But your poor mother lost two," she says, "and both of them were *boys*."

Just then, Bahar sees me behind them. Biting her lip, she tries to grab the aunt's attention, to warn her that she's saying too much, but the aunt is oblivious.

"It's one thing to lose an infant," she sighs, "but when she lost the ten-year-old—"

"That's enough," Bahar snaps. To me she says, "go back out and set the table."

I've prayed with this family on Yom Kippur, sat with them at seders, slept outside in a sukkah. I've seen them once a week since I can remember and in all that time, I have not heard mention of a lost son. How strange, I think: in a family where grief is a way of life, no one I know has ever alluded to the greatest calamity of all.

NIYAZ NEVER TALKS to anyone about her affair with Omid. She appears in public with him everywhere, and she seems loyal, even giving, but she won't answer a question about what she feels for him or what kind of a future she thinks she's going to have with a married man. True, you don't need to look at them for long to realize that she is the one in command, that whatever her feelings for him, she needs him less than he wants her. That gives her an undeniable advantage; it's clear she can get him to leave his wife and child any time she wants, but she hasn't done that yet, and this is what perplexes people and drives the gossip about her and Omid: is it because she is kindhearted and benevolent, or because she doesn't want him around all the time?

I've thought about this for a long time—how my father gave so little of himself to Bahar, who needed him so much, and gave so much to a woman who could easily have done without him. I think there was something in the way Bahar depended on him, the way she waited year after year for him to come back, that made him want to leave. I think his indifference, his cruelty, were products of Bahar's weakness.

It isn't what she had wanted to become; it's what he forced her into. But he resents her for it all the same.

❧

WHAT I NOTICE about my parents is that they never touch. They speak to each other if they have to, sometimes go places together, but they never get close enough for their bodies to meet even by chance, or reach for one another, or hold hands. I'm aware of this because I see the way lovers touch on Peyton Place once a week, and I imagine this is what Omid is like with Niyaz. I know he doesn't sleep in the same bed as Bahar, that he has turned his study into a bedroom for himself. I wonder if this is a failure on Bahar's part. I've heard the Arbabs say that "a man who is content in his wife's bed doesn't wander into the arms of other women."

Sometimes, in the morning when he and Bahar are drinking tea in the dining room, Omid will sit a while and light a cigarette, open the newspaper and read quietly as she pours him another glass. Then he'll look up from the paper and talk to her about something or other, and she'll answer in a calm voice, and they'll go on like this for minutes, maybe even half an hour, before he looks at his watch and says, I have to go. On those mornings, I know that all is not lost for my parents and our damaged family.

HE GOES TO AMERICA for three weeks, and when he comes back, he has brought me a suitcase full of gifts—dresses and shoes, little plastic dolls with blond hair and blue eyes, a miniature ladybug charm necklace made of gold, with red enamel wings and emerald eyes. To make up for the time we haven't seen each other, he takes me to the cinema to see an animated film, dubbed in Farsi, about a boy named Mowgli who lives in the jungle with only a bear to look after him. Afterward, he takes me to a restaurant called Chattanooga to eat a banana split. It's the biggest bowl of ice cream I have ever seen, but he tells me that this is a normal-size portion in America, that all the different flavors and the chocolate sauce and whipped cream, what seems like such extravagance to people in other parts of the world, are in fact taken for granted by Americans.

He watches me eat the ice cream. He asks if I'm happy at school, if I like the other girls.

"I wish I had a sister."

He laughs and says that I'm not missing anything by being an only child, that having siblings is overrated. He tells me about his own childhood in the Arbab household, how his mother had dressed him and his brother in white cotton pants in the summer, white wool sweaters in winter, and expected them to keep their clothes spotless at all times. He says he doesn't remember having ever played with, or fought with his brother.

I believe him because I've seen the way his mother looks at me when we go to the Arbab house, and I imagine this is how she looked at Omid when he was a child. She's always sitting in a stiff-backed chair, looking imperious but annoyed. When I go up to kiss her, she offers her cheek, but only reluctantly, and quickly pulls away. Every Persian New Year, she gives me a gold coin.

"Open your hand," she orders, and puts the coin in the center of my palm.

"It's for luck," she says every year. "Now run along."

I imagine she spoke to my father in that same tone, that she displayed the same disinterest, the same boredom that she shows me.

"Did you love your mother?" I ask him in Chattanooga. He looks stunned by the question.

"Why do you ask?"

I feel as if I'm looking in a mirror, seeing myself in Omid. I know what it's like to have a parent who doesn't see you most of the time— even when she's with you. A parent who loves and resents you at once.

Suddenly, I can forgive Omid his indiscretions with Niyaz, his absence from our house. I can understand why he would give up his own family for a woman who doesn't want him all that much, or doesn't want all of him.

I wish for nothing more than to trade places with Niyaz, to *become* her so I can bring Omid home, but I know this will never happen because I'm too needy, too frightened and vulnerable to love him as my mother loves me, as Mrs. Arbab loves Omid: as if he didn't exist.

OMID TELLS HIS FATHER he wants to divorce Bahar.

He says he has tried, but can't force himself to stay in the marriage, that he made a mistake when he was twenty-four years old and doesn't want to pay for it with the rest of his life. He's still a young man—thirty-seven—and he thinks he deserves a chance at happiness even if he *did* fail to see the writing on the wall.

They're standing by the back gates of the Arbab house, next to a car Mr. Arbab has bought that day. It's a black Cadillac with gray leather seats and a wood console, so majestic-looking it is bound to attract many an evil eye. To defend himself and protect the car, Mr. Arbab must baptize it with sacrificial blood. So he has sent Hassan to buy a goat from a man who raises sacrificial animals—goats and sheep and, for lesser occasions, roosters and chickens—in his yard. Now, Hassan is sharpening his butcher knife, and the goat, which has sensed danger, is bleating furiously and pulling at the rope that keeps it tied to a tree a few feet away from the car.

Mr. Arbab is dressed in a suit and tie. He's pacing across the wide carport with the red and green awning. Every time he comes near Hassan, he stops a moment and watches the knife slide against the black stone that is used to sharpen metal. He has known for some time that he would have this conversation with Omid. He has already discussed it with his wife, even, and together they have decided they would let Omid choose the moment. Mr. Arbab paces across the carport once more, stops and lights a cigarette. The goat keeps rising on its hind feet, pulling so hard at the rope that it looks like it may give any minute.

"You mean you've lost your head to that woman," Mr. Arbab finally answers.

Omid recoils.

"It appears she knows how to order you around."

Mr. Arbab has never been especially proud of his son, but he takes particular exception to the way Omid has acted with Niyaz, the way he has eschewed decorum and tact, abandoned himself to his whims, made a spectacle of his feebleness with a woman who, if you disregard exceptionally good looks, is really a high-class whore with a good bit of money and a once-illustrious surname.

Mr. Arbab knows that his son is not endowed with great courage or willpower. He has known this since Omid was a child, from the way he followed his mother around the house and tugged at her skirt, called for her at night from his bed, and when she ignored him, as she should have—every nursemaid and doctor and parent would tell you that doing otherwise will spoil the child—he lay in the dark and cried himself to sleep. Mr. Arbab had wished Omid had the mettle to defy orders, get out of bed and turn the light on and march out of his room like a man, demand attention, risk punishment, but you can't change a person's nature; some men are born frail. You take from God what he gives you and say grace.

The weepy little boy became an aloof teenager with few friends and barely a female companion until when he turned twenty-three and his mother scored for him the match of the decade. "The Baha'i Girl," as the Arbabs called her, would have been the perfect wife and mother and daughter-in-law, if only Omid had managed to keep her. All he had to do was send the girl a few dozen roses and tell her she walks on water, so what if he didn't believe it himself? Who said you have to *believe* the nonsense women like you to tell them? You just say it and go about your business, take seven lovers if you want, just be discreet. Don't embarrass her and certainly don't embarrass *yourself* by letting her leave you halfway to the altar.

Mr. Arbab has locked eyes with Omid and is counting the seconds before his son breaks down and looks away, because that's what happens every time—Omid doesn't have the guts to stare his father down—and soon enough, Omid clears his throat and turns his head.

"We can leave her out of it," Omid says, and the hurt in his voice almost makes his father pity him. "I'm not happy in my marriage."

Across from them, Hassan Agha puts his knife down and calls out for the two other servants to come to his aid. They run over and grab the goat so it doesn't escape when Hassan unties it. The goat struggles violently in their arms, more so when Hassan approaches.

"The damn things always know when they're about to die," Hassan declares, and wraps the end of the rope around his own hand.

"Being happy," Mr. Arbab says, "has nothing to do with it."

He throws the butt of his cigarette on the ground and crushes it with the tip of his shoe, then yells for Hassan not to bother moving the goat too far—it's fighting hard, might as well kill it where it is, all we need is the blood.

He turns to Omid.

"You have a wife and a daughter," he tells his son. "You're responsible for them as I am for mine—as every husband and father with any modicum of honor would be. You can be happy with them or not—it's a life."

It's the life you chose in spite of our warnings, and maybe it's the best you deserve. Either way, you've done enough damage already. It's time you recognized there are limits to what should and shouldn't be done.

They're trying to push the goat to the ground, but it won't go down. So they grab its hooves and pull its legs out from under it till it falls on its side. The two younger men bear down on it fiercely while Hassan runs over to get his knife. Mr. Arbab sees the color drain out of Omid's face, recognizes the revulsion that used to make Omid sick when he was younger, actually vomit his insides out every time they slaughtered an animal in the house.

The goat has seen the knife in Hassan's hand. Instead of fighting, it lets out a long whimper, then lies, nearly still, as it waits. It's strange, Mr. Arbab thinks, how some animals surrender to death when they realize there's no escape.

Hassan knows that it's a sin to make an animal wait too long to be slaughtered. You have to do it fast, deliver the coup de grâce and put the thing out of its misery. He raises the knife and brings it down over the goat's neck. It slits open like a broken dam, blood leaping out of it and all over Hassan's chest and arms. The goat lets out another whimper, then keeps trembling for nearly a minute before it goes limp. Blood streams out of it and onto the ground, outlining the carcass, staining the servants' shoes, flowing toward Mr. Arbab and his son.

One of the men dips his hands into the blood, then walks over to the car. He rubs the blood on the front tires of the car, goes back for more, rubs it on the back tires. They have to wait for all the blood to drain out of the carcass before they can skin and quarter the animal, and then they'll take the meat to South Tehran and give it away to the poor. Their good deed—feeding the hungry—will bless and guard the new car.

Mr. Arbab lights another cigarette.

"Like it or not," he says, "there are things we allow ourselves, and boundaries we don't cross. No one's telling you to give up your mistress, but you have to realize you're a Jew and she's Muslim, you have a name to honor and she's the child of an opium addict and a woman who whored herself for a new husband. I don't like your wife and I don't know what you're going to do with your kid but they're *your* burden to bear and I won't have the stigma of divorce haunting us in this town."

PART IV

I START SECOND GRADE in September. In December, the teacher calls our house.

It's the end of a school day, and I'm sitting with Bahar at the dining table where I do my homework every night. The light above me is dim, the windows fogged over by the contrast between the frigid weather outside and the oppressive warmth of the oil heater that has only one switch—on or off, with no way to modulate the intensity of the heat it generates. Every once in a while, I get off my chair and kneel on the ground, clean the tip of my eraser by rubbing it against the surface of the Persian carpet with the red and blue pattern woven in wool thread that covers the floor. My fingertips are stained from the lead in my pencil; the side of my middle finger that anchors the pencil is dented from the weight it supports. I have written all day in school, then again at home. We have to write a great deal in second grade—math equations, science terms, Persian poems, Arabic phrases from the Koran—but I often end up writing more than the other children because I don't follow the lessons well, don't understand what the teacher has said, and so she'll give me a single sentence, or a paragraph, to write a hundred times—until I learn to pay attention in class.

It's nine o'clock, and my wrist aches. My eyes are burning with sleep and my head longs to rest on the page, but I'm not even halfway through my punishment. I work as fast as I can without letting the speed ruin my handwriting because I know the teacher will not accept the assignment if it's not neat or legible; will in fact double the number of repetitions I have to do the following evening. My main concern, however, is that Bahar will notice what I'm doing, that she will find out I've been inattentive in school and become angry.

The phone—a black bubble with a heavy receiver and white circles where numbers are inscribed—sits on a small end table that marks the end of the dining room and the start of the living room. Bahar picks up on the third ring, beams when she learns that my teacher is on the line. She is effusive in her greeting, but quickly becomes quiet, shifts her weight on her legs, and looks up at me quizzically. As she listens, the smile that had brightened her eyes contracts into a frown. Then she says, "What do you *mean*, she's distracted?"

Next to the end table is a hand-painted commode, six feet long and three feet deep, with narrow, rectangular mirrors, each with a beveled frame, covering the inside. When I was smaller, I used to hide in this cabinet for hours at a time. I'd pull my knees to my chest and watch my own image repeated in a thousand echoes—in each strip of mirror, each beveled edge, each part reflecting all the others.

"What's a seven-year-old supposed to *absorb*?"

On the other side of the commode is a sofa with a wood frame and a pink satin cover, six matching chairs, a coffee table. Next to that is a chest with a glass front, where various items of monetary value and no real use—a crystal rose, a pair of hand-carved candlesticks, an enormous gold coin displaying the image of the Shah, complete with jewel-studded cape and crown—are on display. The sofa and chairs are pushed back against the wall; the coffee table is laden with silver bowls that have not been filled in years. The carpet—a quince-colored silk weave—is so untouched that it glows under the light.

The living room is where my parents would have entertained formally if they had had a real home life. It's where Omid would have sat with his business associates, offered them a glass of Scotch—twelve years old, at least—or a shot of vodka, or if it's after dinner, a touch of Hennessy. It's where Bahar would have sat with her school friends, who would come, wide-eyed and envious, but never forgetting the social graces and expected rituals of a good guest, to admire everything from the chandelier—yes, it was made in Czechoslovakia; my father-in-law had it delivered by hand straight from the workshop to this house; it arrived in three hundred and twelve pieces, took a whole day to assemble—to the tassel-fringed drapery, to the narrow-waisted, gold-leaf glasses in which Bahar would serve tea.

In fact, my parents have used the living room only a handful of times, when the Arbabs and their relatives came by, or when Omid's friends accepted an invitation they quickly regretted, and then they all gave up—this girl is never going to learn, it's not in her blood, you either have class or you don't, there's no faking it these days—and stopped coming to our house.

Bahar hangs up the phone and remains still, her right hand closed in a fist that presses against her mouth, her head bent so that her focus is on the floor. My heart beats louder the longer she retains that pose, because I know she's thinking hard about what to do—that she has heard something shocking and is trying to find her bearings. I know that when she finally turns to me her face will be pale and drawn with disappointment, that her lips will have become blue-pale, that her teeth will be digging into her bottom lip.

The teacher has complained that I'm inattentive and unmotivated in class; that I'm removed and unfriendly in the yard; that I "linger on the periphery but never join."

"What does she *mean* by that?" Bahar asks me back at the table.

I shake my head and say I don't know.

"Why don't you join in?" she insists. "Why are you excluded?"

In vain, I search for an answer.

The other kids don't like me; they don't want me to get close. I go up to them sometimes but then I just stand there, looking, as the four or five other girls talk busily to one another and only glance at me from the corners of their eyes, and when they're done, they just turn around and walk away, they leave me there as if I didn't exist.

I know better than to say this to Bahar.

"I don't know."

"Is it true you have no friends?"

Her voice is sad and accusing.

The question stings like a rush of poison. I look away from Bahar, at the empty salon with the heavy silk drapes and the black phone that used to remind me of our loneliness—because it rang so rarely—and that, today, has borne witness to my inadequacy.

I imagine I'm small again, crouched over in the cabinet with the glass panels, surrounded by a thousand other me's, all of us one dimensional, intangible, safe behind a wall of glass.

"Have you been getting bad grades and keeping them from me?" I hear her ask, but I've already removed myself from the room—left my shame and confusion at the table and taken refuge behind that glass: she can see me, and she thinks I'm real, but I'm not.

"Look at me when I talk to you," she says, and I hear the despair in her voice, know that in a moment it will turn into rage and explode.

"Don't you want to succeed in life? Don't you think I've been shamed enough by your father? Don't you know that we'll be judged more harshly—you and I—because of what he has done?"

There is a knot in my throat that makes it impossible for me to speak.

"So then why?" Bahar is unrelenting. "Why do you want to ruin us?"

At this, her voice breaks. She puts her face into her hands and—to my horror—sobs so that her whole body shakes.

I don't know, Mother. I don't know what confuses me in the classroom, makes me a pariah on the playground. I don't know what it is that surrounds me, invisible, everywhere I am, that separates me from everyone.

Even from my father.

Even from *you*.

SHE TELLS ME I mustn't talk to anyone about the teacher's call.

She says it will be our secret—one we will quickly bury and move on from. She knows I understand the importance of doing well in school, that I appreciate the consequences of failure. She knows I don't want to be ordinary, that I don't intend to relive her already-botched-up life.

Don't tell the kids at school. Don't repeat it to Ruby. No matter what, don't say a word of it to your father. We have more to prove—you and I—than an ordinary mother and child. People think your father prefers that woman to us because there's something wrong with *us*. They think it's *our* fault he's abandoned us. So they're always watching, waiting for a flaw they can point to. We have to be careful we don't *show* them a flaw.

She's particularly conscious of this around the Arbabs. Whenever we're going to visit them, we begin preparing far in advance. We have to buy new clothes, make arrangements for Bahar to have her hair done and her eyebrows threaded, go over the rules of Persian etiquette: say hello to and kiss everyone in the room, whether you know them or not; do not sit down unless you've been invited to; when the food is served, admire it greatly and beg the host's pardon for the enormous trouble you've put them through.

There are other rules as well—ones we don't talk about but which we follow religiously: I never talk to the Arbabs about my mother, or react when she's not in the room and one of my grandparents makes a comment about her. I sit politely, hands on my lap, as Mrs. Arbab refers to The Unmarried Sister as "rotting"—how is your rotting aunt?—or when she says about The Opera Singer, "that singing brother of hers should buy an accordion and get a monkey on a chain."

You don't challenge an assault by an older person, because you have a duty to respect them no matter what. You don't defend yourself, or your children, against an affront by a person your own age, because you must maintain your dignity under fire. You don't disobey a man, even one younger than yourself, because you must prove your ability to follow rules.

It's an unmerciful hierarchy. It obliterates the weak, the young, the rebellious.

We live, each of us, in a shadow land of veiled truths and guarded mysteries. It's like the way houses were built in our part of the world before the Europeans arrived: There was an "outer chamber"—neat, beautiful, furnished as opulently as the owners could afford—where visitors were allowed. And then there was an "inner chamber," where only the closest family could enter, where the women of the house spent most of their lives and where they could take off their veils, speak, and even laugh.

Every person I know has a hidden half.

❧

SUDDENLY, the roses begin to die in our yard.

Decades-old Muhammadi bushes that have lined the base of the yard wall and produced magnificent flowers turn brown from the roots up and wither. Alarmed and slightly offended by this, Hassan Agha blames the harsh winter for the damage and bets on the spring to return his roses to their usual splendor. In the spring, he fertilizes the soil and pulls out the weeds, waters the lawn and the trees, plants new grass. But the grass only grows yellow and brittle, and the grapevine remains bare. Trees that have borne fruit every year stand naked and indifferent, their bark peeling off in dry layers, trunks growing increasingly hollow.

Hassan then suspects that the water he's using for the plants is contaminated—probably on purpose, probably by British functionaries who have forever engaged in the most unspeakable forms of intrigue in Iran and who are not above poisoning the water just to deprive us of our beautiful Persian gardens the way they are robbing us of our oil. For thousands of years before the British arrived, Hassan always says, people drank from wells and washed with water that flew in gutters. Day-old infants were bathed in unfiltered water and lived to old age. Suddenly one day, everyone was told that well and river water were unsafe and contaminated—you must drink only what comes through a copper pipe, at the end of a plastic hose or a metal faucet, and so what if those cunning bastards have mixed something in with the water? Something that makes plants die and women behave in unseemly ways? That makes hundred-year-old trees keel over and die, and sends a person's wife into the street where the most sordid rumors are allowed to hatch, with no concern for how that can obliterate a man's pride?

Hassan can't get Ruby to stay at home and can't revive our plants, and so he blames British spies or the black plumes of exhaust fumes that rise behind every car and bus and taxi on the street outside and that form a nearly permanent cloud over downtown Tehran. He wonders if some jealous neighbor is creeping into the yard at night, spraying acid over the lawn just for the pleasure of seeing it wither. He accuses everyone who has ever commented on the beauty of the roses of having cast an evil eye upon them, but in the end, all he can do is stand by and see the garden die.

I'm watching him one afternoon as he waters the plants. I'm sitting on the steps that lead from the yard into the ground floor of the house. Bahar is in her room, sleeping. Ruby is off "buying a tub of butter." I'm bored, and though I've asked a number of times, Hassan won't let me help him with watering the lawn.

He's barefoot, his pants' legs rolled up, his eyes so focused on the task before him that he hardly reacts when the doorbell rings.

Hassan goes on with his work as if he hadn't heard a thing. His skin is dark and toughened by the sun. His feet are calloused and bony. He's so thin you can see each of his vertebrae through his shirt.

The bell rings again.

"Go away," he calls out, assuming a traveling salesman is at the other end. "We don't want anything."

He fans the air with the hose, letting the water fall in an arc onto the soil. He has no tolerance for people who come to waste his time, offering God-only-knows-what from the back of a mule or the trunk of their car.

There's a third ring, and now Hassan is positively mad. He curses the person at the door as loudly as he can, threatens to greet him with a horse whip if he doesn't go to hell right away.

I know I shouldn't, but I run down the steps and open the door.

A man stands before me in a shiny gray suit with enormous sweat stains around the armholes. He looks dirty and hot, as if he were melting in the sun. He has a fedora in one hand and a battered suitcase in the other. As soon as the door opens, he puts the suitcase on the ground next to his foot and sighs, like a traveler who has come from far away and cannot stand to carry his load for one more second. Then he looks at me with sudden recognition and says, "It's *you.*"

I've seen this man before, but only from a distance. His name is Chamedooni, and he's The Tango Dancer's newest tenant. He's always wearing the same clothes, and he carries the suitcase everywhere. He sells what he claims are "rare and exotic items—talismans that, if used properly, will unlock the gates of good fortune and give you the world and all its forbidden fruits." He sells a yellow oil that he swears will cure baldness, a candle that, if left to burn in a room all night, will rid the air of evil spirits. He sells counterfeit passports to women who need to leave the country in order to escape abusive husbands, the names of surgeons who will repair, for a fee, the broken hymens of girls who have lost their virginity before marriage. Mostly, he sells the hair of dead women.

He buys the hair at the cemeteries in Tehran and neighboring cities, cuts it off the corpses of young girls who have died of disease or of a broken heart and have ended up naked on a stone slab, like Sleeping Beauty before the prince. He has to bribe the undertakers to let him get to the hair before they wrap the body in a caftan shroud, and he knows he's committing an unpardonable sin by seeing the girls naked and by touching their hair—defiling them for eternity and causing them to be banned from heaven—so he does his best to treat the hair with respect. He cuts it off carefully and ties it with a ribbon before he folds it into the suitcase, and then he takes it to the hair-dressers and wig makers in Tehran's upscale salons. It isn't his life's ambition, he tells the hairdressers, to turn a poor girl's chastity into adornment for rich women; it's just something he took up, a decade ago, to help him through hard times.

He leans toward me in the doorway and whispers, "I'm glad you answered." He wipes the palms of his hands on the front of his jacket.

They leave a wet trail that glows on the shiny fabric. "I've been wanting to talk to you."

He smells of formaldehyde and harsh soap and plastic, of cold, stale places—like the empty water storage tank in my grandparents' house on Cyrus Street, where birds fly in through the tiny hatch, and can't find their way out, flail madly about till they break their wings or their neck and fall to the ground. I try to hold my breath, but I'm afraid I'll offend him if I pull back, so I remain in place, frozen, and watch him force a smile that barely parts his lips. His hands are dirty, his fingernails lined with grease. He is more pathetic than frightening, and I know I shouldn't have opened the door for him, shouldn't be speaking with him alone.

He cranes his neck forward and looks around the door into the yard. He can't see Hassan, but he can hear the water running.

"It's about that boy," he says.

"Who's there?" Hassan yells from across the yard.

I leave Chamedooni in the doorway and run to Hassan.

"Tell him to get lost," he says when I tell him someone with a suitcase is at the door. "Just shut the door and come back."

But when I go back to the door, the man has already opened his suitcase and is searching through a pile of odd objects of assorted sizes and colors.

"I've heard about the troubles with the yard," he tells me too loudly, his voice breaking in places. He's breathing hard as he speaks, and I can see that his hands are trembling slightly.

"I have for you the perfect solution."

He pulls out a plastic bag with green and black letters written in English across the front.

"This is called Miracle Plant—" he says the name in English, again too loudly, like the announcers who advertise stuff on the radio. "It's guaranteed to turn any desert into the Garden of Eden."

He glances quickly from left to right and behind him at the street. Then he leans toward me and whispers something so quickly, I don't understand him at all.

When I don't react, he becomes flustered.

"They use this in Hollywood," he yells, "in the gardens of movie stars and other important people."

Then he leans toward me and whispers, "I've seen the boy with the bicycle."

He pushes the bag into my hand.

"Take this to Hassan Agha, your able gardener, and tell him it's the cure for all his troubles."

He's playing a charade.

"I know you see him too, because you're always on that balcony, looking at the street," he whispers.

Sweat falls from his jawbones onto his shirt. He wipes his eyes with one hand and takes a breath.

"I want to tell you I think he lives in this house," he says, suddenly winded, as if the very words have taken his breath away.

He searches my face.

"I *know* you see him," he insists. "I *know* you do."

LATER THAT DAY, I find Bahar working at her Singer sewing machine and tell her about Chamedooni.

"He kept talking about a boy," I tell her.

Bahar is running a red organza sleeve through the machine. She's holding the sides of the fabric down with both hands, watching the needle go up and down, and she barely seems to hear what I've said.

She finishes the stitching and lifts the needle off the fabric.

"What boy?"

The sleeve is inside out. She turns it over.

"I'm not sure," I say. "There's a boy who's in the alley a lot. He has a bicycle. I think that's…"

Bahar turns ashen. I sense that I've said something wrong and wonder if I should backtrack. I know she doesn't want me looking at the Alley from the edge of our dining room balcony.

"When did you see this boy?"

It's too late for me to deny anything. "I see him all the time," I stammer.

"What does he look like?"

"Like nothing special. But Chamedooni was saying he thinks the boy lives here."

Bahar's eyes fill with tears. Her mouth is half-open, her lips nearly white. I realize she's reacting to more than my disobedience.

"Do you know who the boy is?" I ask.

She shakes her head—no—but her eyes have already betrayed her.

Yes, it's he, of course—The Ghost Brother—but I don't know this yet and won't find out for some time.

He has dark eyes and pale skin, and I can tell he's impecunious because he wears the same old shirt and rotting shoes even in the dead of winter. I see him shivering in the Alley late at night or early morning in winter, or sitting in the shade of The Tango Dancer's house in summer. And I have never thought he's anything but a real person, never had a clue that he is long dead, that he comes to June Street because his own parents keep chasing him away, that they're afraid he will bring back to them the same dreadful luck that caused them to lose him in the first place. He inhabits a world of in-betweens—a world in which he can see, but isn't seen; where he is forgotten but can't forget. He chases Bahar because she was the first person who saw him when he came back from the dead and he thinks she might see him again.

He has followed Bahar out of Cyrus Street and into the very place she thought she would be safe from him.

I don't know any of this the day Chamedooni comes to our door. Nor do I know that even as I tell Bahar about the man with the crooked teeth and the suitcase full of miracles, I am losing my own connection to the world.

ONE AFTERNOON, it's nearly dusk, I hear my parents screaming in the next room. Bahar is upset because Omid has been somewhere with Niyaz—a party thrown by someone who is not related to the Arbabs by blood, but who is close enough to be considered family. This—that he has taken her to a family function—is a violation of the terms of the truce, albeit a tacit one, my parents have made with each other. It has also upset the Arbabs—we're not this kind of people, we don't display our mistresses in public, we respect the sanctity of family and tradition. Omid knows he's overstepped the boundaries but doesn't seem regretful or ashamed, won't apologize to his father or offer an excuse to Bahar.

"You have a *daughter* for God's sake," Bahar yells at him inside the house. "You don't care what happens to *me*, but what about *her*? How is she going to find a husband after the shame you've brought us?"

I'm too afraid of the fighting to go in, too worried to walk away or ignore what I hear. I've heard the same words, the accusations and insults and threats—*damn this town, if you push me I'll leave the country and never return*—countless times before and I've never become accustomed to them, never stopped trembling at the first scream, praying through all the exchanges that it will end, that Omid will leave the house or Bahar will go into her room and shut the door, so that by the time one of them finally does walk away, I feel like a wounded soldier left to guard the ruins of her own sanctuary.

From my bedroom window, I can see the maple trees that line June Street—how their leaves have turned orange and yellow and red, how they carpet the ground on both sides of the street. I remember walking on the leaves when I was younger, delighting as they crackled under my shoes. It occurs to me I haven't heard that sound—of dry leaves being crushed—at all this fall.

It gets dark out, and my parents are still fighting. On the street, a few men have lit a fire in a metal barrel and stand around it, smoking. They feed the fire with bits of wood and garbage and with heating oil that is sold by the gallon. Ruby comes out of our house in a bright red dress, with her hair loose on her shoulders, and takes a cigarette from one of the men. I can only see her back, but I know that she's smiling, that she's talking fast and watching The Tango Dancer's house, hoping for Artemis to emerge from it.

"What about *us*?" Bahar is pleading with Omid. "What'll become of *us* if you leave?"

Something about the despair in those words makes me want to scream. I feel an unfamiliar sensation, something bigger and more gripping than either hope or fear: a rage so powerful it ignites my heart, my chest, my arms and hands. I look at the fire outside and wonder what it would be like to pour the heating oil over the dry maple leaves on the sidewalk, let the fire spread. I imagine the entire length of June Street on fire. Our yard on fire.

I wasn't like this—ruinous—by nature. Left to my own devices, I believe, I would have chosen tenderness over rage, forgiveness over revenge.

OMID'S RECKLESSNESS with Niyaz is a warning to Bahar that he's preparing to leave us for good. She has tried everything she knows to avert this disaster and realizes she's about to fail. She decides it's time to confront Niyaz.

Up till now, she has avoided running into Niyaz. She says it's because she wants to maintain her dignity, refrain from engaging in a catfight or becoming the butt of other people's jokes—I'm not a shrew, not shameless like that Muslim woman, my people have lived quietly and without scandal for generations, they may not be the richest in the world, but they're solemn, they keep their poise even in the face of tragedy, I'm damned if I'll let that whore strip me of my pride.

This is not entirely true. Her parents may guard their reputation like it's the last drop of water in a hot desert, but they are no strangers to disgrace. Her father comes from a line of traveling musicians, who because of their profession, were relegated to the lowest ranks of society. Every generation in the family was forced to do the same work because they all bore the mark of the family's shame—to engage in the kind of activity that aroused men's passions and drove women to prostitute themselves. They were like the clans of undertakers in each community—despised, but necessary.

Bahar's father managed to escape this legacy because he came of age at a time when Reza Shah allowed the Jews to live outside of their ghettos. He also introduced, for the first time in the country's history, the idea of having an official, registered surname. He created government offices that issued birth certificates for newborns and for older people as well. You could select any surname you liked, regardless of whether it matched that of the other members of your family. So Bahar's father had moved from the ghetto to Cyrus Street and adopted a name—Jahanbani—that gave no hint of his past, and he thought he could convince some rabbi to take him on as a pupil. But there's more to a person's legacy than a mere name. You can feign ignorance of the traveling kamancheh and tar players of your past all you please, but there will always be people who remember you when, who will bear witness to what you've been. My grandfather had chosen a name no one in the ghetto had heard of, and for a while, he had managed to study with a rabbi who had come to Tehran from some faraway province. Soon enough, however, younger men wouldn't stand up to show respect, as was the custom, when he came into a room. Older women covered their faces with their scarves when he looked in their direction. Mr. Jahanbani recognized the signs of being designated undesirable and stopped pretending.

So when Bahar says she's loathe to confront Niyaz out of a sense of decorum, she is telling only half the truth. The other half is that she fears the inevitable comparison, fears she'll lose to Niyaz in the eyes of anyone who can see, and perhaps in her own eyes as well.

But in the days after Omid's appearance at the home of the Arbabs' family friend, Bahar realizes that drastic action is required. She tells me we're going to find Niyaz. We're going to stand our ground and tell her that Omid is not hers to keep, he has a wife and a child who need him and they're right here, before you, miss, they're real people with real pain, this isn't an episode of *Days of Our Lives*, you don't get to wreck a life and avoid burning in hell, just let him go, you can always snare another man, a richer one than Omid, no doubt, that kind of thing is easy for the likes of you.

There's a beauty shop that has, of late, become terribly popular with all the rich wives. Bahar has never been to the salon, but she has been introduced to the flamboyant owner, Fareed, more than once, and he always acts as if he's meeting her for the first time. Bahar imagines that Niyaz would go there on Thursdays, because Thursday night is when all the big parties in Tehran happen. She calls the salon for an appointment.

The woman at the other end asks for Bahar's surname. She hesitates when Bahar answers.

"Which Arbab?" she asks, cautiously at first, in case Bahar is someone she needs to respect.

"I'm Omid Arbab's wife."

The receptionist covers the mouthpiece with her hand, but doesn't bother to hold the phone away as she asks someone else, "Do we know Omid Arbab's wife?"

There's a frenzy of chatter on the end of the line. Then the woman returns.

"He's busy this week."

Bahar knows this is a snub, that whoever is informing the receptionist at the salon has declared Bahar not important enough to be seen by Fareed.

"I don't mind waiting."

The receptionist gets annoyed.

"We don't do that."

"Why not?"

"Because we don't," the woman snaps.

Bahar gathers her breath.

"Take down my name," she commands. "I'll be there on Thursday."

FAREED'S BEAUTY SHOP occupies the entire second floor of a two-story building in Tehran's upscale shopping district. It's a large, airy space with bay windows and velvet curtains, white Roman columns with gold-leaf touches, Louis XIV furniture, and marble floors. When we arrive, the windows are open, and a young boy is mopping the floor, humming to himself as he works. He nods a greeting, but quickly turns his attention back to what he's doing. Bahar and I wait by the unattended reception desk. After a while, we hear the clicking of heels, and then a woman appears in a black dress and dark sunglasses. She's carrying a cup of Turkish coffee in one hand, a deck of cards in the other. A burning cigarette dangles from between her ruby-red lips. She doesn't react when she sees us. She puts the coffee and the cards down on the desk, puts the cigarette onto the edge of an ashtray, then goes around and takes her seat across from us.

"Yes."

It's not a question, not an invitation of any kind. It means, state your business and be off.

Bahar, who has come ready to make peace, stiffens.

"I called earlier in the week."

"Yes," the woman says again.

"I'd like to see Fareed."

The woman takes off her sunglasses and looks at us. She has acne-scarred skin and eyelashes that bear the weight of endless layers of mascara she clearly hasn't washed off in days. Women in Tehran make an art of applying mascara. They spend hours painting every lash, then separating the ones that stick together with the tip of a safety pin. They wait for the lashes to dry, apply another coat, wait again, and apply more. Only then do they curl the lashes, and paint their eyes and the rest of their face. At bedtime, they'll take off the eyeliner and eye shadow, but not the mascara.

"A lot of people want to see Fareed," the woman says. "Do you have an appointment?"

Customers who command respect do not need an appointment to see Fareed.

"He's not here anyway," the woman says, and takes a long drag on her cigarette. She looks at her watch. "It's only ten o'clock."

Fareed's clients are women who go to parties every night, stay till morning, often have breakfast somewhere with friends before they go home. Ten o'clock is way too early for any of them to be anywhere, or for Fareed to be at the salon. Bahar knows this, but she has been up for hours with anticipation; she wants to be sure Fareed doesn't have an excuse for not seeing her; and she doesn't want to miss Niyaz when she comes.

She takes my hand and walks to the waiting area in the foyer.

"I'll wait."

The foyer overlooks Pahlavi Avenue and the manicured lawns and cascading waterfalls of the new park that is the Shah's most recent "gift" to his capital city. During the day, the park teems with families and small children, old men who sit in groups of two and three, playing with worry beads, young girls who are hiding from their parents so they can read a love letter or a book of poetry, agents of the shah's secret police who are there to eavesdrop on every conversation. At night, it becomes the domain of small-time drug dealers and emaciated young men in bell-bottom pants with silver "Peace" signs hanging from their neck, who sit barefoot on the ground, smoke hashish, and argue over the politics of Che Guevara and the philosophy of Hannah Arendt until daylight chases them away like bats. Bahar gives my hand a squeeze.

"Don't let this bother you," she says, almost too loudly. Her fingers are ice cold. "I know how to deal with the likes of her."

I look at the receptionist. She has finished her cigarette and is playing solitaire with her cards. She seems to have forgotten us the moment we were out of her sight, and this comforts me, but not enough: I worry about what will happen when Niyaz comes in, how it will be when she and Bahar face one another. I'm afraid of what the receptionist with the heavy black lashes will think of Bahar and me if there is a scene, that other people who know my parents will witness the face-off and report on it to their friends, that Fareed will be there and ask us to leave. More than anything else, I'm afraid to see Niyaz.

"Let's go home," I beg Bahar, but she's determined.

She is brave, and out of options.

AROUND ELEVEN O'CLOCK, Fareed's clients begin to trickle in. They all wear dark glasses and red lipstick, order coffee and aspirin, ask the receptionist, who knows them by name, if she has heard from Fareed yet. They sit down in the foyer and smoke, eye Bahar and me from head to toe and back again without the slightest effort to disguise their curiosity. They know who we are—many of them were guests at Bahar and Omid's wedding—but they extend no more than a greeting and a nod to us.

Every time someone comes in, I freeze in terror. I don't know what Niyaz looks like, but I know I'll recognize her nevertheless, and that Bahar will too.

At one o'clock, the servant boy takes orders from the ladies for lunch to be delivered from restaurants in the neighborhood. Shortly after that, Fareed arrives in a silk Nehru jacket and baggy silk pants. He's short and stocky, with a thin mustache and plucked eyebrows. By then, there are thirteen women waiting for him, and he sits with them, smokes a cigarette and drinks a cup of Turkish coffee, before he rises with a sigh—let's get this show on the road who wants to be first?

I'm watching Fareed interact with his clients, wondering if he's going to observe any kind of order, to acknowledge that Bahar was first to arrive and should therefore be attended to before the others. Then I see him throw his arms up and smile widely at someone who's just coming in through the door: it's a tall woman in a narrow skirt and high heels. She nods at the receptionist but doesn't bother stopping. She's headed straight for one of the private rooms in the back, where Fareed sees his celebrity clients. I know this is Niyaz because of the way she moves—like someone who's aware the world is watching her and doesn't care—and because her hair is as straight and shiny as a Chinese doll's. When she gets closer, I can smell her perfume and, beneath it, the scent of her skin. She smells like winter.

I look at Bahar; she hasn't noticed Niyaz yet. Then I see the receptionist look toward us in the foyer, see the gleam of triumph in her eyes, and I know all is lost.

"Niyaz is here," she calls out to Fareed, as if he hadn't seen her first. Everyone looks at Bahar.

There's a moment when I feel I don't exist; I've been erased from the world, turned to glass, painted off the surface of all things. I sit still, my hands leaden on my lap, and wait for Bahar to react. The receptionist is still staring at us, the other women have suddenly gone quiet, and even Fareed has paused. Bahar's fingers grip the edge of her purse; her eyes are sewn on the coffee table directly in front of us. She looks like she's waiting for her strength to return, for her legs to move, her heart to beat again. She has to get up, with everyone watching, and face her adversary. She has to see for herself what it is that she lacks so badly, what she *isn't*; what Niyaz has so much of. She doesn't move. Behind her, Niyaz, unaware of the drama she has caused, disappears into a room. Fareed touches Bahar on the shoulder.

"Come with me," he says, extending the only bit of mercy she will receive that day. "I'll have my assistant take care of you."

An hour later, Bahar's hair is teased and twisted and sprayed stiff. She looks spent and exhausted, on the verge of tears. We leave the salon together and stand on the street to find a taxi. I hold her hand, but her eyes follow the traffic around us, and she's far away, beyond my reach.

"You look pretty."

She bites her lip, struggles to hide the telltale quiver of her chin.

"You're prettier than any of those women in there."

We're in this together, I want to say; you're not alone, I'll stand by you, I'll defend you against *her* and anyone else.

But I know what happened at the salon is a turning point in both of our lives—that Bahar was defeated not just by circumstances, but also by her own fears. She has prevailed over a haughty receptionist and a cruel group of strangers, pushed through to the eye of the storm, and emerged, once again, the lesser for the fight.

THAT NIGHT, I stand by the window of my bedroom and watch The Tango Dancer's house in the dark. She's nowhere within view, but I can hear her music. I've never seen the inside of her house, but I imagine her sitting at her piano in her studio, dreaming of her days in Buenos Aires, of the way she had danced. Her eyes are lined in black and her hair shines with the forbidden oil—Ruby has told me this—that she buys from one-eyed pirates who live on the reed-covered islands of the Persian Gulf. They attack the boats that smuggle goods between Iran and its Arab neighbors, steal the cargo, and throw the sailors into the sea to drown.

I have never heard her speak, but I imagine that The Tango Dancer's voice is deep and scratchy, ruined by years of smoking unfiltered cigarettes and drinking hot coffee.

"I like Iran," she tells people, "because it doesn't have too many Iranians."

What she means by this is that Iran is a nation made up of many other nations—a gathering of tribes and cultures and religions that once occupied the better part of the Asian continent; that it's a diverse country, home to a generally tolerant people. She's right.

The second floor of the house is dark except for Artemis's room, where he leaves the light on whether he is at home or not. The other two windows—the Zoroastrian's and Chamedooni's—are shuttered. Behind one of them is a faint, white light, like the reflection of a television screen against a black surface. The panels on the shutter are half-open. Through them, a pair of nervous eyes is staring right back at me.

❧

SHORTLY BEFORE THE END of the school year, the teacher calls our house again.

There's something wrong here, madame, your daughter is either dim-witted or hard of hearing. You may not realize this, but it's evident to all of us here at the school, I suggest you have her looked at by a professional.

The next day, Bahar marches into the school office and demands my records. She tells the principal that my teachers are incompetent and vindictive, they haven't taught me a thing all year, all they do is complain and criticize. She arranges to have me finish the year in another school, where the principal is a friend of the Arbabs. Then she pulls me aside and tells me it's now or never—turn a new page or get used to being a failure all your life. She knows how badly I want to have long hair, so she uses this as incentive: if I do well in school, she promises, she'll let me grow my hair.

She must have known, even then, that there was indeed something wrong with me. She must have seen the telltale signs, must have suspected it with the kind of ghastly dread that only a mother can feel—that desperate, slow-burning awareness of tragedy that lurks behind a child's skin and that no mother can be blind to or wish away.

But if she did know, she never let on to me or anyone else.

She was not indifferent to my pain or naturally averse to the truth. She denied the obvious for so long because she knew she wasn't equal—that *we* weren't equal—to the truth, that it would destroy us the minute it was allowed to roam in the open. You have to have lived that life, contended with those limitations, to understand her conundrum. In some parts of the world Truth will set you free. In most others, it's a sentence you may not outlive.

PART V

ALL SUMMER LONG, Chamedooni watches our house. He hovers around our front door with his suitcase full of promises, stands at the corner bus stop like a sentry at his station. He lets the buses come and go without climbing into any of them because he's too busy keeping an eye out for the boy with the bicycle. At night, he hides behind the shutters in his darkened bedroom and watches me.

People say that in his youth, Chamedooni was a "person of substance." He comes from a family of crypto Jews in Mashad—a city in northeastern Iran where, in the mid-nineteenth century, the entire Jewish community was forced to convert to Islam. After that, the Jews practiced their religion in secret, aware that if discovered, they would be put to death. To keep from assimilating, they promised their children to one another at birth and married them off at very young ages, so that generations later, even after they had been liberated from their oath of conversion, Mashadi Jews were surrounded by an aura of remoteness and mystery that set them apart from Jews in other parts of Iran.

After the Second World War, Chamedooni's father brought his family to Tehran and opened a rug and antiques business. They lived in an alley off Cyrus Street, but the store was on Ferdowsi Avenue, which was popular with British and French and American "advisers" who were sent to Iran mostly to tell the Shah how to run the country. Compared to other Jewish young men in South Tehran, therefore, Chamedooni lived a privileged life.

He was further blessed when, upon finishing high school, he passed the college entrance exam which was deliberately designed so the greatest majority of applicants would fail. Chamedooni was not among the smartest students in the land; everyone knew this. He didn't have a father who could *buy* him a place on the admissions roster. And he certainly wasn't good-looking or charming enough to have ingratiated himself to one of the powerful women in the Shah's inner circle. How he had burrowed his way into university remained a mystery even to his parents, until he had been there for a year or two, and demonstrated, by the way he got himself into some very public trouble, that his being admitted was nothing less than God's design—that He arranged this merely to ruin Chamedooni's life and bring eternal grief to his family.

First, he declared that he was going to study sociology—as if that were something you needed to go to school to learn. It's a scam, I tell you, why can't a person just look around and glean whatever he needs to know about "society," for God's sake? What kind of a job does that get you anyway? Other people's sons are becoming doctors and engineers, what are we supposed to say when someone asks what *our* son is doing with his life? Say he's studying *society*?

Undaunted by his parents' opposition, Chamedooni made matters worse by joining every student organization that would have him. Against the dire warnings of his elders—sooner or later they'll remember you're a Jew and stab you in the heart—he accepted invitations to lunch and dinner and all-day hikes with Muslim friends. He went to other kinds of gatherings as well—secret ones where young men and women read the works of Marx and Lenin and called the Shah "a Western lackey" and an "American stooge." He even brought home some of the leaflets handed to him at those gatherings—something that scared and offended his parents beyond their wits. They reminded him that the Shah was the best thing that had ever happened to Iranian Jews; that he had protected and defended the Jews at his own peril. They also reminded him of the secret police who watched every citizen in every corner of the country and certainly in Tehran, of all the spies who were spread across schools and universities, who rode taxis and ate in restaurants, shopped in stores and worked in factories only so they could report the smallest infraction—a word, a book, even the appearance of disloyalty—against the regime.

The secret police—SAVAK—had earned its reputation by living up to and often exceeding every citizen's worst fears, and it did not fail to catch up with Chamedooni either. One morning in the third year of his studies at university, two men in tailored suits and Italian ties picked him up off the street and drove him to be interrogated at "an undisclosed location." For months after that, his parents looked for him all over town and in the city morgue as well. They knew without needing to be told that their son was being held by the military police. It happened all the time—a person vanishing off the street, only to turn up months later, dead and floating in a river, or with a dozen bullet holes in his face and chest, or hung by the neck from a helicopter. Sometimes, the "missing" would be tortured but not killed, so they could go home and spread the word about what had happened to them, scare other foolhardy souls who may be tempted to defy the Shah's rule.

Chamedooni never spoke of the eleven months and nine days he had spent in solitary confinement in a basement at Evin prison, but you could tell, just by looking at him, that he had suffered great horror and, in the process, lost half his mind. He went in a young man with too much confidence and a sense of invulnerability; he returned paranoid and imbalanced, unable to hold down a job or tolerate living with anyone else, convinced that he was under surveillance every minute of the day.

He couldn't live with his parents because he was sure the house was surrounded, and he couldn't work in any one place because that would make it easier for SAVAK to find him. He moved into The Tango Dancer's because he believed the rumors about her being an undercover Nazi doing the bidding of foreign governments, and therefore thought she would be immune to prosecution by SAVAK. Even then, he continued to be obsessed with the memory of other prisoners he had met during his ordeal, and so he went looking for them at the morgue every day.

At the morgue, he met many people with many sorrows, and that is where he got the idea of selling "cures" for every ailment that afflicted humanity. He began collecting herbs and pills and heavily perfumed oils to remedy physical illness, prayer scrolls and talismans and little bottles of blood from sacrificial beasts to tend to emotional needs. He hunted for books and letters, phone numbers of hard-to-find professionals in uncommon fields. He kept a log of policemen who could be bribed in every neighborhood, of hospital nurses who would agree to raise a dying patient's dose of morphine without express permission from the doctor.

For one of those patients—a woman who had lost all her hair and lay in bed looking like an overgrown fetus in a cotton gown—he agreed to find a wig. The woman had red hair, which wasn't common, and didn't look natural in synthetic fiber, so Chamedooni went to the morgue and started searching. He knew the importance of hair to a woman's chastity. He knew about Samson and his powers, about the ghouls and warriors in Persian mythology who could be summoned instantaneously if a single strand of their hair was set on fire.

What he didn't know was that he would fall in love with the young girl whose hair he stole that first time, that he would go looking for her long after she was buried and her hair had been made into a wig. He didn't know that, in time, he would become obsessed with seeing the pale faces and naked bodies of all the other girls who lay, prone and supine—his to admire or mourn, rob or grant mercy to—all over the morgue. He gave a few hundred rials to the indigent undertakers who washed and minded the dead, and then he was free to roam around— the charming prince in a sleeping kingdom—but he didn't realize that he would carry the dead with him when he left, see them in his sleep and waking life, seek the texture of their hair and skin in everything he touched.

He didn't realize that they would haunt him—those women who were forever denied entry into paradise because Chamedooni had defiled them—and that sometimes, they would bring with them their dead sons and husbands and still, Chamedooni would go looking—for that red-haired girl he had stolen from, and for all the other ones as well. That he would look for them—contrite and repentant—hoping to restore for them the piety he had taken away, and that he *kept* taking away from others, in spite of his own best intentions.

OMID HARDLY SLEEPS at home anymore. He stays with us only if Niyaz is out of the country, and even then, he spends most of his time alone in his room. There, he'll sit at his desk and read, or go over his papers. Or he'll stand by the window and smoke while he listens to the radio. I know this because I go to him whenever I can—when I feel that he'll let me approach and that Bahar won't resent me for it—and that's how I find him, in the early morning or the middle of the night. When I ask him what he's looking at, he shrugs and says, "Nothing, really," but I know this isn't true; I recognize the longing in his eyes when I've caught him off guard and I think it's Niyaz he's thinking about.

Some nights, I dream I'm standing on a narrow stretch of road that is as long as the horizon; I'm wearing a white dress he has bought for me, and the white shoes that he has once admired. I'm waiting here because I know Omid is about to arrive, that he'll see me and stop, decide he loves me more than Niyaz.

I wake up from the dream and walk the length of the corridor to his room. If he's away, I go in and lock the door behind me. I go through his drawers, search his closet. I'm looking for something, but I don't know what it is. I stand before the vanity mirror. I'm only nine years old, but I pretend I'm Niyaz—just as tall and pretty—and that I'm wearing the black dress and white pearls she wore the day I saw her at Fareed's.

He's not going to abandon me. He hasn't forgotten me and doesn't prefer anyone to me. It's only Bahar he doesn't want, only *her* he hides from in this room.

ON ASSASSINATION DAYS, the entire country shuts down. We stay at home with the doors locked, and listen to the sound of processions going past our house. Men of all ages, dressed in funeral clothes, march in groups and wave black mourning flags. In Farsi and Arabic, they chant prayers for their dead prophet and for his martyred disciples. To prove their grief and devotion, they beat themselves and their young boys with heavy metal chains or with machete-like blades. Their clothes tear and their faces and bodies get drenched in blood and still they march, striking the metal against their forehead until they crack their skulls and fall, unconscious, to the ground.

After dark, the processions over, the city slips into a silence ripe with danger: raw nerves and pulsating anger and millions of young men ready to die for a cause—any cause, just name it and we'll be there, it's our duty, the least we can do in the service of the holy Imams who gave their lives for us. Anyone with a sense of self-preservation knows to stay off the streets and out of the way of those men. But self-preservation does not sit well with Ruby, because she's a Kurd: they're brave and adventurous, they raise their daughters like boys, let them go to school and teach them to ride and shoot guns and even go around without covering their hair and face. As soon as the last procession has turned the corner away from June Street, she wraps her chador around her waist and goes outside to wash the blood off the sidewalk.

"This blood makes me sick," she claims, though my mother suspects that she's outside hoping to see Artemis. "I feel like fainting every time I set eyes on it. By morning, it'll smell like a rotting carcass. I wish those men would kill themselves once and for all and spare me from doing this again next year."

She's washing the blood one night when a taxi pulls up and deposits The Opera Singer outside our house. He's unshaven and disheveled, and he looks disoriented. He stands before Ruby without saying anything. He clears his throat and strains for words, starts and stops, then starts again. "The Pigeon Sister has hung herself."

She went up to the roof with a piece of rope. She tied one end to the railing, the other end around her neck, and stepped off the ledge. People saw her from a hundred meters away, dangling like a straw figure, her legs loose and shaking like those of a marionette, the hem of her dress puffing up in the wind like a balloon, but no one thought she was a real person—it must be a joke, or a scarecrow; something to scare the birds away. It wasn't until her children were walking home after school, when they saw the body and recognized their mother's dress, that anyone realized what she had done.

Her suicide offends her psychiatrist husband to such an extent, he refuses to pay for the burial or to sit shiva in his house. He tells his son and daughter they may attend the funeral and the week of mourning at their grandparents' house, but that afterward, they are not to see their mother's relatives again. Because he knows this will embarrass the in-laws, he sends the children to Cyrus Street in the care of Jadid-al-Islam and his daughter-of-a-mullah wife.

They arrive early one morning in the white Mercedes Jadid-al-Islam has bought with money he recently inherited from a dead cousin. He knows he's despised by the cousin's wife and children for taking what would otherwise be theirs, but he feels justified because he's only obeying the law that rewards converts to Islam with all their relatives' inheritance. He's adamant that his conversion had nothing to do with this law or the prospect of earning easy money. He says he became Muslim because he was visited by an angel who told him that only those who loved the prophet Muhammad and revered his son-in-law, Imam Ali, would be spared the fires of hell. He says the angel had blond hair and pale skin, "like Doris Day," he says, "only without the bob." She appeared one day as he was walking around Imamzadeh Saleh, in Tajrish, north of Tehran. There's a thousand-year-old maple tree there with a trunk so large someone has built a whole store, of normal size and proportions, inside it. It's such an unusual sight that people travel to Imamzadeh Saleh just to see it, which is what Jadid-al-Islam was doing when he saw the angel. He says she followed him out of the hollow tree trunk and back to Tehran, visited him once or twice in his sleep, and she was beautiful and convincing enough that he went and gave up his "infidel" status once and for all. Is it his fault, really, that along with the invitation to paradise, he gets to collect his relatives' inheritance here on earth?

I have seen The Pigeon Sister's children before, on the rare occasions when their father allowed them to visit our grandparents' house for Sabbath. On the morning of the burial, the boy, who's younger, comes into the courtyard first. He's short and pudgy, his cheeks flushed amber. He digs his hands into his pockets and mumbles to himself without looking at anyone in particular, just leans against the yard wall kicking at gravel and looking as if he's doing his best not to cry.

His sister is wearing a black dress that must have belonged to her mother, because it's clearly too big, and she has a black scarf draped over her head and hiding her face almost entirely—a shrunken shadow in a pair of patent leather shoes so new they still squeak when she walks.

It's strange, how a person carries around the shadow of those that matter most to her. You can always see it—that presence, or its absence—in the eyes, in the movements of the hands, in a person's laugh. You can see it—if an old woman had a father who loved her when she was a child; if a middle-aged man lost his first love; if a teenage girl has a best friend she knows she can run to. You see it in the way people move and speak, in the subjects they choose and the things they avoid, in the way they appear solid or hollow, certain or plagued with doubt.

When she was alive, The Pigeon Sister's children clung to her—one on either side, holding her hand, and she between them with her limp body and transparent eyes, like a blind woman being led to safety by a pair of midgets. As troubled and insipid as she was, she had managed to provide safe harbor to her children. They sat with her, eyes downcast, at the seder table; fell asleep with their head on her lap at dinner. They whispered in her ear the things they were too embarrassed to say out loud—that they were hungry, or cold, or too shy to accept an offer of tea even though they wanted some.

The day they come to bury her, The Pigeon Sister's children carry her shadow. It's still protecting them—that visceral knowledge, however false, that they can run to her when all this is over, bury their faces in her chest and cry and tell her how terrible it has been to see her dangling from the rope, taken down and hauled away like some beast, wrapped like a cheap shroud and thrown into the earth in that cemetery where the Jews have buried their dead for hundreds of years, stacking the corpses on top of each other because the land is so small and the mullahs wouldn't allow the cemetery to expand, and where some of the headstones are so old, they disintegrate at the touch.

WE SIT SHIVA on Cyrus Street. Men and women stay in separate rooms and cover the windows and mirrors with black cloth. The women wear all black, and spend a good part of each day cooking meals that are served to any number of visitors who happen to call. The men grow beards, smoke incessantly, drink bitter tea, and eat peeled cucumbers with salt, whisper to each other it's a real tragedy that man is responsible for his wife's death but what are you going to do? He's the kids' father, and besides, you can't tell a doctor he killed his wife.

In the room where the men gather, my father sits in his custom-made suit and imported leather shoes and does his best to avoid getting into a conversation or having to answer any questions. He feels the weight of everyone's stares all the time, and he knows what they're thinking, knows what they say about him the minute he walks out of the room to get a breath of air or to take a break from the endless rounds of prayers in which every male next-of-kin is expected to participate. He has never hidden his lack of regard for Bahar's people, but he makes a point of being at the shiva every day because he's truly saddened by The Pigeon Sister's death, and by the effect it has had on her family. For the first time since he has known them, he is able to see his in-laws as real people who have more than their fair share of sorrow. He feels a compassion for Bahar that is entirely new to him. He has witnessed her anguish for years without comprehending the cause of it, but with this, he feels real empathy for her. He wants to comfort her, but they've been strangers for so long that he doesn't know how to reach out, so he comes to the house first thing every day and sits quietly through the prayers, eats the food that's offered, and in the evening, makes sure he's the last to leave.

My mother never forgave me for this, but I believe Omid was a kind person at the core. Even when I was angry with him, when I resented him for his ruthlessness with Bahar, I couldn't condemn him entirely, because I thought I knew how alone he had been as a child—as alone as I was—and this made me forgive his transgressions. I watched his hands, those long fingers that touched me so rarely, that reminded me more of his absence than of his love, and thought of all the times they *had* held me, the tenderness they *were* capable of. I watched his eyes—*my* eyes, people said—and though I was ashamed of this before Bahar, saw myself in them every time.

The day he took me to Chattanooga, we came out of the restaurant and walked a few blocks to his office, where he had some papers to pick up. It was a freezing afternoon in late fall, on a crowded city street, and we had to fight a relentless wind that tore at our hair and shrieked in our ears. We stepped over an old man who was sitting on the sidewalk with his legs stretched out. His clothes were torn and dirty, and his beard was matted and long, and I could tell he hadn't slept on a bed in many years. Next to him on the ground was a glass Coca-Cola bottle that had been emptied of its original contents and filled with a clear liquid—bootleg *arrack* mixed with rubbing alcohol, the last resort of addicts who couldn't afford the real thing. He wasn't an unusual sight, so we passed him, Omid holding my hand, and I would never have thought of him again except for what happened next: Halfway up the block, Omid stopped, as if struck by a thought, and walked back to the man. He took a pack of Marlboros out of his breast pocket and gave it to the man. Then he shook hands with him the way you would with an elder who deserved respect.

"Why not money?" I asked later, and he said, "It might have embarrassed him."

How was I to square this gentleness I saw in him with the ruthlessness he extended my mother?

❧

EVERYONE WE KNOW COMES TO THE SHIVA.

Jadid-al-Islam arrives every morning without his wife and children, and has the decency to leave his *aba* at the door. Eschewing the chairs, he takes his shoes off and sits on the ground with his legs crossed the way it's done in mosques, plays with his worry beads and talks to other men about the soaring price of land and the maddening blackouts that are a result of an electricity shortage in Tehran.

Omid's parents have skipped the burial and appear at the shiva looking uncomfortable and almost in pain. They can only stay a few minutes, they say, they have another engagement, one they cannot possibly miss. Even though the room is already dark, Mrs. Arbab won't take her sunglasses off. She uses it as a barrier between herself and the others. Mr. Arbab takes a seat next to Omid and says, "Here we are." Here we are, you've finally done it, reduced yourself to the ranks of your wife and her family, and dragged us in the mud for good measure.

Bahar's parents are so honored by the Arbabs' presence, they almost forget their grief for a moment. The Seamstress offers them tea and dates. Her husband keeps telling Mr. Arbab that he shouldn't have put himself out, it wasn't necessary, I'm sure you have much more important affairs to look after. Their presence at the shiva makes me an automatic target for the envy of my cousins and the other children my age. They stare at my clothes with disapproval, ask me questions with tightly set lips, nod at my answers as if they were taking notes for another conversation—one in which my words will serve as proof of my father's vagaries. Everything they say is loaded with reproach because they think of me as an Arbab—haughty and rude and willing to step on a young woman's heart as the Arbabs have on Bahar's. Part of me wishes I could belong with my mother's family. The other part is glad I don't.

The Tango Dancer comes on the third day and sets in motion a whole new round of rumors and speculation about her hidden life. She hadn't heard of The Pigeon Sister before her death, and doesn't know anyone else in Bahar's family. She has never even *spoken* to Bahar all the time they've been neighbors. But she's doing only what custom demands, what any decent neighbor would do. She has even gone so far as to shed her customary white outfit in favor of black, but she still wears the three dozen bangles on her wrists, and a pair of enormous hoop earrings as well. In spite of the prohibition against makeup or any kind of adornment during shiva, she has painted her eyes and braided her hair into a single strand that reaches down to her waistline, and she dominates the room without saying a word or even moving—just sits there with her back straight and her hands clasped on her lap, looking at Bahar's parents and nodding at their grief as if she hadn't the slightest idea what they think of her or how they condemn her ways and habits. I, on the other hand, revel in watching her.

I'm afraid to say this to anyone, but I love The Tango Dancer's music, love the way it aches and arches and makes me want to cry without knowing why. It's completely different from the Persian pop and traditional music I hear on the radio. It feels alien, melancholy, out of place in every regard. People dislike it, Bahar has told me, because it can corrupt women who listen to it—compel them to "do things" with their bodies that they would never have done otherwise.

Perhaps.

But I think the real reason people hate The Tango Dancer's music is that it sounds visceral and impulsive. And that it's bold—unafraid like the woman herself.

RUBY CALLS ON THE SAME AFTERNOON as The Tango Dancer, in a too-tight black dress with her hair loose around her face. Her affair with Artemis has heated up to the point where she no longer feels the need to hide it from anyone, even her husband. For months, people have seen her go into and out of the yellow house, always dressed in those skimpy clothes and tacky evening shoes, and they know it isn't music lessons she's taking avail of. They've mentioned this to Hassan a thousand times, directly and otherwise, but he keeps playing dumb because he has no idea what else to do. He knows—he's always known—that Ruby is waiting to find someone better so she can leave him. He knows if he confronts her with the rumors, he'll only force her to make a decision—to choose between him and whomever she's seeing at the time. And he knows he'll lose.

But the matter between Ruby and Artemis has gone further than any previous affair. She thinks he's going to marry her, that he's in love with her—he's said as much once or twice, in the heat of passion or on the few occasions when she has withheld her affections from him—and though she's aware that all men are pathological liars and no-good bastards, she believes Artemis when he says he wishes she weren't married so he could make her his own wife.

At the shiva, Ruby hands Bahar an armful of poet's jasmine and says, "May you always remember your sister with joy." She stays in the women's room during her entire visit, never once betraying an inclination to retire to the kitchen where another maid might feel more at home, and on the way out, insists on shaking hands with everyone as if she were their equal.

On the last day, Chamedooni ventures in.

He lugs his suitcase through the crowd of children who sit, bored and restless, in the yard, and up the front steps of the house, into the men's section. He makes a beeline for Omid, whom he has never met but whose hand he shakes vigorously—my condolences to yourself and the Mrs., I would have come sooner had I known, I only just found out, it's a tragedy, really, may her soul rest in peace. His hand is wet with perspiration and his eyes are bloodshot and darting about as he moves on to greet other family members. He circles the room and sits down next to Omid, who has been polite but not friendly, and who clearly has no idea who Chamedooni is. Embarrassed, he puts his suitcase on the ground between his legs, and sighs. He pretends he's listening to the prayers, but he must feel ill at ease because he keeps perspiring into his shirt collar, wipes his face every few minutes with a yellowed handkerchief, and says "Amen" too loudly. Because of him, a pall has fallen over the room, and even the rabbi seems to have lost track of the prayers and slowed his recitation.

The men pass a tray of black tea and dates, and a second one of peeled cucumbers with salt. When Omid goes outside to smoke, The Opera Singer uses the occasion to sit next to Chamedooni.

"Nice of you to take the trouble," he says, offering tea.

Chamedooni mumbles softly and takes a glass, hunches over it to avoid eye contact. Without asking, The Opera Singer drops three pieces of hard sugar into the man's tea, then passes the tray. His expression of familiarity, when the two have never met, terrifies Chamedooni. He slurps his tea and winces because it burns his mouth, but he sinks farther into his chair, brings his chin closer to his chest to hide his face. He's thinking The Opera Singer is a SAVAK agent, that's why he knows Chamedooni, he's been waiting for him all day, and now he's going to signal his friends and they'll pounce on him like a pack of wolves, drag him away to Evin, where Chamedooni has decided he will kill himself rather than submit to more torture.

He heard about The Pigeon Sister from Artemis, who's heard about it from Ruby and mentioned it in passing, and he's come to see Bahar and Omid because they're neighbors, and he feels a certain affinity for them (he, too, was once a person of substance). He had expected to be received more warmly by Omid, but now he's trapped, he can't get up and leave, because it would be rude, and because he thinks The Opera Singer will chase after him; and he can't keep sitting there, because he feels the weight of everyone's questions—who are you and what do you have in that briefcase you guard so closely? The Opera Singer releases him from his misery.

"Thanks for coming." He slaps Chamedooni lightly on the knee. "You probably have a million things to do."

Outside, he puts the suitcase down and takes a deep breath. He looks around for Omid, and when he doesn't find him, he picks up his suitcase and descends the steps into the courtyard. Then he notices me sitting on the edge of the fish pool, and breaks into the largest, most delighted smile I have seen.

"*There* you are!"

He rushes up to me and bends so we're at eye level.

"What a sight for sore eyes," he says. "What a beautiful girl you are." I'm petrified. He touches my hair, the side of my cheek.

"You have magnificent hair," he says. "You should grow it long."

Tears have welled up in his eyes. He stares at me some more. Then he says, "I'll give you anything you want for your hair. Anything at all. Just name the price."

I hold my breath that day and wait till he goes away. For a long time after that, I will do my best to avoid Chamedooni. But the day will come when I will find myself alone and desperate, with only the devil to bargain with, and then I'll remember The Pigeon Sister's shiva and what Chamedooni has said, and I'll go to look for him, to beg for what he has promised me by my grandparents fishpool.

ONE FRIDAY, I'm in the living room with Bahar, listening to an old vinyl record Omid had bought years ago in France, when we hear screaming in the yard.

We run to the window and look out: Ruby is standing barefoot by the greenhouse, pounding her chest and letting out one deafening shriek after another.

We run to her.

"God help me, please!" she screams. "Strike me dead or save me! Oh dear God, help me, help me, help me!"

When she sees Bahar, her eyes glaze over.

"Oh, miss, you should have seen it," she cries. "You should have seen the little monster; it was grinning right at us. I wanted to scream but couldn't. I thought I'd lost my mind."

She sits down cross-legged on the ground, puts her head into her hands. She's sobbing with genuine emotion—without the calculated grief and measured despair she normally uses to manipulate Bahar into letting her do what she wants.

"I know why it came," she cries, rocking back and forth. "I'm a sinner, and it's finally caught up with me. That's why it came. But I wish I had been blind. I wish I hadn't seen it, because now I'm damned forever."

She had been "spending some time" with Artemis in the greenhouse, she says. They had closed the door and were "catching up" when she looked up through the glass wall of the greenhouse and saw a boy riding a bicycle on the other side. She thought he must be one of the neighborhood brats who had sneaked into the yard, and she couldn't have him intruding on her privacy with Artemis, so she went to the door and yelled for him to go away.

"The minute he heard me, he went mad," she says, breaking into tears again. "He started riding around like a trapped sparrow. 'Get the hell out of here,' I yelled, but instead of aiming for the yard gates, the damn thing charged *me* instead."

He rode toward her, then at her, then straight *through* her into the greenhouse. She knows this because she was in the door frame when he came at her, with her body blocking the entrance almost entirely. Artemis saw this as well, and it frightened him so much that he lost his voice and had to run—nearly naked—into the Alley and back home.

"It was a jinn for sure, a real-life jinn, and he lives in that greenhouse, I swear it. That's why the place is dry like a desert—because the damn thing is breathing his foul fire-and-brimstone breath over the trees all the time, and now he's going to possess *me*, I just know it. I'm going to become crazy and afflicted because I saw him."

People who are possessed by jinn do and say things that are entirely beyond their control.

"And besides," Ruby wails, "this one's a Jewish jinn. That's why it's turned up in a Jew's house. Who knows how a Jewish jinn acts or what it wants from a young Muslim woman?"

I look at Bahar and, to my amazement, see that she's crying without a sound. To put her mind at ease, I tell her this must be the boy I see on the street sometimes, that he isn't a jinn at all, just a kid who probably has nowhere to go. The light is bouncing off the glass shell of the greenhouse, making it reflective like a mirror. He must still be in there, I tell Bahar, come look for yourself.

There is a waft of stale air—like from inside a tomb—then the smell of dead rats. There are some empty ceramic pots on the floor and a long, black hose hanging from a hook and cracked from dryness. Bahar walks in, cautiously, and looks around. She sees no one—no boy; no little red people with sharp ears and long tails; no black, bald, one-eyed ghouls. Behind us, Ruby is reciting an Arabic prayer that apologizes to God for any unintended heresy on her part, and assures Him that He's the One, the Only One, mighty and kind and please, God, save us this day from the foolishness of these Jews.

But then we see the bicycle tracks: they swirl around in the thick layer of dust that covers the stone floor, and they stretch from the door all the way to the edge of the glass wall.

﹡

I SPEND MY NIGHTS half awake, rankled by the memory of the day I have had at school, the awareness that I am perceived as odd by my teachers and by the other children at my new school, that I am once again failing to perform, or understand, or connect as well as I should.

I can read well enough, and retain what I have read, play the words and phrases back in my mind until I have memorized every one. I can recite entire poems by heart, finish my arithmetic homework in no time at all. My handwriting is neat and careful, the pages of my workbooks forever filled with clean, straight lines and digits and letters that look like they were engraved on silver. And yet: you must be stupid, you're dense as a donkey, you write twenty pages when I've asked for two, or you don't write at all, you're sitting here looking at me but you might as well have slept through the entire lesson.

In class, I stare at the blackboard so intently my vision becomes blurred. I press the pencil between by fingers till they ache all the way to my wrist, and rush to take down every word the teacher says. Still, I manage to miss too much. Sometimes, when I realize I don't know the answer to a question we have already gone over, that I can't solve an equation we have already learned, I'll be caught in a panic so fervent and immediate that I have to ask to be excused from the class, to run to the bathroom and lock myself in one of the stalls and try, with all my energy, to remember. I stay there terrified and cold, praying to God to help me out this one time, let it come back to me just this once, and from now on, I'll study more and absorb better.

When I emerge, trembling and exhausted, from the bathroom, so much time has gone by that the teacher often sends me to detention in the principal's office, and the other children laugh at me, call me "loose-pants Yaasi" and ask what I ate in the morning that has made me stay in the bathroom for so long.

I'm afraid that Bahar will find out about my failures, that the teacher will call or send a note. I'm afraid, too, that Omid will leave us once and for all because I've disappointed him. I've heard Bahar predict this a thousand times: "One of these days he'll just take off with her for America." I've seen Bahar stare at herself in the mirror, lean forward and examine the fine lines that have begun to appear around her eyes and mouth.

"I'm getting old," she says.

I pray for Bahar to stop aging. I pray for better grades, for Omid to leave Niyaz. Mostly, I pray for the courage to become what I should have been in the first place.

THE PRINCIPAL OF OUR SCHOOL is the daughter of a Qajar prince who, years earlier, had lost his kingdom to the Russians, seen his belongings confiscated by Reza Shah, and escaped with his life and a few of his children to exile in Paris. There, he lived in genteel poverty and near-total isolation, writing his memoir, *The Forgotten Prince*, in French, and having it published by a friend who took the trouble out of respect for a former royal and who later lied to the prince about the number of books he had managed to sell—less than a hundred, and all of those to friends and family members—while the author, aided by a walking stick he had bought in a pawnshop but which he claimed had been given to him by the king of Thailand, strolled up and down the city's rain-soaked boulevards until he contracted pneumonia and died.

After his death, the prince's daughter returned to Iran and married a cousin, declared she was not going to have children because she couldn't tolerate noise and disorder, then proceeded to found the Golden Door, a small, coeducational elementary school that she operates like a watch factory and supervises with an eye for the minutest details. She hires every one of the teachers herself, drops in on every classroom every day to make sure things are managed as she has ordered, and walks around the school yard at recess with a black leather horsewhip that she does not hesitate to use on any student who arouses her anger. During the lunch hour, when some students go home to eat and others gather in the basement commissary, she comes into the office to check on those who have been sent to detention.

Whenever she finds me there, she looks at me from high above her noble cheekbones, her thin lips forever painted in bright red, her large bust balanced ever so delicately over a waistline and hips that remain narrow even into her old age. She shows me none of the repulsion she demonstrates for unruly boys who have talked in class or fought on the playground, or the icy disdain she shows girls who have forgotten their homework.

She has admitted me to the school because she knows Mr. and Mrs. Arbab, and for that same reason she spares me the more humiliating punishments she exacts so frequently on other troublesome kids. I'm not made to stand in the office corner with my face to the wall and my hands raised above my head for hours at a time, or displayed at the morning all-school assembly as a repeat offender. I'm not beaten at the playground with the whip, or administered twenty strikes of a razor-thin ruler that leaves red welts or tracks of blisters in the palm of other children's hands. Once, when I have been sent to detention three days in a row, she puts on her eyeglasses and examines me through the half-frame as if looking at a specimen in a microscope. It's the middle of the morning, the last week of winter, and the office is cold and dark; it smells of her perfume and of cigarette smoke. The principal observes me for a long time.

"There's something *wrong* with you," she concludes softly, and puts her glasses down.

She's wearing a tight, knee-length skirt, a close-fitting blouse, and high-heeled pumps so fine they look like the plastic Barbie shoes most girls bring to school and show off to each other at recess. They bring clothes and hairbrushes and even a closet or vanity mirror for the dolls, describe at great length how their parents have bought these treasures for them in America, and then they open their book bags and take out even greater riches—scented erasers, Mickey Mouse rulers, thin, metal cases that hold a row of colored pencils that stand shoulder to shoulder, like perfect little soldiers in a Technicolor dream.

I long to be let into these girls' circle, to smell the erasers, to run my fingers across the beveled surface of the line of pencils. My own father, I want to tell the girls, has been to America twice. The first time was before he married Bahar. The second time, he brought me clothes, an enormous box of chocolates with the picture of a cable car in San Francisco, a coffee mug with two red hearts and the words "I Love Beverly

Hills" printed in bold black letters.

The principal circles her desk and sits behind it on an antique chair with a carved wooden back. She writes a note and hands it to me without a word. It's permission to go back to class, and it should make me feel relieved and grateful, but it has come too easily and too soon, and that only means she has bigger plans for me than simple detention in her office.

"Go on," she nods when she sees me hesitate. "I'll talk to your grandparents about this."

"It's *your* fault," Bahar is screaming at Omid. "You've abandoned us, this is what happens to a girl who has no father; she's shamed by you, that's why no one will be her friend, they look down on her, talk about her. What did you *expect* when you run around with your mistress all over town? "

We're in the dining room—I at the table, she and Omid a few steps away. She was reviewing my schoolwork when Omid walked in, and now they've forgotten I'm here.

"I want her checked out by a doctor," Omid says in a low voice, his index finger jabbing the table to emphasize his point.

The principal has called the Arbabs, who have in turn called Omid. The Arbabs are concerned, and also embarrassed. Omid is alarmed. Bahar is afraid she'll be blamed for whatever is wrong with me.

"She's distracted at school because she's upset by what *you're* doing," Bahar tells Omid. "How am I supposed to explain *that* to a doctor? What if they say she's hysterical? Say she's *mental* and ruin her reputation for good? How are you going to answer your parents *then*?"

At this, Omid hesitates. He knows that a label, however false, can mark a woman for life. People remember these things, and tell others. They think of it every time they see you or your family, especially your children. It will become the thing that defines you and your descendants, the biblical curse you won't be able to escape.

"It may be nothing," he says, softly now, the doubt shimmying in his voice. "Maybe she needs glasses. Maybe she has tapeworms."

It's true that tapeworms can make a child restless and inattentive. They wake you up at night, interfere with your appetite and the way the food is absorbed in your body. They make you walk in your sleep, make you feel melancholy. There's a girl in my school who's paralyzed in the right side of her body. She goes around in a wheelchair, but she has a twin sister who is healthy and beautiful and very popular. The half-paralyzed girl would have been beautiful too if her face weren't so lopsided and deformed. Her family claims she became injured in an accidental fall—she had tapeworms, walked in her sleep, and fell off the balcony in their house. Other people say she was born this way, that her parents have invented the tapeworm story to protect the healthy twin against allegations of genetic imperfection. She comes to school with a servant who carries her up and down the stairs in her arms, takes her into and out of the bathroom. The girl is pleasant but quiet, and she has a grown-up's sadness—the kind that doesn't lift, isn't forgotten or abandoned by a small distraction or a bit of good news. Sometimes, when I see her sitting in her wheelchair on the side of the yard where the other girls play dodgeball, I think she might have thrown herself off the balcony on purpose; that she might have been born with that sadness, tried to escape it by falling, and instead, found herself trapped in her body forever.

"Whatever it is," Omid finally says, "we can't afford to ignore it."

He leaves again at nine o'clock, having ordered Bahar to take me to the pediatrician the next day. It's snowing outside, and the house is cold. Bahar goes to the heater to warm her hands. After a while, she lies on the ground next to the heater, like a refugee from a terrible war, and falls asleep.

By the time I finish my homework, the dining room window has fogged over. I wipe a strip of the fog with my hand and look out. The sky is a deep purple. The yard and all the trees are sparkling white.

I see a shadow on the snow and lean closer to the glass. I cup my face with my hands to get a better view of the outside: the boy with the bicycle is standing on the balcony, shivering in his cotton shirt and rotting shoes. I turn around to see if Bahar has seen him as well, but she's still sleeping next to the heater. I know I shouldn't let the boy in, but I can't imagine leaving him outside as he is. He's imploring me with his eyes, his breath making white question marks in the freezing night air. I unlock the window and run to bed.

THE PEDIATRICIAN'S OFFICE is in a one-story building on the side of a crowded alley in downtown Tehran. The waiting room is dimly lit, the walls paneled with fake wood. There's a clock above the door that ticks every time the minute hand moves, a ceiling fan that jerks every time it has gone full circle. I sit on a chair with a pink vinyl seat, my feet dangling, my hands tucked under my thighs. I think about Bahar's instructions on the way over: listen carefully to what the doctor asks, make sure you answer everything, don't talk out of turn, don't speak too quietly or too loudly, don't tell him anything that makes you sound really sick.

He gives me a full body exam, takes my temperature, puts me before an eye chart. He has known me all my life, known Omid since *he* was a child, and yet he asks me a whole host of questions he has never asked before. He wants to know about school and my friends, what television shows I like to watch, if I ever go to the amusement park, the ice skating rink, the public swimming pool at the Darband Hotel. Do I play with my cousins, do I help my mother with the dishes, do I have a hobby, like collecting stamps or embroidering handker-chiefs.

His questions make Bahar nervous. More than once, she answers for me and the doctor doesn't seem to mind this—parents always answer for their children, they know best, they can get to the heart of the matter and save the doctor's time. He just nods as he listens to her, then turns to me with another question. He's an old man. He has thin, gray hair and a spine that is curved at the neck, pushing his head a few inches ahead of his body, like a turtle's. He has the longest eyelashes I have ever seen. They make him look like a caricature, like someone who has put on a disguise to entertain the children he sees.

He pats me on the back—well done—and tells me I can get off the examination table.

He turns to Bahar.

"She may have fluid in her ears," he says, "but I don't see anything."

She doesn't understand. What does fluid have to do with stupidity?

"How long has she been like this?" he asks.

Bahar is impatient.

"Like *what?*" she snaps. "She's just distracted."

The pediatrician doesn't answer.

"We thought maybe she has some ache or pain she's not telling us about. There's nothing *wrong* with her," she insists.

The pediatrician raises his gray eyes at Bahar and says, "There's some hearing loss."

He waits for the words to sink in. "A significant degree."

Bahar is ghost-pale, immobile.

"It may be a temporary thing," the man says, but without conviction.

Bahar jerks forward. "Of course it is. Give her some penicillin." She's hostile, almost rude.

The man pediatrician a prescription pad out of the pocket of his lab coat. He writes in long, cautious strokes, making sure each letter is easily legible. He's not in a hurry. When he's done, he doesn't tear the sheet out of the pad. Instead, he asks, "Has there been hearing loss in the family?"

There is a long silence. Bahar's eyes are radiating fear. Her mouth is slightly open, and she looks like she's never going to breathe again.

"What kind of hearing loss?" she asks.

"Deafness."

At this, she snaps.

"Of course not," she nearly screams. "You've known the Arbabs for decades. Why would you even ask such a question?"

Yes, it's true, he knows the Arbabs and their family history; he's been in practice for nearly fifty years, and all the Arbab children have been his patients. But it's not the Arbabs he wants to know about.

"On the mother's side?"

Incensed, she grabs my hand.

"No, sir," she says. "Just give me the prescription. *We* haven't had that kind of problem either."

We leave the office without saying good-bye or scheduling another appointment. Outside, night has fallen and the street is teeming with traffic. Bahar and I stand on the sidewalk and watch the cars' headlights paint yellow streaks across the dark. Cold air stings our lungs and face, turns our fingertips to ice even inside our gloves. We have to walk to the next intersection to wait for a cab, but we're both glued in place, as if something were pulling at us from behind, back into the doctor's office, to those questions and the reason he posed them.

"I'm not coming back here again," Bahar mumbles to herself. "Stupid old man has lost his mind."

She looks at me.

"Don't repeat his questions to your father," she orders. I can tell she's afraid, that she's hiding something important. I nod and inch closer to her, and then we begin to walk, down the alley and through the intersection, onto the long stretch of street at the end of which, I suddenly know, is nothing but despair.

BAHAR GOES to the Sorrento Café to look for The Opera Singer. She finds him sitting alone on the roof with his iced coffee and stack of old newspapers, listening to the late-afternoon news on a crackling transistor radio he has borrowed from one of the waiters. He knows there's nothing true in the version of news people are allowed to listen to in Iran, but he likes the announcer's voice, likes to practice enunciating words and phrases as he hears them on the radio. The sun is setting slowly over the city, fading into the haze of pollution and noise that rises from the street. The café has been empty since after lunch, but now it's beginning to fill again with young men and women who stop here on their way home from university, slip into the darkened restaurant with the tinted windows through which they can look out without being seen.

Bahar sits down across the table from her brother, runs her hand through her hair, and sighs deeply, as if trying not to choke on her own grief. She looks up at the waiter who's appeared out of nowhere, looking combative, expecting that she, at least, will order something, justify her brother's occupation of the table for half a day.

"Bring her a Coke," The Opera Singer commands. "Don't put too much ice in it."

He feels a tightness in his chest and is surprised at the way he feels—the extent to which he is moved by the sadness he sees in Bahar. He has always thought of himself as separate from his family—someone who was meant to exist only within that small and vaunted constellation of movie stars and ballet dancers and famous musicians, who, he has slowly come to realize, have stopped waiting for him to join them on the stage. Nevertheless, he finds himself touched by how alone Bahar looks, chagrined by the memory of how different—how much more hopeful—she had been only a few years earlier. He thinks he knows what she has come to talk about, so he tries to break the tension by getting to the point.

"I hear your husband's moving out."

She turns so white he fears she's going to faint. He realizes this is the first she has heard about Omid moving out, so he reaches for her hand across the table and lets out a fake laugh, pats the back of her fingers because he has no idea what to say from here on. The waiter brings the Coke, and she takes a sip of it without looking at The Opera Singer.

It occurs to him then that he's not at all in the mood to see someone else's pain—he's had an armload of it recently with The Pigeon Sister's death, and he resents Bahar bringing him her problems as if he were a rabbi, or a judge, or some elder in the community who might be able to dispense useful advice of any kind.

"You *did* insist on marrying him," he says, not bothering to disguise the edge in his voice.

She nods, then looks up. There are lines around her mouth and eyes, he observes, and her hair is turning gray.

"That's not why I'm here," she says.

He feels suddenly deflated.

He's grateful that they won't have to talk about bad marriages and stray husbands, but he's not relieved. She has never just dropped in on him before. She must have something heavy on her mind.

Behind her, the sun is setting in a yellow-white halo that softens the contours of her face and shows off the shiny streaks of brown in her hair. The Opera Singer thinks she's not so bad-looking, really, she's actually quite pretty, at least in this light. Why the hell is Omid in such a hurry to leave her?

"How is Yaas?" he asks, just to fill the void.

She answers with a question: "Why do you suppose he keeps coming back?"

The Opera Singer looks startled. He pauses a moment, then goes on as if Bahar hadn't spoken at all. "She's getting big. Must be—what? What grade is she in?"

"Why does he come back?"

He knows what she's asking but can't understand why. He gives up. "Dunno." He shrugs. "Why do you ask?"

"What do you think he wants?" Bahar insists. She has brought up The Ghost Brother as if he were something they chatted about in everyday conversation.

"*Why* are you asking?" he snaps.

The Opera Singer realizes he's about to be interrogated about a subject he has no desire to discuss. Aggravated, he opens his newspaper with as much noise as he can make, and starts to read. She's still looking at him.

"How should I know?" he says from across the paper. "I'm not a medium." He keeps reading.

"How old was he, when they found out?"

The Opera Singer is ten years older than Bahar. They both know he remembers the circumstances of The Ghost Brother's death. But it has been years since he discussed it with anyone, and he really would prefer to leave it that way.

He puts the paper down again and says, "Look here: I didn't sign up for this today."

She's not going away.

"I don't understand why people become sentimental after they lose someone," he says, more out of frustration than to reason with Bahar. "They start to search their past for clues as to why something happened, like there's any logic to this world in the first place. Like you can cull meaning out of loss. Make sense out of senselessness."

His words bring tears to Bahar's eyes. He wishes she wouldn't cry, can't stand to see her like that, so he softens.

"He always *was* an obstinate little bastard," he says, sighing.

Below them on the street, cars are spewing black exhaust fumes into the air. Drivers honk incessantly at one another, creating a cacophony that won't cease till near midnight. Half a dozen men are burning scraps of wood in a tin can for heat. The Opera Singer feels the smoke reach the back of his throat, and covers his mouth with a handkerchief—to preserve his vocal cords. As much as he wants to resist getting drawn into Bahar's grief, he can feel his own heart fill with sadness. He puts down the handkerchief and leans toward her with earnest compassion.

"Let it go," he whispers. "There's no solace in knowing."

ACROSS THE STREET in The Tango Dancer's house, Chamedooni has begun to act in an increasingly erratic manner. He has always been distrustful and afraid, but more and more, he displays signs of paranoia or some other kind of madness that must be related to the fact that he's from Mashad—those Mashadi Jews intermarried so much, they have genetic defects you can't even find in medical books. He's so afraid of being pursued, or watched, or kept under surveillance that he has put not one, but two padlocks on the door of his bedroom, installed metal bars outside his window. Still, he checks the place every night for signs of a break-in. He thinks he sees footprints in the carpet where there are none, jumps at the slightest sound, keeps his light off whenever possible at night so he can't be watched from outside. He won't eat any food he hasn't prepared himself, burns any piece of paper that may bear his name, discourages people from coming close to him when they speak.

It isn't just SAVAK agents and government spies that are after him, Chamedooni is convinced. It's worse: he's haunted by a whole army of ghosts—the women whose hair he has stolen for a pittance and sold to the wig makers in Tehran's high-end hair salons. Their men would have punished them for this loss of virtue, except that the women are already dead and can't suffer much more, so the men haunt Chamedooni as well. They follow him from the street into The Tango Dancer's house, lie in his bed, rise like smoke above the Zoroastrian's book of prayer. They've come to demand blood, and they're not going to leave, no matter how much he repents his sins and how sincerely he begs forgiveness. He thinks The Ghost Brother is one of those stray ghosts, and that's why Chamedooni is always watching our house—because, like Ruby, he has seen the boy in our yard.

Yet for all his paralyzing terror and sincere regret, Chamedooni can't stop himself from stealing hair.

He's as remorseful as a person can get when a once-simple interest takes over and ruins his life, and he'd like nothing better than to wake up one morning and be able to resist the pull of the bus that heads south, then west, from June Street and toward the morgue, but he can't. He comes home every night exhausted from the hunt where *he* is the one pursued. He stays in his room with the lights off—so the ghosts can't find his window in the dark—eats his dinner in the glow of the television screen. He sits in the only chair he owns and has the same food for every meal: plain yogurt mixed with walnuts and cucumbers and sprinkled with dried mint leaves. He makes the yogurt himself—to reduce his chances of being poisoned—mixes in the other ingredients, and scoops it out of the bowl with a piece of flat wheat bread that he's rolled into the shape of a cone. He follows that with a glass of tap water, then a glass of black tea sweetened with so much sugar he can barely taste the tea. After that he watches one of the two television channels where the late-night programming consists of government propaganda masquerading as news, or traditional Persian music played by a reed-thin, opium-addicted flute player, or poetry recitations by a heavyset woman with doe eyes and beehive hair, who wears beaded evening gowns and pronounces every word as if it were the last one she'll ever utter.

Chamedooni is barely aware of what is being said on TV, because he's too busy making pledges and taking oaths that he will never again step inside the morgue after that day. He swears on the Torah and on the spirit of his dead father who went to his grave cursing the day he allowed his son to go to university. He writes a declaration, signs it, posts it on his wall right above the TV. He throws his bus money into the toilet and flushes it away, and all along he knows he's fighting an already-lost battle: the only place he really feels alive, where all his senses are sharp and his heart races with excitement, is among the dead.

At midnight, when both channels have stopped broadcasting, Chamedooni falls asleep in his chair. He's afraid to go to bed because he doesn't know which hideous ghost might have lain in there while he has been out, and so he stays in the chair till morning with his arms limp at his sides and his head drooping over his chest, his entire figure lit up by the blue-white screen so that he looks, from the distance where I watch him through the blinds, like a ghost himself.

BAHAR TAKES ME to another doctor, and then a third. Suddenly, we're in and out of doctors' offices all the time, answering the same questions, taking the same hearing tests. If we run into people we know at any of these offices, Bahar takes pains to explain that we're there for a routine checkup.

In between doctors' appointments, she takes me to healers in the old Jewish ghetto and to fortune-tellers in the Armenian quarter. An old man in a dusty backyard adjusts the bones in my neck and promises a quick and complete transformation. Another one rolls dried herbs into cigarette paper and instructs Bahar to blow the smoke from it into my ears. A Parsi woman from Bombay recommends that I drink my own urine. An Iraqi midwife turned witch doctor asks Bahar the names of all the people we're in regular contact with. She writes the names down on the shell of a raw egg, and throws that into a bed of coal burning red inside a brazier. And then, because nothing we have tried has been effective, Bahar resorts to the most feared of all possible cures, and takes me to be seen by a psychologist.

"I'm thinking it may be a hysterical hearing loss," she tells the psychologist on the day of our visit. "I've heard of people fainting from hysteria, or going blind, so I thought you would be able to tell us if this is the case, show us the way to a cure."

The psychologist is sitting behind a brown wooden desk, wearing a suit and tie like he's at a business meeting. He has a bald head and black-rimmed glasses, the ironic stare so common among middle-aged Iranian men of some education who believe themselves so vastly superior to women that they don't bother to communicate but the most essential information.

He asks some questions, then tells Bahar he wants to talk to me alone. She resists this—there's nothing she can tell you that I don't already know; I'm her mother, for God's sake; we can't have children keeping secrets—so he gets up from behind his desk and comes to her.

"Let me show you the waiting room," he says. He opens the door. There are a few other people waiting. "We have lots of magazines, and you can relax for a few minutes."

He sees her out, closes the door, and comes back to his desk.

"Don't be afraid," he tells me. "You and I are going to have a friendly chat."

He pushes his chair away from the desk and puts his feet up. His stomach bulges against his jacket, so he opens the button to make room. He wants to know what's weighing on me, he says, what makes me sad.

"Nothing," I say.

He stares at me through his glasses.

"Nothing," I say again. "I'm not sad."

Where we are from, children have no right to be sad unless they have suffered a legitimate loss—a parent's death, say—and even then, they must keep their grief under wraps, make sure it doesn't interfere with their manners or their studies and doesn't impose on the adults who, because they have lived longer, own the right to grieve.

"Listen to me, dear," the man wipes his glasses with the edge of his jacket. "I know your parents aren't happy to bring you here. It's always a last resort—a visit to someone like me. People think it means they're insane."

He stops and looks at me. "I'm telling you now I may be able to help you, but you have to tell the truth."

His voice is soft and measured, difficult to hear. I think he's said I have to tell the truth, but I can't be sure, and this scares and confuses me. He may have said, "You have to sit up straight." In Farsi, the same word is used for "truth" and "straight"; the words for "tell" and "sit up" are very similar.

What if I respond to something he hasn't said? Prove that I'm indeed going deaf?

I sit up straight. I see that he's becoming irritated, but I don't know what I'm supposed to say to him or why he doesn't relent.

"I *am*..." I say, too unsure of what I've heard to complete the sentence. I can't tell him about my hearing loss, or my parents' troubles, or our desolate, haunted lives.

"Tell me what's making you uncomfortable."

Is it my ears, or the way he speaks, or my panic at being alone and failing with this man that makes me so confused?

Again, I don't know if he's said "comfortable" or "uncomfortable," so I can't answer him. I start to cry. He puts his feet down on the ground and leans toward me across the desk.

"I'll give you my word," he says, "that you can trust me. You can tell me anything and it will stay between the two of us. Nothing you say here will leave this room."

So I told him.

I realize it was wrong, that I had no right to talk to a stranger about the people who were closest to me. I did it because I thought it might make me stop crying, or give me back my hearing; because I thought, stupidly, it might make a difference to what happened in our home, between my parents. Mostly, I did it because I believed the man when he said he would keep my secret.

I told the psychologist about my parents' fighting, Omid's affair with Niyaz, how I was always afraid he would leave us for her, how Bahar expected me to bring him back. I told him about the maid who wanted to leave us, the boy who couldn't be chased away. I told him about the jinn that killed our plants, the cruel husband who drove my aunt to hang herself, the frantic neighbor who was chased by ghosts.

I said all this in as few words as I could, tried to make it look as normal as possible. He listened and asked questions, nodded and listened some more. At the end of the hour, he told me I had permission to leave, but that he would see me again, that he and I had lots more to talk about.

"We're going to be good friends," he said.

Bahar waits till we have left the office. Then she says, "I heard everything."

For a minute, I feel as if I'm turning into ice.

"That can't be," I protest.

She turns her lips up and shrugs. "Everyone else did, too."

I feel my chest burning up, my hands tightening into fists. I want to assault her right then, or to obliterate myself.

"You're lying," I scream.

She shakes her head again.

"Everyone in the waiting room heard you."

I'm stunned. I mutter, "He said no one would know."

"Right," she smirks. "And you *believed* him."

I see the faces of the women in the waiting room, how they looked at me when I came out.

"You're lying," I say. "He was a doctor. He promised me."

"You told him all about your father and me," she offers proof. She's seething, stabbed in the back by the daughter she has always known would be her "worst enemy" and who has proven herself worthy of the title.

"But you *took* me there." I start crying. "You *told* me he could help."

She stops, bends down, and brings her face to within an inch of mine.

"You spoke too loudly," she says. "*You* can't hear yourself, but everyone else *did* because you're so loud."

THE NEXT DAY, Mr. Arbab summons Omid to the house on Jordan Avenue. It's Friday, and the cook has made lamb kebab with saffron rice and broiled tomatoes. After lunch, they sit on the terrace to drink tea. Mr. Arbab has a smoker's cough and a slight tremor in his right hand, but he's otherwise strong, more deliberate and forceful than most men his age. Normally, he talks with the tone and emphasis of one who is accustomed to being obeyed, but on this day he appears mild and reflective, more empathetic than judgmental.

"There was a man in the ghetto, way back when I was a boy, before the Jews were allowed to move out," he says, and the very words shock Omid because he has never heard his father talk about his own boyhood, or admit that he had lived in the ghetto in South Tehran. It's this way with most Jews who have moved up in the past fifty years—they're so ashamed of their ghetto past that they deny they ever lived there, or that their parents lived there, or that they even knew where the ghetto was. If you press them about their beginnings, they might admit to Cyrus Street, but that's as far as most are willing to go.

"He used to clean out the septic tank in our house. He came every morning with a basket strapped to his back. He emptied our tank with his bare hands, went from house to house till the basket was full, then dumped the contents in some field outside of town. People avoided him because he was so dirty and smelled so bad; he was practically *najis*—untouchable—the way Jews were to Muslims."

He takes a sip of his tea. He knows Omid is wondering why he's being told about this man, what this story has to do with the real reason he has been called to the house.

"The thing is, he had been *born* into this work. Some jobs—the best and the worst ones—were inherited by each generation in a family.

This man was doomed to do this work because no one would give him another job, or buy anything he might have to sell to make a living. That's how it was in the ghetto: whatever you did, good or bad, belonged to your children. Your good name opened doors"—he pauses for a second—"and your mistakes ruined your progeny."

He stops and drinks his tea again without looking at Omid.

"When Reza Shah opened the ghettos, the Jews were ecstatic. Anyone who could afford to left immediately. The septic tank man, on the other hand, refused to leave. This astonished us. We thought he'd be the first to run away, shed his burden, and live where people didn't know him. We knew he despised his work, and yet he wouldn't change his name or deny what his family had done for generations."

Finally, Mr. Arbab looks at his son.

"So I asked him. He said, 'I may be impure, but I'm the guardian of my father's name, and I will carry it with honor."

Mr. Arbab looks over the yard, at the white mulberry tree with the enormous leaves, at the way its branches have spread so perfectly over the nearby fountain, allowing patches of sunlight over the water while keeping the rest in shade.

"If this is about *her*," Omid says, "I don't want to talk about it."

Mr. Arbab throws a furious glance at his son. They have always been strangers, but their relationship has become more strained since the day he told Omid he may not divorce his wife. Since then, Omid rarely comes to visit, and he avoids his father outside of the office. They speak when they have to—about work—then quickly part. Mr. Arbab has the upper hand—he controls the money—and Omid hates him for this. He has denied Omid happiness with Niyaz, all for the sake of protecting the family's good name, and he doesn't care what this does to his son at all, doesn't mind losing Omid's affection, because he knows what is wrong and right and where to draw the line. There are things we allow ourselves, and boundaries we don't cross.

"It's not about *her*," Mr. Arbab says.

One of the women in the psychologist's waiting room is a friend of a friend of the Arbabs. She's told people what she heard, and they, in turn, have told the Arbabs. Omid's father has tolerated much in his lifetime, but he cannot stomach having his name sullied by a ten-year-old and dragged through the mud by his son's family. Still, that's not the reason he has called Omid.

"Listen to me once and for all," he tells Omid, his right hand shaking as it raises a cigarette to his lips. "I've done some things in my life I'm not proud of, and I've forgiven *you* much as well, but I've never compromised where our honor was on the line."

He puts the cigarette down on the edge of the ashtray and, for the first time in Omid's life, allows something other than disapproval to seep into his voice.

"I don't know how you got yourself into this trap," he says, the words pulsating with something resembling affection, "but you have a daughter who is practically deaf, and a wife who'll be no one if you leave her. To turn your back on them as you have, to go around with that woman pretending all is well"—he pauses to catch his breath— "that's something I don't want to be remembered for."

THERE ARE THINGS we allow ourselves and boundaries we don't cross. There are transgressions for which one will not be forgiven, crimes that indict not only the perpetrator but also those related to him by blood.

You can be unfaithful to your wife, but you can't divorce her. You can take away her dreams, but you can't stop providing for her. You can despise, but not disobey, your father, dislike, but not dishonor, him. You can pretend your child is not ill, but you can't abandon her.

For every sin, a virtue; every cruelty, a measure of mercy.

NIYAZ IS IN AMERICA when she receives Omid's letter.

"Forgive me," he has written, "but I must uphold my duty before God."

He writes about a child who needs his attention—Niyaz remembers having heard about her in the past; she's going blind, or deaf, or something equally tragic, Niyaz recalls—and that he feels he must devote himself to her, look after her and her mother until they find a cure.

It's this kind of interdependence that Niyaz dislikes about Iranians—they're always with their families, traveling in packs like a bunch of penguins. They do everything by committee, make every decision communal. Even after they're grown men and women, they don't become separate people. They live each other's lives as if it were one great tragedy they signed on to at birth. They get married but don't leave their parents' care until the parents are too old and the children take charge of *them*.

Niyaz has no sympathy for Omid or his child, can't see what he could do for the girl if he stayed with her mother. She's annoyed that he hasn't talked to her about this in person, that he waited for her to go to America and then wrote a letter, but she knows this is because he'd never be able to do this face-to-face. At any rate, the letter doesn't alarm her much. She reads it twice and throws it away. She doesn't write back, or call Omid in Tehran, or contemplate any of the other senseless acts that jilted lovers engage in so often. She knows Omid will come back to her—sick child or not. Whatever he may think of himself and his ability to rise to certain occasions, Niyaz knows his limitations.

OMID TELLS BAHAR he wants to start over.

He looks spent—devastated—as he says this, but he confesses that he has failed Bahar and me, promises he will do whatever possible to turn himself into a real husband and father.

Bahar cries tears of sorrow and relief—tears of that bitter joy that belongs to those who have given up too much on the road to victory.

They have rented a house on the Caspian shore, in a village nestled between the sea and acres of rice fields. We pack for the trip at night because we're going to leave early in the morning. At four-thirty, Omid comes to my room and wakes me. In the kitchen, Bahar pours tea into slender glasses and tells me to drink fast, we must leave soon to get to the seashore by sunrise.

We drive across narrow mountain roads, above valleys so deep the end is invisible, through long, narrow tunnels made of stone, beside a lush jungle where white tigers live. We stop once, to buy a bucket of blackberries from a peasant boy who has picked them only minutes earlier. He's barefoot, his face and neck scratched, his hands bleeding from the thorns and branches he has had to clear to get to the berries. At sunrise, we come upon rice fields where the water, still as glass, shines like yellow gold. Then we reach the Caspian.

IT WAS THE SEA, I thought even then, that brought my parents together. It's as if Bahar had always known this—that they would have to travel away from their life in order to find happiness. That's why she told him about the Caspian that day when they spoke for the first time. She had told him about a happiness she hadn't experienced but knew existed. It was all a matter of faith, The Opera Singer would have said, and I thought, that summer when my parents and I became a family for the first time, that he would have been right.

Omid and I swim in the sea every day on the beach outside our rented house. At midday, we retreat into a straw hut that has been erected on stilts dug into the sand. Little boys, younger than me, sell trays of steaming rice and broiled meat that their mothers have cooked. Old men with rotting boats and crooked oars bring us the fish they have just caught. They gut each fish with one slice of a knife, pour its insides on the sand, cook it over a fire they've made in an empty ten-gallon oil can.

Bahar emerges from the house with glasses of iced cherry nectar, quince-seed juice, cantaloupe juice. She's wearing a cotton dress, large sunglasses—Jackie O glasses, they are called in Tehran—straw sandals.

In the afternoon, I sleep on the floor of the hut, under a sheer cotton blanket of the kind woven by local women on old-fashioned looms. My hair is matted, my skin covered with sand and salt from the sea. I close my eyes and feel I'm still being rocked by the waves.

When I wake up, the air is sticky and humid. The sun is still out, but rain is falling in perfect, shimmering drops. It's a golden rain, each drop the color of the rice fields along the shoreline. I come out of the hut and onto the sand. I feel my heart expand with joy, and I think it has something to do with this sea, this beach, this rain that I can hear—

I realize suddenly, and to my astonishment—that I can hear so well, as clearly as I once did and as I haven't for a long time.

Even today, I hear that rain in my dreams.

THEY RETURNED from the Caspian with new optimism. They talked about going back often, about spending more time together at home. I remember Bahar singing as she made dinner, setting the table with flowers and sugar-coated almonds in pastel colors and golden saffron rice. Even after I started fourth grade that fall, Omid came home early on Thursday afternoons to watch Peyton Place with Bahar and me. Friday mornings that spring, he drove us to the Karaj River. We hiked toward the snow-covered peaks of Alborz, ate fried eggs and yogurt in coffeehouses built along the water. My cheeks would sting from the cold mountain air and my hands would become numb from the icy water and Omid would take them into his own, hold them till they were warm, and I could see the relief in Bahar's face, see her thinking, it must be true—that family triumphs over all, that blood pulls harder than desire.

It doesn't.

We're driving back from Karaj one Friday in late spring when he reaches for Bahar in the passenger seat, brushes her hair out of her eyes, and says, "I can't go on."

I can't do this anymore I've tried but I'm dying inside I need to leave this wasn't meant to be—you and I—you must know it too.

Stop, she screams, and her voice echoes in the car. Stop it, Yaas can hear you, have pity on *her* if you don't have it for *me.*

Omid pleads with her. "Hear me out."

He tells her it was all a mistake, that he never should have married without love, that life without Niyaz is nothing more than an endless, empty wait. This is not something he has chosen; it's what he's doing because he has no alternative.

I remember his voice trembled when he spoke. I remember that Bahar sobbed next to him all the way home. I remember thinking I had become invisible from the neck down, that I had no legs to tremble, no stomach to churn with anguish, no heart, even, to break.

PART VI

AT THE END OF THAT SUMMER, Artemis, the "Persian Ringo Starr," gets the big break he's been waiting for all his life.

He has been working in the shoe store for nearly fifteen years, playing the drums at weddings and bar mitzvahs once every few months, usually because a musician friend has felt sorry for him, or is unable to perform, and has asked Artemis to fill in. He hardly gets paid for those performances, and barely makes any money selling shoes—which might be touching, even admirable, for an artist in his prime, struggling against the odds, but Artemis is nearly forty years old, graying at the temples and much too wide at the center for the fitted shirts and low-waisted trousers he still wears. It's not clear if he is any good at the drums anyway, because he makes so much noise when he plays, you can hardly escape with your hearing intact. But you don't have to be a musicologist to glean from his circumstances that Artemis is a step or two short of achieving the Beatle-like fame he aspires to—that he is, in fact, quite unlikely ever to leave the Alley of the Champions or the second floor of the yellow house where he lives alongside a love-struck Zoroastrian and a haunted Jew, above a South American maybe-spy who avoids sleep for fear of dreaming of her Nazi parents' prey.

The only person, other than himself, who continues to believe in Ringo's potential, and banks her own name and entire future on it, is Ruby. She started sleeping with him out of pure lust, she has confessed to Bahar, which isn't a bad reason to sleep with anyone, especially a "boy" as handsome and impressive as Artemis, but she has, over time, fallen in love with him—so much so that she's willing to wait as long as it takes, support him with her own meager earnings if she has to, just for the pleasure of seeing him succeed. Then the two of them will leave South Tehran together, get married or "live together"—she knows people do this in America because she reads Bahar's *Modern Ladies* magazines—in one of those suites on top of the Tehran Hilton where rich Jewish and Muslim men keep their mistresses.

The fact that she's married doesn't once interfere with Ruby's fantasies about Artemis. She has already abandoned Hassan in her heart if not on paper. She hasn't told him a thing about what she is doing, and he has never confronted her. He goes about his duties with more-than-usual obsession and spends all his free time trying to revive the garden that is clearly beyond hope. He must still think there is a chance for Ruby to leave Artemis, Bahar says whenever the subject comes up; he must think he can outlast the other man.

At this, Ruby always laughs, throws her head back, and shakes her hair.

"Right!" she says. "And the Shah's wife is going to leave *him* for the one-eyed street sweeper."

She has even gone so far as to buy herself and Artemis matching pendants, two gold letter R's—Ruby and Ringo—intertwined so that they each look like a person in profile facing the other, and she wears hers all the time, even to bed, without regard for what Hassan might think.

But for all her faith in his potential, when success does come to Artemis, Ruby will be the person most taken aback.

They have been carrying on as usual, she dropping in on him in the afternoon and staying two or three hours, going back again sometimes at night or in the early morning when she brings him freshly baked bread and handpicked peaches. One Friday night on Cyrus Street, The Opera Singer looks at my mother and says, not without a hefty dose of envy, "So your *maid*'s lover finally made it."

Bahar has no idea what The Opera Singer is talking about. She says she can't imagine what would constitute "making it" for a person like Artemis.

"He's clearly delusional," she says.

The Opera Singer is indignant.

"I agree. The guy's a fat mule. But so are the people who've picked him for their band."

Bahar is perplexed.

"What people? What band?"

Iran's national television network has started to produce local programming. Among those programs is a music variety show where Iranian singers and musicians dress and dance and act like American pop singers. The show is wildly popular, and it nearly guarantees anyone who appears on it certain fame.

"The backup band for the singers who come on the show."

Rock-and-roll drummers, especially ones with a name like "The Persian Ringo Starr," are in short supply in Tehran. The ones that the show does manage to find, quickly leave for America, seeking record deals and sold-out concerts.

"It's slim pickings," The Opera Singer explains Ringo's selection.

Bahar is still incredulous. "Ruby would have mentioned this."

The Opera Singer laughs bitterly. "Ruby wouldn't *know* about it," he says. "*You* know what it's like." He stops himself there, but it's too late. Stricken, Bahar looks down at her hands.

"Yes," she whispers. "I know what it's like."

"What I *mean* is, she'd be the last person he would want to tell. You don't actually think Mr. Ringo Starr is going to haul your Kurdish maid— a married one at that—out of her station and up to where he's going?"

Bahar looks at her brother. She feels hurt by what he has said— about how she had found out, later than most others, that her husband was cheating on her—and she feels sad for Ruby, but most of all, she feels pity for The Opera Singer. Why is it that some people's dreams, hopeless as they are, happen to come true?

"Take my word for it," The Opera Singer concludes. "The only way Ruby's going to know about this is if someone other than Artemis tells her, or when she sees him on TV. By then—mark my words—he will have vacated his room and vanished where she can't follow him."

He was right.

❧

I WILL SEE HIM AGAIN—the boy outside our window.

He comes back almost every night, stands on the dining room bal-cony, or in the yard, or on the street directly under my window. His eyes are soft, and they wrap around me till I can't look away. I realize they're watching me all the time, that they want something from me, but I don't know what that is, or why the boy keeps returning. He must be aware that he is not welcome in our house by Bahar, because he hides from her doggedly, comes in like a beggar through the window in the dark. I've learned about ghosts and jinn from Ruby, heard about that house on the Avenue of Faith—the one people say is haunted by robber ghosts: they walk through the house even as the owners are at home, take what they want, and leave without being detected. The only person who can see them is an old opium addict who lives in the kitchen of that house, and who can believe him anyway? How is one to know what he's really seen and what he's hallucinated? Meanwhile, the house on the Avenue of Faith, once among the most magnificent in the city, has been stripped of all its contents, even the rugs and the curtains, and still the robber ghosts keep coming back. I wonder if the boy on the bicycle is one of those ghosts.

One night in fall, my parents are away. Ruby, who is supposed to be watching me, has sneaked out to see Artemis, and I'm alone in the dining room, doing homework. When I see the boy in the yard, I don't wait for him to come to me; I go outside to meet him.

It's past midnight, and I'm barefoot and in my pajamas. There's no snow on the ground, but the earth is hard and cold, and a sharp, dark wind cuts through. I see the boy shiver in the wind and realize that I'm shivering as well—from the cold, perhaps, or from the excitement of the encounter. I have no idea why I've come to him.

He smiles at me, and I notice for the first time that his front teeth are chipped and that he's missing a tooth in his lower jaw. He must be about my age, I think.

"What do you want?" I ask.

I'm surprised by my own voice. It's as if it didn't belong to me, as if I've heard the echo of someone else's words in the bare, empty yard.

He keeps smiling, but his eyes don't move, so I know he hasn't understood my question. I notice, too, that he must be older than I had thought: he's as tall as a ten-year-old, it is true, and he has the hands and the facial bone structure of a child, but there are lines around his eyes and on the sides of his mouth that I have seen only on people my parents' age. You'd have to get close to him to see this, but it gives his face a strange and unsettling imprint.

He shuffles his feet now, and I fear he wants to run away.

"What are you looking for," I ask again, "when you come here?"

There's a moment when I think he's going to speak, but then the moment is gone and he's still standing there, smiling widely as if to say he means no harm. I look at him—eager, earnest, wanting to do right—and, suddenly, see myself. Then I understand: The Ghost Brother is my double.

❧

BAHAR TAKES ME to a young doctor who has just finished his studies in America. After the physical exam, he calls us into his office to talk. He's irritated that I have no medical file to help him explain my history, but Bahar hasn't kept records of any of our visits to other doctors, because she doesn't like what they have told her.

"Do you have hearing aids?" the doctor asks.

He has directed the question at me, but Bahar rushes to answer. "We don't need hearing aids."

He raises his eyebrows at her.

"Do you know what hearing aids are?" he asks her.

He's polite but arrogant—one of those Iranians who has studied in the West and therefore believe that they, and what they know, are light-years ahead of everyone and everything in the East.

"Yes, I do," she snaps. "I'm not ignorant."

"Then you must know that your daughter is nearly deaf."

Bahar is aghast. She glares at the doctor, breathless, and fights to regain her composure. When she speaks again, her voice is thin and fading. "That's why we're here. So you can cure her."

He sighs and leans back in his chair.

"I don't know if there's a cure for this," he says, looking at me. "There may be nerve damage, or some genetic issues. The important thing right now is to help her hear as much as possible—in case she gets worse."

He must realize how frightening his words are, because he's smiling at me as he speaks. "I'm not saying that it will happen," he tells me. "I just think we should prepare for the future."

I'm ten years old. I don't know what constitutes "the future"—how far away it is or when it will arrive. To me, the future is the next day, the next hour, the next breath.

Bahar stands up and signals that the visit is over.

"No hearing aids," she spits. "I won't let her become a pariah."

The most important thing, Bahar told me after we had seen the young doctor, was that no one find out. She told me this after we had seen the young doctor. She sat before me that day, in our house on June Street, so many worlds away from the Square of the Pearl Canon, in my room with the floor-to-ceiling window that overlooked the ramshackle houses and down-on-their-luck residents of the Alley of the Champions, and tried to explain why I had no choice but to hide. From where we sat on the bed, I could see her image reflected in the mirror with the etched-glass frame that hung on the far wall. Always slender, she had grown bone-thin and pallid in those months. Her movements, once certain, had become small and tentative. And if I had looked deeper into the mirror, if I had pulled myself away from the words enough to study her face, I know I would have seen the doubt, the question that hung in her eyes every time she spoke to me in those days—do you understand what I've said, did I say it loudly enough, will I be able to reach you, later, when words no longer have a sound?

She told me the story of her own deaf brother.

He was born hearing, but slowly went deaf. He stopped going to school because he couldn't understand anything the teachers said. His parents tried to keep him at home, but he rode away on his bike into the street every day. The car that hit him had honked repeatedly, the driver crying, "Get out of the way, boy, pull over, pull off the road."

And still, The Ghost Brother kept pedaling.

His family had kept his deafness a secret because they wanted their daughters to have a chance at a good marriage. It was the wisest choice, what anyone else with a brain or heart would have done under similar circumstances. You hide your losses and try to prevent greater ones, and sometimes, you actually get away with it.

THE LAST DOCTOR we go to works at the American township in the southern city of Abadan. Bahar and I make the trip—seven hours in the car and a night in a small hotel—because we have heard that the American doctor, someone called Toni Gomez, can diagnose and cure ailments that are outside the range of expertise of Iranian doctors. We're sitting in the waiting room when a woman walks in with her sick child. The woman is slight and wiry, dressed in a yellow padded suit that's much too warm for Abadan's searing climate. She wears a little pillbox hat, high-heeled pumps, a pair of pearl earrings that look as if they have been kept in a drawer for a decade before she has taken them out and put them on to impress the doctor. She walks in clutching the top of a cracked leather purse, her face and neck already shiny with per-spiration. Behind her is an enormous young boy with large, flat hands and mad eyes. He rocks back and forth as he walks, makes whimpering sounds that the woman ignores. When she sees Bahar and me, she smiles and utters a greeting. She speaks Farsi with an accent, and she has slanted eyes and flat cheekbones, like a Mongolian without the dark skin. Gently, she directs the boy to a chair in the farthest corner of the room and helps him sit down. She sits next to him and pats his leg for reassurance. Then she balances her purse on her lap and smiles at us again.

"It's a hot day," she remarks in Farsi, and now I can tell she's not Mongolian at all, because her accent is too heavy and her manners too foreign. "I'm glad the doctor is working."

She opens her purse and takes out a handkerchief, dabs the mois-ture from her hairline and the back of her lip, her neck, the top of her chest. Her fingers have left wet marks on the top of her bag. She wipes those off as well, then puts the handkerchief away and snaps the bag shut.

"I'm from Korea," she says to Bahar as if to explain the warm clothes, or the accent, or even the boy. "My husband is American. An engineer at the refinery."

Bahar nods politely, says, "We're from Tehran."

We sit quietly for a few minutes. The air conditioner buzzes like a swarm of metallic bees. The boy rocks back and forth in his chair and mumbles incomprehensibly. I'm worried that the woman might address me next—ask me my age, or my name, or my reason for visiting the doctor. I'm afraid that I won't hear her well enough to understand the question—that her accent will make it impossible for me to guess what she has asked.

The boy's voice is becoming louder and more urgent.

"He likes to talk to himself," the woman explains. To my horror, she's looking at *me* as she speaks. "Sometimes, he gets angry."

I nod to say I understand, but I know she can tell this isn't so. I feel intimidated, even threatened by the boy—by his bulk and his eyes and the tension in his limbs, by the way he looks as if he could go off at any moment.

"I was able to constrain him when he was younger," the woman says. "Now, he's so much bigger than me. So the doctor has him on medication to keep him calm. We come every six months."

It occurs to me that the woman is volunteering too much information, that she's setting herself up for the possibility of being asked questions she won't want to answer.

"His name is Bryan," she says to both Bahar and me, and her voice becomes smaller and more faded—like a trail of ants that march out of her mouth and straight down into the cavity of her neck.

"He was born in the States. I thought I should give him an American name," she forces a brave smile.

Bahar nods. I try to look away.

"I'm from Korea," the woman repeats. "I met my husband there. He'd been married twice before already."

Her family had been against the marriage. You can't trust a man who's failed two wives already, they told her, but the woman had thought this was different—she was born lucky and destined to go to America, why else would fate have brought her together with this man?

"I thought my son would be lucky as well," she says, and looks over at him.

He had been strange from the outset. He wouldn't let her hold him when he was a toddler. He grew too fast, but didn't learn to speak. When he became angry, he would hurt himself and anyone near him.

"So we come here every six months for medication to make him calm," she explains.

An eternity passes. I keep praying for a nurse or the doctor to come to the door, call us in, save my mother and me from being embarrassed before a stranger. Bahar, suddenly dragged into the confidence of this woman she does not know, nevertheless looks drained, exhausted by the enormity of a mother's suffering. Out of nowhere she says, "My daughter is losing her hearing."

Her words hang in the air—six little flowers that glow purple in the heat and that stun me with their simplicity. With their weightlessness. Their poison.

The woman turns to me, looking wounded, but she spares me the question. We remain quiet for a beat.

"I used to fight with my husband a lot when I was pregnant," she says, picking up the narrative of her own life because she knows, now, that Bahar will understand what she's saying. "I think this is why my son became ill—because I was unhappy when I carried him. I think it made his brain go bad. I think it's my fault."

She says this in an even, matter-of-fact tone. Her eyes are still and her lips curl around each word like a bright, silk ribbon, and it's only if you see her fingers pressing against the leather of her handbag, leaving a trace of perspiration that trickles down to her knees, or if you see the way she jabs her face and neck with the handkerchief, that you can imagine the tumult inside her.

"I think I never should have married in the first place," she says, and at last, her eyes fill with tears. "People ask me why I don't cry," she says, her eyes resting directly on me. It's as if I'm a duplicate of her son—as if we're all the same, all of us flawed children who come into this world only to break our mothers' hearts.

"They think it means I'm happy, that I've kept going in spite of this because I don't care that much about my son. They don't know that I don't cry because I have no tears left."

She swallows hard, then declares, "I'm not lucky, and neither is my son—no matter how American I made him."

We sit in total silence. Just when I think she's not going to speak again, she looks at Bahar and asks her the strangest question: "But *you*," she says, "*you're* so pretty. How could something so bad have happened to *you?*"

TONI GOMEZ, we soon learn, is a woman. Her real name is Antonia. She had come to Abadan as an army medic in charge of looking after the many oil workers and contractors sent here by the U.S. government, but she stayed after the term of her service expired and now takes private patients. In her lab coat and her high heels, she looks like a cockroach—tiny head, skinny arms and legs, squeaky voice—and she is just as tough. She speaks some Farsi, some Arabic, because Abadan is close to the border with Iraq, but her English is fast and barely comprehensible to Bahar or me. On her office wall is a clipping of a Farsi-language newspaper with a picture of her in an American army uniform. She's standing erect, and she has made a point of looking away from the camera just enough to indicate that she is not one to be distracted by frivolous tasks like being photographed.

With me, too, she doesn't make eye contact. While she examines me, she asks the usual questions without looking at Bahar or reacting to anything she says. She does a hearing test on me, makes us wait for another hour. Then she calls us into her office.

She's sitting at her desk, reading a file. She looks up at us and closes the folder. "Get her hearing aids," she says. "She's at 30 percent now. I bet you anything she'll be deaf in a year."

⁂

THAT NIGHT I LIE AWAKE, alone in my room with the arc-shaped window, and listen to Bahar talk to my father on the phone. We have driven straight back to Tehran from Toni Gomez's office. In the car, Bahar has held my hand but looked away to hide her tears. When we arrive, Ruby meets us at the door and shakes her head in disapproval. I told you to leave it alone, she says to Bahar, the child is what she is, you can't fight the will of God. She picks me up in her arms—you're too small, you weigh less than a six-year-old, your mother should stop taking you to doctors and feed you a little instead—and carries me up to my room.

"The trouble with rich people," she says as we climb the stairs, "is that they think they should be immune to the will of God."

She says this in a voice so diminished by grief, it is barely recognizable. It has been months since Artemis became a television star and left the Alley without a word to Ruby, and still she hasn't bounced back from her disappointment. She goes through the motions of everyday life without any of the daring and recklessness that had been her hallmark since I've known her.

"Somebody needs to tell you people to wake up," she mumbles.

I put my head on her shoulder and close my eyes. When I open them again, I'm in bed, my room lit only by the glow of the street lamps outside. I think I can hear Bahar's voice. It's dense and muffled, as if filtered through cloth. It isn't far away so much as muted—devoid of the ring, the chime I had once heard in every word.

It's that ring, that miraculous glowing of sound, I will mourn most deeply after I have lost my hearing. It's the resonance of language, the emotions that give each word its unique shape as it's uttered, that shimmer with joy or break the heart—it's those emotions that I will miss the most.

"I won't accept it," she says on the phone, and I close my eyes again, pray I will fall asleep and bury that day and everything that's happened.

Near dawn, I feel a breeze and open my eyes to find I'm standing barefoot on the dining room balcony. The air on my face is dry and cool—a far cry from the heavy, humid air of Abadan—and it takes me some time to remember that I'm back at home, in Tehran: I have no inkling how I got from my bed onto the balcony.

I must have walked in my sleep—chasing the light.

I'm drowning here. Look in the dark and see me.

THE MOST IMPORTANT THING, Bahar had said, was that no one find out.

I had believed her, guarded our secrets until they became my only companions, until I was so alone, I felt like one of those cardboard figures in my English-language workbooks—this is an arm; this is a neck; this is a girl. I had thought that denial and silence would protect my mother and me, but then I saw The Ghost Brother and began to wonder what had brought him back.

He had helped his parents keep the secret of his deafness, shielded his sisters from the judgment of an unforgiving world, made himself invisible so that others could live more easily. His silence protected his family, but it robbed *him* of the story that he could have left behind— the one that defined *him*. Without it, he was just a boy who had died young. He existed only because he had broken his parents' heart, taken from them all the laughter they might have been capable of. If he was remembered at all, it was only in the context of other people's lives—as an absence, someone who *wasn't*.

I'm terrified of angering Bahar, or earning her disapproval, or causing her to feel betrayed; but I'm even more afraid of becoming a ghost. I would rather be like The Tango Dancer, I think—despised and ostracized but ever present, willing to forgo the smaller mercies of an existence that depends so entirely on conformity, that exacts obedience and punishes defiance by casting the guilty forever out of the tribe. I would rather have nothing, than live in fear of losing what I have.

What is a life, at the end, but a story we leave behind? What if that story were never told?

THE NEXT TIME BAHAR is out running an errand, I go into my room and take out the little box filled with gold coins that Mrs. Arbab gives me every Persian New Year. I'm eleven years old; I have eleven coins. I empty them all into my pocket and, when Ruby's not watching, leave the house.

For over a year, I have managed to avoid Chamedooni whenever he comes to our door or waits for me on the street, but now I run the length of the Alley to the yellow house, praying he'll be there when I arrive. I stand, panting, at the door, and try to muster up the courage to ring. Any minute, I know, someone will see me here and tell Bahar. The Tango Dancer opens the door.

Her eyes are dark and stormy—like the waters of the sea of Oman, I imagine. Her fingers are adorned with many rings; her body is slim and taut. She has on a floor-length dress with ruffles. The dress is black, the ruffles bright red. I imagine they flare when she's dancing, making her look like an upside-down rose.

She's waiting for me to speak, but I have no voice. She must recognize me because she asks, "Are you looking for Ruby?"

Ruby hasn't been to the house since the day she went there to see Artemis and found his room bare and empty.

I shake my head. My right hand is clenching the coins in my pocket, but I can't bring myself to take them out, or to tell her I'm looking for Chamedooni, for the cures and wonders I had laughed at only a year ago. I've come because I have nowhere else to go, no one else I can plead with for the thing that was mine but is being taken away.

"Did someone send you here?"

I shake my head again. I can tell she's losing patience.

"All right, then," she declares, "spit it out or go away."

Because I can't answer, I take the coins out of my pocket and hold them to her. She frowns.

"What are you doing with all this gold?"

There are no edges in her voice—just pure wonder.

"I've come to buy something from Chamedooni."

"Buy what?"

I hesitate. I'm embarrassed to say the words, because it would be an admission that I'm flawed and doomed. I'm also afraid she will tell my parents, give them a chance to stop me before I've got what I want.

"Hearing aids." The words feel like daggers in my throat.

I see something move in her face, like a storm cloud shifting to reveal a much gentler sky. She hadn't looked cruel or angry before—just impatient—but now that's all gone.

"So it's true, then," she whispers, almost to herself, "what people say."

I feel like I'm going to cry. I hadn't realized that people had been talking about me, that they knew I was going deaf. The Tango Dancer notices my shock and adopts a different tone.

"Do your parents know you're here?"

I shake my head.

"Won't they buy you the hearing aids?"

I shake my head again.

The Tango Dancer's smile, then, tells that she knows about this—about being a child and at the mercy of one's parents. She comes down on one knee, looks at the coins in my open hand, and takes only one.

"This is more than enough," she says. "I'll give it to him."

I thank her. She stares at me with those black eyes and says, "Don't thank me. I'm not doing you a favor."

I put the rest of the coins back in my pocket. I know I should leave, but I don't want to. I want to go with The Tango Dancer into her house, sit next to her in this place that has closed itself off against the world, learn to be brave like her, to defy the others as she does.

"Now you remember what I'm going to tell you," she says gently, her face still close to mine. She waits to make sure I'm paying attention.

"There's such a thing as too much hope."

I don't say anything.

"It's like a black hole: you fall in, and there's no bottom. That's why Chamedooni is the way he is: he can't tell the difference between what's possible, and what's not."

THE HEARING AIDS ARE OLD—I can see that the minute Chamedooni hands them to me—and don't quite fit my ears.

He has shown up at our door early one Friday morning when he knows most people will be asleep. I've been up since five, looking at the Alley, and when I see him come out of the yellow house, I know he's heading toward me. I run down the stairs and open the door before he has a chance to ring.

He looks tired and dirty, a sweat ring already forming around his shirt collar.

"I brought you these," he says, holding out his hand.

I stare at them—a pair of tiny gray mice—without daring to touch.

"I had to find ones small enough to fit you," he says. His lips are purple, his teeth black at the gum line. With his free hand, he reaches forward and pushes my hair back behind my ear.

"Such pretty hair," he says, "and it's good that you've grown it long. It'll cover these so no one will know."

Since Bahar stopped cutting it, my hair has grown down to the middle of my back. It's straight and shiny as I had always wished, but she has me tie it in a ponytail every day.

"Do you know how to use them?" Chamedooni asks.

"I'll learn."

He must think what I've said is amusing, because he smiles and says, "You *do* that." He hands me the hearing aids.

"And something else," he adds. From the inside pocket of his suit jacket, he takes out the gold coin I had left with The Tango Dancer. "You should keep this."

"It's payment for the hearing aids," I protest.

He smiles.

"Such a precious girl," he says, and touches the side of my face. His eyes turn glassy; his lower lips trembles. He runs his hand down over my back, onto the front of my chest, between my breasts, and rests it on my stomach.

"Such a *beautiful* girl," he says again, terrifying me. "And such glorious hair."

I run into the house and put on the hearing aids in front of a mirror. Then I go out on the dining room balcony and listen. I hear sounds I haven't heard in months, or perhaps years—sounds that stun me with their clarity and reverberation, that echo in my ears and make me light-headed with joy. I tell myself I've been cured, I don't care what Bahar says or what other people think, I'll never give up these little gray mice, I'll wear them for the rest of my life.

❧

BAHAR NOTICES the hearing aids right away, and she's so stunned, she doesn't even try to snatch them away.

"What's this?" she asks, staring at my ears. "Where did you get them?"

I'm determined to stand up to her. "I bought them from Chamedooni," I say. "I used my own money."

"You mean from that filthy old man with the suitcase?" she balks. "Have you really lost your mind?"

I've only had the hearing aids for a few hours, but already I feel different—less afraid—so I can respond to Bahar without my usual trepidation.

"I'm going to wear these all the time," I say. "I'm even going to wear them to bed."

I've braced myself for her anger, for screaming and threats and dire consequences. Instead, I see my mother fold with sadness. She sits on the ground, in the middle of the room, and puts her face into her hands. I want to go to her, but I stand still because I know this is one fight I can't lose.

"Do you know how ugly they are?" she asks after a while. There's no malice in her question, I realize. She's not angry with me. It's the circumstances we're caught in that she hates.

"I'll cover them with my hair. You should be happy for me." You should be on my side, cheer for me, offer me more than a flood of despair and words that sting.

"Do you really think they'll work?" she asks.

FOR HER TWENTY-NINTH BIRTHDAY, he brings her white lilies.

He hands her the flowers and kisses her on the cheek—happy birthday, he says, and they each look away from the other. He looks like someone visiting a patient at hospital—uncomfortable, embarrassed, eager to leave. He takes off his overcoat and gloves, shakes the bits of snow out of his hair. He's still a young man, but he looks worn out.

He rubs his hands together and looks around for something to do. He looks relieved when he sees me. How you've grown, come, let me see you. I kiss him on the cheeks. His skin smells like snow. His eyes rest on my ears, but only for a moment, and then he looks away.

"She wears them all the time," Bahar says, because she has seen him look at my hearing aids. He already knows this—they've had more than one conversation about it. She has tried to enlist his help in convincing me to give them up, but in vain.

"That's all right," he says, his voice muted and shy.

"She's wearing them to school," she pleads, "to *bed*."

"Let her be."

I'm so grateful to Omid for this, I grab his hand and put my eyes to it.

"But you know they're not going to do any good," she says. "Once she goes deaf, they're not going to do a *thing*."

She has said this many times, but I don't believe her. It may be true for other people, but I have a plan: I'm going to use the hearing aids for as long as my own ears are good, and in that time, I'm going to memorize all the sounds, so that when I do go deaf, I can play them back for myself like a piece of music stored on a vinyl disk. Every morning when I leave home, I listen to the sound of traffic, of children crying as their mother drags them by the hand, of one-legged Gypsies and hare-lipped prostitutes trying to convince strangers to give them money. I memorize the whipping of the flames inside black metal barrels around which a group of men warm their hands; the popping of the charcoal in the brazier where street vendors broil lamb testicles and cow livers on metal skewers; the sound of a couple laughing at night as they pass a bottle of arrack between them.

At home, I learn the sound of the car door closing at the end of the yard when Omid arrives in the evening, of Ruby's laughter, of the phone ringing, scissors cutting through a piece of fabric. I memorize the sound of my mother's voice even as it becomes dimmer and more hollow—a beating heart that still glows red but that I know will lose its color for me unless I save it in my mind.

She tells him she's made dinner and he says he'll stay, walks up to the dining room heater and warms his hands. Other households in Tehran have long ago installed central heating and air-conditioning. They are equipped with electric dishwashers and washer and dryers, electric stoves that make obsolete our older model, which operates with a tank of gas that's delivered to the house once every few days. In our house, the clock stopped the day my father met Niyaz.

We sit at the table—Omid at the head, Bahar and I on either side— and eat. I'm wearing my newest outfit—a navy blue and white pleated skirt, a white shirt with red and navy blue buttons. Halfway through dinner, he puts his fork down on his plate and draws a breath.

"I'm leaving," he says.

The room becomes so cold I can feel my knees tremble against the chair. I look at Bahar and see that she's frozen stiff, her eyes burning, her hands limp.

We wait for Omid to say more—I'm leaving for the night, but will be back later. I'm going on a trip with a friend. I have business to take care of; I'll be back in a few weeks.

"I'm leaving for America in a few weeks. I'll have the office take care of all your financial needs. I don't know when I'll be back."

I look at him and pray that it's not true, that he'll say so any minute, reach over and take my hand and reassure me that I've understood incorrectly.

Did he realize, then, how much I needed to believe in him?

I get up and say I have to go to bed. I walk away without waiting for permission, leaving my parents—two corpses—staring at one another silently. At the window, I stop and put my face to the glass, press my forehead—so cold, it nearly sticks to the frozen glass—toward the darkness outside. I can tell it's going to snow all night because the sky has a deep purple hue. I watch the snow that lines the top of the brick wall surrounding our yard, that turns the trees fluorescent white, that lies on every inch of ground beneath me, on the edges of the railing around the balcony and on the outside frame of the window.

He lived with us for a while longer but in my mind, that's the night my father left us for good.

✎

"WAS SHE PRETTY?" Bahar would ask me often after I had seen Niyaz at Fareed's salon. She had walked by us so quickly, and Bahar hadn't dared look at her. Afterward, Bahar was haunted by the significance of that moment—by all the things she could have learned about Niyaz if only she had looked, the words she could have said, the way she could have changed what happened to us from then on.

Was she pretty? She would ask me, and it made me feel like a traitor, the spy who brings to her master news of impending demise. I told her I didn't remember, that I hadn't really seen Niyaz either, that she couldn't have been so special if she had failed to leave a strong impression. Bahar would nod, but I knew she didn't believe me, that she interpreted my reticence as a sign of complicity with the other side. You must think she *was* pretty, and that's why you don't want to talk.

Was she pretty?

I don't know if Niyaz was pretty. I remember she was tall. That she made you want to stare at her forever. She might have been the most beautiful woman in the world, but to me, her image evokes only loss.

THE DAY AFTER OMID announces that he's leaving, Bahar decides that we're going to do our spring cleaning early. It's still snowing outside, but she tells Ruby they'll take down the curtains, wash all the linen, clean the windows with old newspapers dipped in water and vinegar, empty the closets and lay mothballs and start to put away our woolen clothes.

Ruby shakes her head.

"It won't stop him from leaving." I don't know who has told her about Omid's announcement, but I doubt it was Bahar. It seems Ruby knows everything that happens in our house without being told.

She has grown thin and quiet since Artemis left. She sleeps in The Triangle most nights, because she can't bear to be near her husband, and she doesn't go on her afternoon travels into the streets anymore.

"You can scrub the house till your fingers bleed," she says, "or you can lie in bed all day. None of it's going to make a bit of difference to what your husband wants to do."

I tell Ruby I will help wash the floors—I'll bring the water and the towels, and together, we'll be done twice as fast. She shrugs. "If you want."

We get on our hands and knees, wet the towels in the bucket, and wipe the black stone floor of the staircase. The water turns gray almost immediately, so we have to change it and the towels frequently. We're nearly finished, our bodies and clothes covered with dirt and dust, when Bahar comes into the foyer.

"What are you doing?" she asks when she sees me on all fours.

I can tell from her tone that I've done something wrong.

"I'm helping Ruby wash the staircase," I say, and show her the dirty towel as evidence. She recoils.

"Who told you to get yourself so dirty?"

I put the towel on the ground and stand up. I try to brush myself off, but she sees my legs and screams again.

"Look what you've done to your knees. You look like a street child. You're filthy, *look* at yourself."

She grabs my wrist, turns my hand palm up, and shakes it in my face. "Look at your nails." I see that they are lined in black.

"Do you think I gave up my life for *this*? So my daughter could look like *this*? So she could wash floors?"

I try to pull my wrist away but she holds on. I pull harder, and at the same time, push her away with my free hand.

"Let go," I scream.

She grabs my hair.

"Look at this." She pulls. "Look how dirty your hair is. I'm going to cut it once and for all. I didn't raise a daughter so she could do a maid's work, or look like a maid, or walk around with this hair."

I make my hands into fists and slam them against my mother's chest.

"Let go," I scream, pushing her with all my might.

She falls, gasping, to the ground. She's sobbing, her face in her hands, her legs splayed, yet I find myself wanting to attack her still. I stand above her ready to assault, and scream again. "Let go!"

WE NEVER CLEANED the house after that. We let the dust settle everywhere in layers till we could draw through it with our fingertips.

EVERY DAY THAT WINTER, I feel the silence rise around me. I fight it as well as I can, fight the isolating terror of what is to become of me once Omid leaves and I can no longer hear. I fight to keep my hope, to hold on to every illusion I have mustered up in the previous months about being able to hear—through memory—even after I have gone deaf. I realize that my teachers have stopped expecting me to know or understand: that the other children hesitate to tease me because they have learned what is wrong with me, and they pity me; that Bahar has stopped taking me out on errands—because she's embarrassed of me.

Every day, I hear less. Every day, I watch for signs of Omid making true on his promise, packing his bags and walking out our door for good.

He's not leaving us both, I decide. He's leaving only Bahar. He dislikes her for all her faults: she has been selfish to hold on to him this long; unreasonable to expect him to give up a woman like Niyaz only to return to Bahar. It's *her* fault that he's leaving.

I KNEW IT WASN'T TRUE, but I had to believe it nevertheless. To save myself from despair, I had to believe that I mattered, that I was good enough for my father to want me.

It's not much, I know, but it's all I have to offer in my own defense.

I was seven years old when I started to go deaf, nearly twelve when the silence became complete. In that time, I saw my mother fight the deafness in the only way she knew, watched her suffer not only *my* loss but also her own—to have a child you thought was well and to learn she is not. I did realize, yes, that deafness was about to separate me from her for good, and this is why I hung on to every word that fell from her lips in those months. What I didn't know yet was that for me, being deaf would mean losing not only my hearing but also the *memory* of sound. I didn't know yet, in those months when blaming my mother was all that stood between me and the terror of being forever abandoned, that the day would come when I would see a word on Bahar's lips, know what it means, *say* it, even, with my own voice, but be unable to recall the music of it. It would be a greater loss—this loss of memory—than the deafness itself. When I went deaf, I became an exile in my own land; when I stopped remembering sounds, I felt I had never existed at all.

What do you do with a loss you can neither cure, nor accept, nor overcome?

ONE SATURDAY MORNING in mid-spring, I find Omid in his room.

He's sitting on his bed with his tie and jacket off, but he's still wearing the shirt and trousers he had on the night before—so I know he has just come home.

"Come in," he says when he sees me at the door.

I sit across from him on his bed, look out at the dead maple trees in our yard. The same plague that has killed our trees has spread to June Street and the Alley.

"You're up early," he says. His eyes are bloodshot; his skin pasty white.

Out of nowhere I say, "Take me with you."

He has just gotten up to hang his jacket, but he stops what he's doing, remains still for a long minute with his back to me. When he turns around, he looks as if he's been stabbed in the heart.

"What did you say?"

He comes back and caresses my head, pulls me to him.

There is a hole in my chest the size of an ocean, I want to tell him. It has been filled with fear all my life, but I'm tired of being afraid and I don't want to be on the losing side so I've decided to betray Bahar and save myself.

"I want to go with you to America."

His hand trembles on the back of my head.

"I'm not going to forget you," he says. "I'll come back often, and I'll send for you to come visit."

I know he's lying, that he'll forget us the minute he leaves.

"I want to go with you," I plead.

Even as I say this, my heart tears at the thought of leaving Bahar, of how devastated she will be when she learns that I, too, have abandoned her. I know it isn't fair—to leave her when I've been the shackle that kept her tied to her life. I know it's cowardly. Omid takes my face in his hands.

"Whatever happens," he says, "I'll make sure you're all right."

That's not enough for me. I hold on to his hands.

"Take me with you," I beg.

He closes his eyes. His hands are trembling. He's biting his lip.

"Fine, then," he says, so softly I'm not certain I've heard him right. "We leave a week from today."

LATER, I WOULD LOOK BACK at that morning and wonder if my father had indeed said what I thought I heard. I would wonder if I had dreamed the entire scene, or missed a word or two in his speech, or interpreted a sound incorrectly. By then, I heard so little, even with the hearing aids, that I had to rely on my own intuition, or on the context, in order to fill in the empty spaces between words.

"Fine then. We leave a week from today."

I believed him.

It's strange to say, but no less true—I believed this man who had forsaken me in his heart long before he left me physically; I put my faith in him though he had already proven himself unworthy of trust.

I believed my father and gave him my faith because I wanted to, yes, but also because, like my mother on her day of courtship, I thought I could take a chance, leave the others behind to perish, and by so doing, change my own luck for the better. It's what Bahar had done when she left Cyrus Street, what Artemis did when he abandoned Ruby. It's what Omid was doing to Bahar and me, what Bahar's family had done when they denied The Ghost Brother's truth.

They have a different burden—the weak, those who are subject to the will and whims of the strong. They have to choose between two bad options: to be loyal and perish, or to betray others and save themselves. It's not the kind of choice that is comprehensible to people who live in places where borders are fluid and obstacles are surmountable. It's not an American kind of choice, not the kind of challenge that can be fathomed in countries where green-eyed young women from small towns and ordinary families can walk into an ice-cream parlor and, just like that, become movie stars.

This is why, I think, Americans remain so composed at funerals— why they don't succumb to the tearful displays and abject grief that are so common in the East: for them, reality is never final, never immutable. They know they can beat anything—even death. Maybe *we,* in the East, cry more because our reality is more bitter.

It's like what The Opera Singer used to say: sometimes, truth alone will not suffice.

Memory does not often serve the truth. I have learned this. I know I might have heard a vow my father never uttered, held on to the pipe dream of a promise he never made. But imperfect as it may be, memory is all I have to help me bear witness.

❧

I AVOID BAHAR ALL WEEK. I leave for school before she has woken up, hide in my room with my homework when I return. On the few occasions when Omid is at home, I avoid him as well: I fear that a casual remark, even a look, might give away our plans, or alert Bahar to my intentions. On Friday night, when she goes to see her parents, I tell her I want to stay home. I bring a suitcase from the basement to my room and pack.

I take my best clothes, two pairs of shoes, the winter coat I bought the year before. I pack my gold coins, my pajamas, the rubber bands I use to tie my hair. At the last minute, I also pack my schoolbooks and notebooks, because I can't fathom being without them, in a strange country without Bahar, alone in a house on the edge of a cold ocean, in a town where my father has come to forget his sins. *Our* sins.

I know Omid will come home that night because I've checked his closet and seen that he hasn't packed his clothes yet. I know we'll leave early in the morning, when it's still dark, because that's when all the flights take off from Tehran. I hide the suitcase under my bed, set my alarm clock for four a.m., and lie down to wait for Omid. I've left my bedroom door open so I can see the light in the hallway when he comes in, and I'm sure I'm not going to fall asleep until then because my heart is beating so fast, it makes my chest ache.

I try to imagine sitting in the car with him, in the dress I've picked for the trip. My legs will be cold against the leather of the seat and my fingertips will be numb and in my heart, I'll condemn myself for eternity.

She wouldn't have done the same to *me*.

When the alarm rings, I jump up and wash my face, change quickly into my travel clothes, peek into the hallway. I tiptoe past Bahar's door, knock softly on Omid's. I don't hear an answer, but I go in anyway, prepared to wake him up if I have to so we don't miss the flight.

The room is empty.

The bed is still made and the closet is full of clothes and nothing has been touched, or moved, or packed.

I stand, confused, and try to make sense of what is before me. It's clear he hasn't been home at all, but I don't know what this means, what I'm supposed to do from here on.

I feel something move behind me and turn around to see Bahar standing in the doorway. She looks at me with a mixture of suspicion and bewilderment—what are you doing dressed? Why so early? What do you want from him?

She's saying something, but I can't make out the words. Suddenly, I remember the suitcase in my room. I wonder if she has seen it—figured out what I'm up to. Her lips move, but I can't hear a thing. They move again, and then a third time. I can see that she's screaming, but I don't hear a single sound.

I must have forgotten my hearing aids in my rush to get ready, I think. I feel for them in my ears. They are there, all right, but useless. I take them out, one at a time, and try to raise the volume. I'm anxious to get back to my room and hide the suitcase, frantic to find out where Omid has gone, but I can't understand what is wrong with the hearing aids and why I can't get them to work.

Bahar's lips are still moving. I put the hearing aids back into my ears and strain. I stare at her mouth and try to glean what I can't hear. Suddenly, I know why she's screaming: she can tell it's happened. I've lost my hearing entirely.

PART VII

HE DIDN'T KNOW, then, that the door would close.

He didn't know that fires would rage in the night—ten million fists waving in the air, black banners hanging from every rooftop, red carnations in the barrels of every soldier's gun while, behind closed doors, priests in black robes laughed at the folly of a people who, given the choice, had opted for servitude over freedom.

We are a people who believe in God.

He didn't know—my father when he left me waiting for him that morning in Tehran—that the borders of our country would soon close, making it impossible for him to return or for me to join him in America. That the Shah, believed invincible only months earlier, would escape the country only to wander the globe, looking for a new home. That mobs of terrified Iranians would storm the airport in Tehran, press at its gates hoping to escape, and find them locked. Through the chain-link fence, they would see planes sitting idle on the tarmac, lined up, motionless—like little aluminum toys. Within months the black banners on people's rooftops would become veils on their women's heads; the red carnations in the soldiers' guns—offerings from the rebel mobs who had called the soldiers "my brothers," had convinced them to switch sides—would adorn the graves of young men and children sent to fight Saddam Hussein's soldiers. And all along, the mullahs in black robes would deliver to those who defied them precisely the kind of justice—swift and deadly—that they had promised. Hiding in their homes, the people who had invited the mullahs to rule the nation would suddenly realize why, when given the choice between the Shah and the mullahs, they had opted for the greater of the two evils.

We are a people who believe in God.

He didn't know that the mullahs would divide—men from women, foreign from native, Muslim from Sunni—the world in order to conquer all; that they would divide the sea: they would draw cables across vast portions of the Caspian, hang sheets, like the sails of a sinking ship, that would separate men from women as they bathed. The wind would lash at the sails, rip them off, and carry them away, but soon, they would be replaced.

We are a people who believe in God.

Even years later, after the borders had reopened, my father would find it impossible to come home without risking his life and freedom. He was a Jew who had lived too long in America; he could have been a Western spy; he certainly qualified as Zionist; he might have been arrested, tried, and convicted in one of the mullahs' sham tribunals: two hours long, without evidence, or attorneys, and then the accused would be taken onto the roof, and shot. I don't think he would have left Iran without me had he known we would never see each other again. I don't think he would have given me up so easily had he known it was forever.

You can define a person by his actions, or you can define him by the choices he *would have made* had he been aware of his options.

I don't blame Omid for leaving us to go to America with Niyaz. I don't believe he chose his allegiances, that he had a chance, really, to do right by his wife and child. But I do blame him for denying Bahar the independence he so adored in Niyaz, and I blame him for lying to me before he left.

I lost my father the same way I lost my hearing, the same way I lost my mother's trust: they slipped away when I wasn't looking, without warning or explanation, until each absence became a link in a chain of questions that would go unanswered and prayers that never stood a chance.

ON THE PLANE, Niyaz holds Omid's hand and closes her eyes, listens to the hum of the engines and the sound of other passengers' chatter. They take off at dawn, travel through daylight, then darkness, and arrive in America when it's light again.

Outside the airport, wind lashes the palm trees and shakes the cars parked along the curb. Niyaz bends her head to protect her face from the gush of unexpectedly warm air that assaults them. Her hair shines in the sun. Omid puts his arm around her, and together they walk to a rented car.

The highway is empty, the asphalt silver in the mid-morning light. They drive down a street called Sunset Boulevard—like the one in the film Bahar loves so much, with William Holden and Gloria Swanson. Bahar has never been to America, but she has decided that Sunset Boulevard is her favorite street. She likes the name, she says. It evokes a journey toward an open horizon where the sun will set every day, so that no ending is ever permanent, no darkness impenetrable; a street that rises and ebbs past gated mansions where tightfisted old windows live within wood-paneled walls and shutters that are forever closed against the sun. It evokes a woman, a strong, determined woman who won't accept the death of her dreams.

Niyaz fiddles with the dial on the radio, finds a station she likes, and turns up the volume. They drive past nightclubs with neon lights, and crowded parking lots where skinny young men dressed in black stand with no apparent purpose. Farther out, they see boarded-up buildings and dilapidated storefronts where startled-looking mannequins with missing limbs stare out at passersby. They go through neighborhoods with wide sidewalks and tiny, one-story homes where no one has lived for decades, then onto an endless stretch of road with nothing in sight but water, until they reach a stone castle with gray walls and painted turrets.

There's a bridge here you can cross only once.

The house is cavernous and cold. Niyaz walks in first, and her footsteps echo against the bare floors. The rooms are dark, the furniture covered with white sheets that look like tired ghosts. There's a green lawn on the other side of the window, a blue pool, rows of lush, leafy trees around the edges of the yard.

Omid is tired but filled with joy. He can hardly remember the house on June Street with its broken glass doors and dead roses—or the pale sketch of a girl with red hair and spotted skin. He has already forgotten the young woman who smiled at him one morning on a crowded city street and, without making any demands, gave him her life. They are all illusions—just a string of tales he has heard long ago and that no longer serve a purpose.

Once upon a time in a land of no tears.

WHEN SCHOOL STARTS in September, I don't go back.

There's no point in pretending I have any purpose in a classroom where I can't hear a word, and so I stay at home, watch from the balcony as other children in gray and white uniforms get on the bus in the morning with their books, return in the afternoon and walk home. I sit in my room and read and reread my old textbooks, go through the stacks of Bahar's serialized novels in the basement, memorizing every word. I help Ruby with her chores, help Hassan Agha water the barren lawn. I stop letting The Ghost Brother into the house when he comes begging, because he reminds me so much of what *I* have become. I stop watching Chamedooni through my window at night because I resent him for having failed me with the hearing aids that stopped working.

I can't tell when The Tango Dancer plays her music, but every afternoon when I see people shutting their windows, I play in my mind the songs I had once heard. I do the same with the radio—the children's program at seven in the morning, the cooking show at ten, prayers at noon—the announcers' voices forever constant from here on, the words they utter singularly fixed in time. I don't ask Bahar what is going to happen to me because I don't want to know. I have no idea if she ever found out that I was going to leave her. What I do know is that she stops looking at me from that day on. Her eyes avoid me as if to guard against some unspeakable pain. When we're together she looks everywhere else—to my right and left and all around me—but not *at* me. I have the feeling that I'm made of glass—invisible but for the contours of my body and the red hair that has grown down to my elbows, and which she no longer seems to find offensive.

She communicates with me by writing, and she insists that I answer with spoken words because she wants to make sure I preserve my speech. She doesn't ask why I keep waiting for a call from Omid—

an explanation, an apology, an assurance that he didn't mean for things to turn out as they did—even though the phone is of no use to me, or why I keep writing to him though I have no address to mail the letters to. I save the pages—lined notebook paper folded into blue airmail envelopes—in my desk drawer and tell myself I'll send them as soon as Omid writes with his information.

Bahar and I eat together, watch television, and sew, and cook together.

She can't let me out of the house alone because it can be dangerous—what if another car lost its brakes?—but once I give up on the hearing aids and stop wearing them, she takes me to Cyrus Street again on Friday nights.

Her family doesn't ask. They don't need to.

I want to throw the hearing aids away, but I don't have the heart. It would mean the end of something I'm not ready to let go of yet—the hope The Tango Dancer has warned about. Instead, I keep them under my pillow, next to the transistor radio and the gold coin Chamedooni returned to me.

I have lost my place in my mother's eyes, it is true, but I still believe she will see me one day because she was once invisible herself—in that fish pool filled with tadpoles and algae, alone with only a vindictive ghost and the dark water that took away her voice.

In the fairy tales I read as a child, I will tell Bahar on that day, the heroine is always damaged: she has spent two decades asleep under a curse, or locked up in a tower. She has lost her mother and been betrayed by her father, forced to promise her firstborn to a gnome, taken into the woods and left to die. Even after the prince arrives to awaken her from her sleep, or breaks into the tower by using her hair to climb to the top, even after the gnome self-destructs and the witch is boiled in the pot she had prepared for the children, the heroine cannot undo the damage done to her. I know this—that I will always remain damaged—but I do believe that I can be real in spite of the damage, that I can find my way through the dark and thorny woods, climb up the valley of The Tango Dancer's despair, and emerge, if not whole, triumphant nevertheless.

I do believe my mother will see me, too, and maybe this is why I like to tell her story: so I can build a bridge with my words, lay the images they evoke, like incandescent pools of light, into a path that will traverse time and undo the past and lead me back to her eyes. Her voice.

THE LAST TIME WE GO to Bahar's parents' house, it's for the fifth anniversary of The Pigeon Sister's death. The family is observing a day of prayers, followed by a dinner that is open to everyone.

All day, I sit on the same chair in the far corner of the women's section, and watch people. I look at their faces, their hands, the way they all move as if weighed down by unspeakable burdens and sorrows so old they have calcified and become one with their bones. I see how they whisper to one another every time The Seamstress or The Unmarried Sister walk into or out of the room, the way they signal to each other with their eyes at the wedding band Bahar has continued to wear even after Omid left Iran, the way they sigh with envy—still—at the sight of her engagement ring.

At dinnertime, I lose Bahar to the commotion in the kitchen, so I take my plate into the yard and sit alone on the edge of the fish pool. From here, I can look directly into the room where the food is being served, so I watch as Bahar goes from one person to another, thanking them for being present, and please, won't you eat something, a piece of fried fish perhaps, or some white rice with lentils—yes, I know, white rice with lentils should not be served except during the seven days of shiva, it's strictly reserved for the time of deepest grief, but my mother forgot this rule when she was cooking for this night, she still mourns as on the first day.

Her cousin Tamar—the one who saved her from the fish pool—is wearing an ankle-length black dress and a knit sweater that reaches down to her hips. She's so tall and long-limbed that she looks like a stilt walker in an overly large costume, but there's something comforting in the way she puts her arm around Bahar, picks an empty plate off the table and hands it to her—take this, stop playing host and eat something. She guides Bahar around the table, piles food on her plate even as Bahar protests that she has no appetite, and brings her outside. They sit on the steps that lead from the house into the courtyard—their shapes illuminated by a faint light spilling out of the rooms, their faces pale against the darkness.

Tamar lights a cigarette and blows the smoke out in three perfect rings. She says something to Bahar that makes her laugh, but it's a sad, superficial laughter—the kind that doesn't undo the pockets of worry lining her face. Tamar takes another drag on her cigarette, balances the tips of her elbows on her knees, and looks away from Bahar toward the fish pool. She utters a few words, and suddenly, Bahar appears struck. Her eyes widen and her hand almost lets her plate drop and she stares at her cousin in disbelief.

Tamar is looking at her now and talking. She takes Bahar's hands in her own and holds them as she speaks—there, there, it's going to be all right, just be strong. Bahar nods and drops her eyes. A minute later, she puts her face in her hands and begins to sob.

I run to her. What happened? I ask, but she doesn't lift her head or answer me. What happened? I ask again, more loudly this time because I have no idea what the volume of my voice is. Bahar is still crying, her face still buried in her hands, and it terrifies me that I can't understand what has upset her so much, can't gauge the size and strength of whatever new adversity has reduced her to sobbing in public, before a group of people to whom she has tried so hard to appear unbeaten. I grab Tamar's arm, feel my nails digging through the fabric of her sleeve and into her flesh. I know that I'm squeezing too hard, that the anxiety and shame I've barely contained all day is suddenly directed at Tamar, but I can't stop.

What happened?

WE DRIVE HOME under a full moon, the city immersed in that cerulean light that I love so much, that wakes me up, sometimes, merely with its gleam. The streets are wide and quiet and long; the few pedestrians still out at this time move slowly and without apparent purpose. In the distance, the mountains look like gray lines sketched across an incandescent plain.

In her room, Bahar takes off her black dress and high heels, puts away the diamond ring she has worn that day in order to imply to people it isn't true, what they have all heard—her husband hasn't left her for good. She pulls the pins out of her hair and shakes her head to let the strands loose, then sits down, on the edge of the bed where she has slept alone for so many years—sits down with her hands on her lap and her face caved in and no idea, I can tell by looking at her, what to do next or how to move on from this moment.

Omid has had a child with Niyaz.

It's no longer just an extramarital affair. They have begun a new family together. They have a girl they've named Samar. It means "fruit of one's labor," the kind of reward that comes to those who work hard and wait. She has her mother's looks—this Samar—and her father's name, the luxury of being born in a place where her gender is not a curse.

She has the same surname as I, but none of the disadvantages. She doesn't have red hair or freckles, I imagine, won't look small and undeveloped, won't grow up feeling like she's a shadow. She won't be deaf, won't be stupid, won't disappoint her parents: she's American, this girl who has been conceived, I feel, to correct the mistake that is me.

I go to Bahar.

"Look at me," I say out loud.

I've come to tell you what I've never dared say in the past—that I love you in spite of my flaws and I know you love me too. That I'm sorry I failed you, sorry I couldn't bring Omid back. I'm sorry it all went so wrong, but I want to tell you that I tried, and that I'll keep trying, always, until you and I can both be proud again.

"I'm going to get better," I say, as if this would correct what has already happened, erase from the world that other child who has made *me* disposable.

"I promise you I'm going to get better."

She looks right through me.

I DON'T GO BACK to my own room because I know The Ghost Brother will be there, at the window, waiting with those imploring eyes, that tattered look of an old person whose body hasn't aged, who's condemned to a childhood of perpetual labor, because that's what it has become to him—the playing, the bicycle rides, the mischief that kept him amused when he first found himself alone on the borderland. He stands behind the glass and stares at me even if I draw the curtains and close the shutters, even when I tell him to go away, I hate you I wish I had never seen you, I won't become like you no matter how badly you want that. I won't become like you.

I haven't said this before, but in Farsi, the word "despair" is spelled Yaas.

Just like my name. The meaning varies depending on which letter "a" is emphasized—where the accent is placed—in pronunciation. I have always known this, of course, and it has struck me as unusually cruel—that the same four letters can convey either the beauty of poet's jasmine, or the hideous face of despair. I know my parents knew this too, when they named me. I think they knew that, like my mother, I would forever stand on the edge of a precipice.

Only I, unlike Bahar, didn't have the mettle to keep fighting.

I go into the room where Omid used to sleep before he left. I have never done this before, but I climb into his bed and under the covers with my clothes still on, lie there and gape at the emptiness of the room, the way it feels uninhabited—hollow. It's as if Omid had never stepped inside this space at all, as if he brought nothing of himself every time he walked in, lay down to sleep, said a word.

I close my eyes and try to recall the sound of his voice, the way he laughed, or uttered my name. I have memorized those sounds a thousand times over the past year, but already, they're far away and out of reach.

There is a pair of scissors on Omid's dresser. I pick it up and stand before the mirror. My hair is tied in a ponytail. I open the scissors at the nape of my neck and press hard to close them. My hair is thick, and it almost breaks the scissors, so I open the ponytail and try again. I cut piece by piece, lay each one down on top of the dresser until I've got it all—I've cut off all my hair and I look like a boy again. I try not to let it bother me, but it stings nevertheless, so I brush the hair quickly and take it into the foyer where the afternoon paper hasn't been opened yet. I wrap the hair in the newspaper, walk downstairs, and leave the house.

The Tango Dancer opens on the second ring. She has dark rings around her eyes and looks exhausted. I wonder how many nights she has gone without sleep, how many records she has played that I haven't heard. I wonder if it's loneliness that keeps her from sleeping, or a thirst for life she can't quench, or the sins of her parents she can't escape. I wonder if she remembers herself at age twelve.

When she notices my short hair, she looks stunned. She touches the ends and says something that, to me, looks like "What have you done?" She keeps touching the jagged ends, repeating the phrase, and then she sees the parcel in my hands and gasps.

I give her my hair.

"This is for Chamedooni," I say, and run away into the dark.

Hope, she had said, is a black hole with no bottom.

Back in our house, the brown heater in the dining room is dormant and cold. Behind it are a can of heating oil and a box of matches that sit idle all summer, until the weather turns and we light the heater again. I pick up the oil, tuck the matches into the pocket of my dress, and go onto the balcony.

It's nearly dawn. The morning breeze has carried a trail of dry leaves and paper into the middle of the street. The beggar woman with the two sons who help her ask for money is just arriving at her usual spot on the sidewalk near the yellow house. Two men in work clothes walk from the bus with their chins tucked into the collars of their shirts, looking tired even before the day has begun. The Tango Dancer has closed her door and turned off the lights.

The sun is just rising over Tehran. The city is still a charcoal sketch—a faraway land in a book of children's stories—of old brick houses and narrow alleys dotted with cars the color of hard candy, but it's beginning to breathe and move with the first light, the sky changing from cobalt to gray and then stark, blinding white, breathing life into what is now a watercolor painting against mountains glowing silver-blue at daybreak. I pour the heating oil in a circle around my feet and light the match.

The fire bursts into life instantly. It surrounds me like a vertical tunnel of heat and light, catches the lip of my skirt, climbs up my legs before I can step away. I turn around to free myself of its reach, but my entire dress is lit up, and sparks fly from me in every direction. They land on the balcony door, on the metal railings, on the dry persimmon tree below the dining room. The tree flares in one breath, and then the flames fan their own wind, leap onto the next tree, and suddenly there are dozens of trees burning like torches in the yard and outside in the Alley.

I see Hassan Agha running between the trees with his arms flailing about and his face twisted in a scream. I have been careful to close the balcony door, to keep the fire contained, but I had no idea that it would spread so fast, and now it has blocked my view of the inside of the house, so I can't tell if Bahar and Ruby have awakened, if they're going to be able to escape in time. To warn them, I bang my fist on the glass until it breaks.

Hassan has turned the hose onto one of the trees, and he refuses to back away, to abandon his garden and save himself. The two workmen from the bus rush into the yard to help him. I'm horrified by what I have done, and I scream Bahar's and Ruby's names until I gag on the black smoke from the flames. Then all at once I see them running out of the house. They're coughing violently and stumbling as they run, but they keep looking behind them at the house, and this is how I know that they're looking for *me*—that they've been looking for me since the fire started. They could have run out and saved themselves from the start, but instead they've searched the inferno for *me*. Suddenly, I know that I matter.

PART VIII

A THOUSAND TIMES since the day of the fire, I've had this dream: It's daylight, and I'm standing alone at the edge of the Square of the Pearl Canon in Tehran. Before me is the Avenue of the Departed with its green maples and shady sidewalks; behind me is the Caspian village where my parents and I once found happiness.

I'm waiting for Bahar to traverse the Avenue of the Departed and arrive at the square—for the moment when she'll turn the corner and find the destiny she has so faithfully awaited. I've come to warn her of what lurks behind this turn, to save her from the good fortune that will augur such devastation in her life.

She's walking toward me with her head in the clouds, so that I have to call her name, to make her look down and see me.

I open my mouth to tell her she mustn't take another step in the direction of the Square. I want to tell her what will become of her if she doesn't change course, how her story will end in heartache, how there's nothing but grief at the end of this journey of hope.

Just then, I hear a sound behind me and turn to see rain falling over the Caspian. It's a glowing, golden rain—sunlight in every drop—and the music of it stuns me into silence. Bahar is watching the rain as well, her face beaming with joy and optimism, and that's when I realize I'm not going to tell her what I had come to say.

I can tell her what lies beyond this border—the distance between what is and what *should* be—but by doing this, I realize, I would deny her the daring that makes her believe in a better fate, the trust that will drive her to close her eyes before her suitor and imagine that the world will have changed when she opens them again.

I can tell her what Omid will and won't give her, but by doing that, I would take from her the purple flowers she will put on a windowsill in a room where the paint is barely dry, the carpet of pink and red rose petals on which she will dance one night in her white lace gown.

I can tell her what awaits her in the house on June Street, how all the glass and mirrored doors she has found so striking will reflect only her unhappiness, how the open spaces that at first let in the sunlight and the stars and the scent of Muhammadi roses will become portals through which The Ghost Brother can return to seek revenge, but by doing this, I would take from her the possibility of escaping the mud brick walls and constricted walkways of her childhood home, condemn her to a life of solitude, or of oppression even greater than what Omid will exert.

I can tell her what will become of our days at the Caspian, how the trust she will place—once again—in my father will be betrayed, how she will go on to lose him, and I to lose my hearing, but to do this would mean to deny her the green of this sea, the gold of these rice fields, the sound of this rain.

ACKNOWLEDGMENTS

THANK YOU, David Poindexter, Scott Allen, Karan Mahajan, Dorothy Carico Smith, Khristina Wenzinger, Julie Burton, Melissa Little, and everyone else at MacAdam/Cage, for giving to this book from the heart.

Barbara Lowenstein, for your loyalty and wisdom.

Adrienne Sharp, for your guidance and friendship.

David Boul and Tom O'Briant, for your faith and courage.

Thank you, Alex, Ashley, and Kevin, for bringing light into the darkest night.

And thank you, David, for watching over me as I've stumbled across the winding brick road.

"In her stirring fourth novel, Nahai explores the struggles of an Iranian family in the tenuous decade before the Islamic revolution… a poignant tale of a 'damaged family.'"
Publishers Weekly

"Nahai's story of a haunted Jewish family in Tehran during the shah's last years possesses the dark beauty and harsh lessons of a fairy tale…Nahai's poetic and cathartic drama speaks for all silenced women, for all who are tyrannized."
Booklist (starred review)

"…both a riveting family drama and compelling historical fiction…The multiple ways Jews and Muslims intersect is also clearly presented, offering a fascinating glimpse into Persian life prior to the 1979 insurgency. Richly detailed, emotionally intense, and tremendously moving, this work is highly recommended."
Library Journal

"Gina Nahai's beautifully written novel *Caspian Rain* is evocative and poetic, with striking images that remain in the mind long after they are read. It is also a heart-wrenching examination of the tragedies of women caught in the net of gender, history, family secrets, and the unbending laws of high society. But ultimately it is a celebration of the human spirit—the moments of joy and courage and risk-taking that make all our lives worth living."
Chitra Divakaruni, author of *Mistress of Spices* and *Queen of Dreams*

"Lovers of the art of storytelling should know Gina B. Nahai. Much more than a fascinating, page-turning glimpse into the tribes and classes of Iran, *Caspian Rain* is an exquisite novel which, like a Ghost Boy on a bicycle, will continue to magically haunt its readers long after its ending."
Sandra Tsing Loh, author of *Depth Takes a Holiday* and *A Year in Van Nuys*

"Gina Nahai, a gifted storyteller with a unique and powerful voice, invites us into a strange, unsettling but ultimately beguiling world, a place of both pain and enchantment. Remarkably, she allows us to glimpse the hard realities of life in contemporary Iran in a new and unaccustomed light while, at the same time, she shows us that the innermost truths of the human heart are truly universal. *Caspian Rain* is both timely and timeless, an important book that comes at just the right time."
Jonathan Kirsch, author of *A History of the End of the World*

"With her fourth novel, Gina B. Nahai establishes herself among the top rank of writers of her generation. In *Caspian Rain*, she brings to stunning life a cast of characters that continues to haunt the reader."
John Rechy, author of *City of Night*

"In *Caspian Rain*, Gina Nahai takes us on a privileged journey into an Iran a contemporary traveler can only hope to know through fiction—an Iran before the Islamic Revolution where women could aspire to independence and dream of larger lives. Through the eyes of her 12-year-old heroine, we see a whole society mirrored, a society enmeshed in superstition but struggling to emerge into modernity. A heroine—and a book—to embrace. I was mesmerized."
Elizabeth Forsythe Hailey, author of
A Woman of Independent Means

"If writers do indeed write what they know, then Gina Nahai has a Ph.D. in the human heart. Her characters inhabit their culture and their time so profoundly that her readers do too; from moments of magical realism to years of anxious drifting and struggling, Nahai's characters are as much in search of themselves as the turbulent nation they live in."
Patt Morrison, columnist, radio host, and author of
Rio L.A., Tales from the Los Angeles River